Jana and Lydia

GREGORY M. HASTY

Jana and Lydia

This is a work of fiction. All of the characters, names, incidents, organizations, and dialogue in this novel are either the products of the author's imagination or are used fictitiously.

Archway Publishing books may be ordered through booksellers or by contacting:

Archway Publishing
1663 Liberty Drive
Bloomington, IN 47403
www.archwaypublishing.com
844-669-3957

Interior Image Credit: Gregory M. Hasty

ISBN: 978-1-6657-0257-7 (sc)
ISBN: 978-1-6657-0258-4 (hc)
ISBN: 978-1-6657-0259-1 (e)

Library of Congress Control Number: 2021902132

Print information available on the last page.

Archway Publishing rev. date: 3/31/2021

This book of fiction is dedicated to the many young women and men who are involved in sex trafficking across the United States and around the world. Sex trafficking is unfortunately escalating everywhere. It is a heinous crime that debases our society, threatens the integrity of our morality, and damages hundreds of thousands of young lives. When trafficking is inflicted on an individual, it affects that person for the rest of their life. It doesn't go away.

The accounts described in *Jana and Lydia* are not intended to sensationalize the undertakings of the girls while in captivity. Instead, it portrays events that occur every day in the lives of imprisoned young women and men. This behavior is common and regrettably part of the daily challenges one must face as a trafficking victim. My hope as the author of this publication is to raise awareness and promote action against these activities. Prayers go out to all of those who are imprisoned and held hostage from their homes and families.

It is also dedicated to the many law enforcement officers who work tirelessly to locate youths who have been kidnapped and forced into sexual bondage. Without their efforts, this civil disease would proliferate beyond our worst nightmares..

One

Friday, June 7, 2019, 9:00 p.m., Central City, Phoenix

Jana walked meekly to the entrance of the Raining Nails Bar in the Central City village of Phoenix. She and her girlfriend Lydia had just acquired brand-new bogus IDs, fabricated by a classmate, and they decided to plunge into the early evening to see if they worked. The two were at an age where their physical maturity coalesced with their precociousness and appetite for adventure. Both were virgins, and they were inflamed with newly developed sexuality, but they didn't quite know what to do with it. They were anxious yet daunted by the enormity of venturing into the sphere of an unknown stretch of landscape they had only read about.

Curious and inquisitive, Jana and Lydia shared a common yearning for male companionship and someone who could gently unveil their hidden sensuality without exposing their naivete. Truth be told, the two girls were probably unprepared to go the distance, but the presence of each other's company fortified their fragile exploits, giving them feigned confidence to press forward.

This was their first try with the IDs. Lydia walked up from the other direction after parking the car and met Jana a few feet in front of the club's entrance, and their eyes met with excitement and a reasonable fear of getting caught. The night was warm, the air stock-still, perfumed by the distinctive fragrance from some nearby junipers. The parking lot was pushing to capacity, and it looked like a busy night at the tavern. Audible from inside was the noise of clinking glasses and a loud hum of table talk punctuated with roaring laughter over a backdrop of Lynyrd Skynyrd.

The doorman watched as they approached and threw the girls a skeptical stare. The two young ladies, both seventeen, walked up to him side by side, looking a little timid, and they gazed up at the brawny black man serving as the gatekeeper to the club. His shirt was unbuttoned to the middle of his chest, showing off pecs larger than their own, accentuated with some silver bling swinging nonchalantly from his neck. The man's shoulders were as broad as a runway, and his neck was like a dense oak tree supporting a larger than normal skull adorned with a closely cropped, thick, black beard and mustache. A bouquet of an overly generous splash of cologne met them with a crisp smack.

He took the IDs and looked the girls up and down, checking the goods along with the IDs. An uncomfortable moment lingered, and the girls instinctively crossed their arms over their chests, shielding themselves. Jana was a slim blonde, about five feet eight, 120 pounds, and she was wearing a snug white tank top with a short green and black skirt riding about mid-thigh, revealing her athletically bronzed thighs.

Lydia was a beautiful brunette, Hispanic, a little shorter than Jana, and clad in an airy blue sundress that didn't leave much to the imagination. Both were attractive, tanned, and bedizened up like models. The doorman looked down at the IDs and then back to their faces, and he slightly shook his head as a hint of a smile emerged at the corners of his mouth. Then he motioned them toward the club, pointing a backwards thumb and giving them clearance to enter.

Jana and Lydia grabbed arms, muting their exuberance, and walked through the tunnel into the club. Once they were out of hearing range of the doorman, they squealed excitedly and hugged each other. They entered the dimly lit barroom and scanned the area, trying to decide the best place to land in the crowded watering hole.

It was their first time in a bar, unknown territory, and they stood at the portal a little longer than customary. A few heads slowly swiveled from the bar to view their entrance, and the two felt conspicuous. Lydia grabbed Jana's hand and pulled her to one of the few open stations available, a dark booth in the corner. They slid into the seats, sitting across from each other, psyched by the intense moment at the front door. Jana took Lydia's hands captive from across the table, and they leaned forward face-to-face, and began talking excitedly while scanning the tables teaming with young professionals, partiers, and barflies.

The air in the bar was thick; lack of acoustics jarred the senses with the sound system leveled on high, and everyone was clamoring over Audioslave and trying to make themselves heard. Scantily clad female servers flitted about, trying to keep up with the landslide of orders, and patrons raised their hands to get their attention. The table maids were nearing a breaking point and afforded the customers only a few seconds to order before jettisoning to the next table.

Spicy chicken wings, fries, and mugs of beer were tossed onto tables with reckless abandon.

One server puffed the hair out of her face as she leaned over a table and took a long, exhausted breath. Then one of the young men at the table reached behind her and gave one of her partly exposed cheeks a caress. The waitress pulled away abruptly, giving him a disdainful eye, and left the table. Apparently, that wasn't the first time she had been fondled. It revolted her, but she was resigned since it came with the territory. Their skimpy attire seemed to invite that sort of behavior, and the owner faced numerous complaints, but he reminded them that their tips wouldn't be nearly as lucrative otherwise.

An overwhelmed busboy was sweating profusely and shuffled from table to table, picking up empties and finished food. The customers treated him as an invisible moving part of the bar's machinery as he went about his business of trying to keep the place clean.

Lydia motioned with her eyes for Jana to look at the table next to them. Three men in their early twenties were chuckling and cutting it up. They barely noticed the two young ladies, distracted as their own self-entertainment accelerated into high gear. Their amusement was only occasionally interrupted by glances at the big screen behind the bar; the Diamondbacks were playing. The two girls giggled and discretely pointed to guys at nearby tables, amused by the tavern's high-octane vibe and overpopulation of available members of the opposite sex.

Sashaying up to their table, one of the servers arrived in a huff. "What can I get ya?"

"Give us two beers."

"Tap or bottle?"

The two looked at each other quizzically, and Lydia shrugged. "Bottle."

"You got it." She wheeled around and was gone with a quick spin, hurrying off to the next table.

The two girls laughed.

"What's tap?"

"Beats me—that's why I went with the bottle!"

More laughter.

Their giggles and excited chatter continued as they admired the nearby table, subtly trying to get their attention. It finally worked.

The most handsome of the three finally looked over, raised his glass, and smiled, exposing his perfectly white teeth and cute dimples.

Lydia was embarrassed, soft-pedaled a smile and diverted her gaze shyly to the table, but Jana returned his smile and gave him an engaging look, locking eyes with him. The two girls giggled and whispered across the table, cutting glances over at him until he rose and made his way over to the table.

Standing above, he said, "I'm Jeff."

"Hey Jeff, I'm Jana, and this is Lydia."

"Hello, ladies. What's going on tonight?"

Lydia said, "Not much … just hangin' out. Our first time here."

"Cool, that's Devin and Ian." He pointed to his comrades at the table.

They offered a brief wave and turned back to watch the game.

"Mind if I sit down?"

"No, not at all." Jana moved over on the bench, giving him room to sit.

Jeff sat down on Jana's side and scooted over close to her.

As their arms touched, Jana thought, *Wow, is he handsome!*

The three hit it off instantly, and before long, Jeff had them eating out of the palm of his hand. He was good at that sort of thing, and they seemed to be receptive to his approach. Two beers down, Jeff ordered another round.

The girls were becoming tipsy and slurring their speech, but they didn't intend to slow down now; they were having too much fun.

Before long, Ian came over and slid in next to Lydia. He picked up the dialogue with her, and Jeff whispered in Jana's ear, trying to communicate over the amped-up White Stripes blasting from the sound system. Jana got tickling chills whenever Jeff spoke into her ear, and her stomach became queasy, feeling an unusual electrical sensation from his closeness.

Jeff went for a gamble and asked Jana if they would like to go outside to smoke a joint.

Jana looked him in the eye cautiously and held up a finger, signaling that a decision needed to be made. She smiled at Jeff, grabbed Lydia's hand across the table, and motioned for her to come closer.

Lydia was unaccustomed to the alcohol and peered into Jana's eyes, not offering much of an answer. "Should we? I'm having fun in here."

"I'd kinda like to, Lydia. He's so cute, and I've never gotten high before. What do you think?"

"I don't know, girl. We just met them. Are you sure?"

"I think so. Let's give it a try. We can always come back if we don't like the scene."

Jana turned to Jeff and said, "Okay, but just for a few minutes."

Jeff said, "You won't be disappointed—trust me."

The four slid out of the booth and left Devin staring at the big screen. He noticed their departure and offered a halfhearted nod as they left.

Jeff gently grasped Jana's hand, interlocking fingers, and led her and the others to his car, which was parked in the darkness some distance from the entrance. Jana felt another strange stimulation, and her body began to quiver as they strode in the darkness. Ian put his arm around Lydia's shoulder, and she uncomfortably acquiesced.

The foursome stopped at Jeff's Mercedes S Class, and he stooped in on the passenger side, reached into the glove box, and pulled out a baggie of weed with several rolled-up joints. He inconspicuously handed a joint to Ian, and he led Lydia to his ride.

Jeff came around to the driver's side of his sleek black sedan and opened the back door—arm extended, palm open—inviting Jana to hop into the back seat.

She thought, *The back seat? I need to be careful.* She climbed in and sat in the middle of the bench. A nervousness gripped her body. She didn't know what to expect from getting high or, for that matter, from Jeff.

Jeff followed her in and sat shoulder to shoulder with Jana. The side of his body touched hers. Mixed feelings of excitement and guarded apprehension clouded her mind, exacerbated by the alcohol she had consumed.

Jeff looked at her with bedroom brown eyes, gave her a comfortable smile, and focused his attention on lighting the joint. He put it in his mouth, lit it up, and took a long draw. He exhaled, filling the car with smoke, and murmured a sigh of satisfaction. Then he handed it over to Jana and held it up to her lips.

She took the lit stick of grass from Jeff and inhaled a short puff, immediately coughing profusely through a nervous laugh.

Jeff laughed with her and urged her to take another hit.

She did.

In a few minutes, after some more puffs and inhaling more deeply, she began feeling the effects, a cloudy, carefree attitude where everything was spacey. Jeff and Jana took photos of each other on their iPhones, posing with ridiculous expressions and emotions, and laughed themselves silly. Time seemed to suspend itself, hanging in hibernation while they frolicked on the buzz of the smoke. She liked the feeling, and Jeff noticed her breezy, unfettered disposition. They made funny remarks about the lights of the club, the traffic driving by, and how strange the people looked walking out of Raining Nails—all thanks to the cannabis. They were laughing so hard they were tearing up, and their sides were hurting from the continuous hilarity.

Jeff is really adorable. His laughter is so contagious too. I wonder if he'll kiss me.

Once the giggles subsided, they looked into each other's eyes—and Jeff closed the distance between their lips. His approach was slow and magical, leading Jana to tremble with anticipation.

When they kissed, she felt sparks inside and a tremor deep within. *Wow, Jeff is a really good kisser.* Aided by the high of the marijuana, she started buzzing all over. As their lips were engaged, she could feel herself becoming dangerously aroused. She began to feel pressure from Jeff gently moving her to a horizontal position on the seat. Jana wasn't sure what she was getting into, but she hesitantly complied as they continued their passionate caress.

Oh my goodness.

The heavy petting continued, and Jana felt a wave of heat washing over her face. She felt like she was losing control of the situation.

Jeff began stealthily moving his hands all over Jana's body.

Jana became nervous and wasn't sure how to slow down Jeff's speeding train. *Should I stop it right now or allow him to continue?* She was torn between the enjoyment of the moment and worries about things getting too far out of hand. *Should I? He's awfully convincing. Wow, we're moving so fast.*

The kissing got heavier, and as Jeff expanded his exploration, Jana became alarmed.

Oh no, this is too much, too soon. Whoa buddy. "Jeff, this is going too fast. I'm not sure I can do this."

"Oh, it's okay, Jana. You're so beautiful. I want to be with you now. You'll enjoy it." Jeff looked her in the eye and continued his fondling.

Jana lurched upward and grabbed his hand, stopping his progress from trying to remove her panties. "No, Jeff! I don't want to." *Doesn't he understand no?*

"It's all right Jana, just relax. It'll be great. I promise."

"I can't. Please stop." Jana reached down and tried to halt Jeff's advance, but he continued to tug on her thong.

What is he doing? No, no!

He pushed the weight of his body on top of Jana, forcing her down onto the seat hoping to continue.

"No, Jeff. Stop. I mean it … stop!" Jana protested and pushed Jeff off to the side, sat up, and pulled her skirt back into position.

Jeff shoved Jana back down and moved back on top of her.

"Stop. I said no!" Jana began to fight, pushing him off of her and yelling for him to stop. *This guy's not gonna quit. What can I do?*

Jeff shoved her back down onto the seat and in the struggle, ripped her underwear off of her hips.

Jana screamed and began hitting him over the head, but he continued his assault. *I have to break free. I gotta get away, I'm about to be raped.*

The struggle became more violent, and it was evident that Jeff was not planning to stop. Jana reached for the door handle and quickly opened the door. The bright interior light beamed down on them, and she wrestled her way halfway out the door. She screamed for help at the top of her lungs as Jeff grasped at her skirt and legs. She wriggled free for a moment and begged for someone to come to her aid.

As Jeff was trying to drag her back into the car, a figure moved quietly toward the open door, stooped down, and belted Jeff over the head with a beer bottle. Jeff reeled and slumped down on the seat.

Jana was in tears as his limp hands finally released the hold on her leg. She stood, lowered her skirt, and looked over at her rescuer, embarrassed, but thankful for his intervention. "Thank you, sir, so much. He got carried away and wouldn't stop. I tried to slow him down, but he kept forcing himself on me. I didn't know what to do. He was tearing at my clothes. I was nearly raped … he was going to rape me! Thank you again. You saved me. I need to leave."

The middle-aged Hispanic man was dressed in all black: black jeans, black cowboy snap-button shirt, and black full-quill ostrich boots. He was short, had deep-set brown eyes, and a pencil-thin mustache. His full head of hair flowed straight back from his forehead and was neatly combed and manicured with a slight scent of oil. There was a trace of empathy in his soft eyes, and he smiled with a warm, comforting turn of his lips.

Jana immediately felt safe and reassured herself that the frightful evening was quickly turning for the better.

Lydia and Ian had been smoking a joint outside Ian's Camaro, leaning against the car, and enjoying the cool evening air after a hot day. Lydia had a view of Jeff's car from the distance, and although she couldn't see too much from her vantage point, she could see the two features disappear into the back seat. Knowing Jana was a virgin, she was hoping she wouldn't go too far with this new acquaintance. She had riveted her attention on the Mercedes for signs of what was taking place. The interior smoked up from the joint they were puffing, and it became foggy as the images of the two slipped away. When the light came on inside the car and she saw Jana struggling, Lydia bolted over to the car to help.

Lydia embraced Jana, and as they hugged, tears of fright fell freely onto her friend's comforting shoulder. She sobbed into her embrace and backed away, sniffling.

"Lydia, I'm so sorry. I never intended for things to get this far out of hand."

"Shh, Jana. It's behind you now. You're going to be okay. Let's get out of here."

Ian slinked back into the bar, embarrassed about his friend's attack on the engaging young lady, and faded into the crowd.

"Lydia, this is the man who saved me—and he couldn't have come at a better time. He stopped this maniac, and I was able to free myself. He tried to rape me, Lydia."

"Hello. My name is Alejandro, but you can call me Alex."

"I was trapped, and without Alex's help, I'm not sure where I'd be right now. This is such a nightmare. I won't be able to sleep for a week." She burst into tears again.

Alex tenderly put his hand on Jana's arm and led her back to the club.

Lydia attached herself to her other arm and they helped Jana along.

Alex said, "Here, let's go inside. Take some deep breaths and get composed while I call the police on your attacker."

Jana said, "Oh, thanks, Alex. I really appreciate all you did."

Lydia said, "Yes, we both appreciate you, sir. It was very timely, and we can't thank you enough."

The threesome approached the entrance and saw the bouncer talking to some inebriated people who were trying to get in. He was pushing them away, and the men were becoming hostile, pushing the large man in the chest and yelling disparaging remarks.

As Lydia, Alex, and Jana walked toward the front door, Jana felt a sharp prick just below her shoulder. She looked over at Alex and saw a syringe in his hand, and that was the last image she saw before losing consciousness.

Lydia saw her friend falling and moved in to help. As she did, another man snuck in behind her. She felt a sharp sticking sensation in her upper arm and collapsed, unable to utter a sound.

The two men quietly dragged the girls to a white van waiting close by in the middle of the parking lot. With help from someone inside, the two men quickly pulled the unconscious young women into the back of the van, jumped inside, and shut the doors.

The driver sped away undetected. There were no witnesses.

¤ ¤ ¤

As the van skidded out of the parking lot kicking up loose gravel, Jeff was beginning to stir. He rubbed his head and wondered what had happened. He sat up in the back seat and looked around in dismay as he massaged the lump on the back of his head. He remembered the beautiful, alluring Jana, the heated moments with her, and their struggle. His last recollection was of her opening the door then everything faded out. Jeff pulled himself together, got out of his car, and stumbled back to the bar.

Ian was sitting with Devin at the bar, and they were having an animated conversation. When they saw Jeff, they abruptly ended their discussion, looked at him, and shook their heads.

"What were you thinking man?" Ian asked.

Jeff said, "Ian, were you around? Did you see what happened?"

"Yeah, man. I could make out you and Jana struggling. What were you doing?"

"That girl was so hot, and I was really turned on. We were getting down to serious business. I thought she wanted it as much as I did. When we were rounding third, she freaked and got agitated and wanted to stop. It wasn't right. She was leading me on, getting me all worked up, and then—out of nowhere—she pulls the plug! I thought she still wanted it, so I kept going … but apparently she didn't. Then she tried to get out of the car, and that's the last thing I remember."

"Dude, this guy was standing with Jana and helped her out of your car. He was staring at you."

Ian said, "He must have hit you with something. Lydia was with me, and when she saw the scuffle, she ran over to see what's up. That's when I got lost and tried to evaporate. Sounds like you got what you deserved, man."

¤ ¤ ¤

The van accelerated toward the highway. At the on-ramp to Interstate 10, they headed south.

In the back of the van, Alex and the two other men caught their breath.

"Alex, man, you got a couple of good ones here. Look at the Anglo here, blonde, really put together, fine as wine, and look at the hooters on this other one."

The girls lay on their stomachs, and the man raised Jana's skirt, admired the view, and started fondling the well-rounded cheeks of her bare backside.

Alex said, "Hey, man, get your hands off of her. You know the rules, Pedro. Once we get them to Raul, he'll decide how we can handle her, but not until then, *comprende?*"

Pedro said, "Yeah, yeah, I know, just trying to get a peek, that's all."

Alex said, "Look, but no touch, now you two get their things and put them in the bag."

Alex pitched Pedro a drawstring bag, and the two men kneeled in the back of the van and removed the young ladies' shoes, earrings, hairpins, ankle bracelets, watches, and rings and threw them all into the bag. They emptied the contents of the girls' purses on the van floor and found cell phones, makeup, coin purses, credit cards, a little cash, and a bottle of perfume.

Alex's underlings split the cash between themselves and dumped everything else, including the cell phones, into the bag. The only thing left on the two drugged females were their clothes. The van shot south on Highway 10, maintaining a constant speed within the limits of the law.

The girls were facedown on the floor, bouncing with each jar in the road, and the men silently stared down at them. Jana's short dress left her cheeks partially exposed. A puddle of saliva pooled by Lydia's mouth as she breathed slow, irregular breaths.

The three men broke open bottles of Modelo from a case purchased earlier and celebrated their conquest by clinking their bottles together over the unconscious girls. They would be paid well for this acquisition, both in cash and pleasure. The big payday would be with the girls—not the cash—since money was plentiful, and there was an unending source at their disposal. These girls were special. They were matured and fully developed unlike some of the younger ones they'd picked up in the past. Beautiful, tanned, and shapely, they were bursting into womanhood, but they were still innocent and unused. That aroused the men as they marveled at the scene at their feet.

After nearly two hours, they were nearing Tucson. Their path would lead them further south to their destination, Nogales, where Raul's operation was headquartered.

Lydia and Jana had known each other since second grade. They had met when their parents had signed them up to play soccer. They had been together ever since, inseparable, and were never seen outdoors without the other. Lydia evolved into a star defensive player on the team and was the best center-back in her entire high school district.

Over time, a soccer player developed life skills and tendencies from the position they played on the field. Lydia was a defender, and her mentality was all about protection and keeping opponents away from the goal. She mirrored those traits in real life, being cautious and pragmatic and evaluating a situation before reacting. In this way, she looked after Jana and protected her at every turn. She was dependable and trustworthy, a person who could be counted on in the clutch. Lydia had solid, muscular legs from her many jaunts up and down the field, and her endurance was unprecedented. Her calves and thighs were rock-hard and highly defined, and her vastus medialis nearly lapped over her kneecaps. She could hold her own with any of her opponents because of her speed and agility and her never-give-up attitude. Her body had matured early, developing much sooner than the other girls her age. She drew stares from all the boys at school, and even some of the male teachers couldn't help but peek at her athletic physique. Her long, dark brown hair spilled past her shoulders and hung near her waist. Her hazel eyes were surrounded by an oval-shaped face without a blemish on her sparkling chestnut skin. She had a cute, diminutive nose, and even as a baby, she was considered one of the prettiest kids who ever graced her part of the city.

She won most beautiful her junior year by receiving a landslide of votes, leaving her rivals with hardly any chance. Now going into her senior year, she was excited to be on the student council and had decided to run for one of the officer positions. She made As and Bs and was a diligent student with hopes of higher education in the nursing field. Her parents were strict and kept a close eye on their oldest of three children. They were well aware of her physical attributes, and it didn't go unnoticed how both kids and adults would ogle at her mature, sculpted figure.

Lydia had been on some dates after her parents carefully screened the callers and granted her permission to see boys her age within rigid guidelines. They required Lydia to check in frequently on her phone. She protected her womanhood with ferocity. A few boys made attempts, but Lydia defended her personal goal with the same tenaciousness she exhibited on the field—and no one ever got close. She was wholesome, dedicated, and a girl you wouldn't hesitate to bring home to meet your parents.

Jana was the polar opposite of Lydia, but perhaps that's why they had become friends. On the soccer field, Jana exhibited early signs of aggression, quickness, and a thirst to score goals. She was relentless in pursuit of scoring, pushing her team ahead of their opponents. Jana was lightning fast and had the instincts of a cat. Sometimes she was accused of having eyes in the back of her head because of her uncanny intuitive abilities. Jana was the team's leading scorer each year and never found a shot she didn't like or fail to take one when she had the chance. She was impulsive and improvisational on and off the field.

Jana was unafraid to venture beyond her limitations and pushed boundaries whenever she had the opportunity. Thank God Lydia was usually around to rein her in, doing her darnedest to protect her best friend from harm, and had on more than one occasion bailed her out of danger. Jana grew quickly and was tall and gangly as a youth, looking down on her classmates from her position high above. Initially, she was clumsy and dorky, and some of the boys even made fun of her and called her Frankenstein. As she developed in junior high and high school, her body became at peace with her growth. Jana's frame finally began to fill out in all the right places, fueled by constant exercise and activity between the lines.

As Jana entered her senior year, she was tall, slender, taut and muscular. Her legs had matured into pistons of steel, carved by the many years of running, and her endurance could match Lydia's. She had a naturally light complexion and bright, stunning blue eyes. Her straight, naturally blonde hair accentuated her eyes, and her long thin face was punctuated with ripe, full lips. Jana's ancestors were Swedish, and the complexion, hair, and eyes chased down the family tree into her seventeen-year-old body on display for everyone to admire. In the summer, she and Lydia spent many hours by the pool, cultivating their tans to further complement the near-perfect physical packages they possessed.

Even though Jana was an only child, her parents were more liberal with her comings and goings, allowing her to go out with boys more frequently and with fewer guidelines than Lydia. The two friends, who differed in some ways, were both dead set on their most precious attribute: protecting their virginity.

Jana was popular with the boys, and there was no shortage of attempts to deflower her, but they were foiled at each pursuit. She allowed them rights to explore the landscape, but she gave them boundaries to work within and wasn't afraid to enforce the limits. Given her size and strength, she was able to police the offenders quite well. Jana was a top student even though a touch of ADD made it hard to concentrate on her studies. Her mind lingered on the guys more than the schoolwork lately, which tended to place second in the active theater of her mind.

These two innocent young ladies laying unconscious, were precariously splayed on the floor of the dark van, going to an unknown destination with unknown consequences ahead. Their parents would be missing them soon when their curfew passed—and the typically punctual ladies didn't show up at home.

Two

Phoenix, Saturday, June 8, 12:30 a.m.

Midnight passed, and neither of the girls made it home. Lydia's parents, Art and Sylvia, made three calls on her cell that went unanswered, and they became concerned since she always checked in or called back when they reached out.

Jana's parents, Tom and Justine, were also up and worried that their only daughter hadn't made it home. Justine trusted Lydia and was comfortable with them going out, knowing that she was in good hands with her best friend, but punctuality was their mantra. The games, the practices, the tournaments, and even school were based on time commitments and schedules, and the two young ladies were robots for time management; they were never late.

Not hearing from either girl raised a red flag for both sets of parents. At twelve thirty, Sylvia texted Justine to see if she'd heard from the girls. She was a little afraid to text the Lincolns at that hour, but the urgency of the situation overruled the social decorum:

S: "Sorry to bother you this late, Justine. Have you heard from the girls? We haven't, a little concerned."

J: "No Sylvia, haven't heard a word. I'm worried too. Do you know where they were going?"

S: "No, I don't. They just said they were going out, but they were dressed to the nines, any ideas?"

J: "Not really, as dressed up as they were eliminates the possibility of a casual meeting with friends. They must have been going somewhere that encouraged fashion. A dance, or a movie, or shopping, but no, this is much too late for any of those type things. If so they would have been home by now."

S: "I'll text some of her friends in my contacts and see if they've heard from her."

J: "Good, I'll do the same, copy me on the texts so I can see who you've tried to contact."

S: "Will do, Justine, thanks, and I'm sure they're fine. I trust our girls implicitly and know they're levelheaded and wouldn't do anything unwise."

J: "Okay, how bout I check back at two if we don't hear any word. Do you mind?"

S: "Heavens no, if we haven't heard from them by two I'm really gonna be worried, let's stay in touch."

J: Thumbs up emoji.

Two o'clock came painstakingly slow, and neither set of parents was able to get a wink of sleep. Jana's dad paced the living room floor, thinking about what could have delayed them.

Justine got copies of Sylvia's texts and contacted six of the girls' other friends who she had saved in her contact list. Sylvia sent out ten texts. A few responses came back, but not nearly enough.

"No, Mrs. Cantu. I haven't been with Jana or Lydia tonight or been in touch since school."

"Sorry Mrs. Cantu, not sure where they might be. "Don't know Mrs. Cantu, that's not like them to be out after hours, let me know if you need anything further."

"No Mrs. Lincoln, haven't seen them."

"Haven't heard from them since seeing them last week, didn't know their plans, sorry Mrs. Lincoln.

"Mrs. Cantu, I'm no help. I haven't talked to either in about a week."

Justine's worry wore heavily on her face.

"Tom, do you think we should call the police?"

"I'm tempted to, but they usually don't get involved unless they've been missing for a significant time."

"Well, I'm going to call them anyway. I need to check in with Sylvia first."

J: "Sylvia, if it's all right with you, I'm going to call the Phoenix police and report the girls missing."

S: "Okay, it's better to start early regardless if they're just innocently detained somewhere. If they're truly missing, Art, and I would like to get on with the process as soon as possible."

J: "I'm sure we'll be hearing from them soon, I hope. I'm calling now just in case."

Justine: "Hello. Who do I need to speak with to report a missing person?"

Officer on Duty: "I'll take a message and have someone call you from Missing Persons. No guarantee you'll hear them until the office opens. It's pretty late, and I'm not sure anyone will be able to respond, but when I get through to them, they'll call you immediately."

Surprisingly, about an hour later, Justine got a call. "Hello, Lieutenant Tatum here, Phoenix Police, Missing Persons, who am I speaking with?"

"My name is Justine Lincoln, and I'd like to report my daughter and her girlfriend missing. Thanks so much for calling us back this late."

"That's okay, I wasn't sleeping very well anyway. When did they go missing?"

"Their hard curfew is midnight, and the girls are both punctual and are never, let me stress, never late. We call them periodically when they're out like this, checking on them, and neither one is returning calls or texts, which is highly unusual."

"What are their names?"

"My daughter is Jana Lincoln, and her friend is Sylvia Cantu."

"Age?"

"Both seventeen years old."

"Where were they going tonight?"

"Well, neither Sylvia's parents nor my husband and I are sure where they went. They were really dressed up, but all they said was that they were going out. We're really not certain where they were off to."

"Mrs. Lincoln, this puts us in a tough spot. It doesn't give us a lot to go on. Could you text me pictures of the two young ladies, and I'll circulate to our on-duty officers as well as put an alert citywide to be looking for them. Can you provide a description?"

"Yes, I can. Sorry we're not much help on their whereabouts. We trust our girls so much that we rarely have to interrogate them on what their plans are."

"I'm not casting any stones on your parenting. I'm just trying to get as much information as possible. Their descriptions?"

"Jana is five feet eight inches tall and weighs about 125 pounds. Shoulder-length blonde hair, blue eyes, very fit and athletic. She was wearing a white fashion tank top with a green skirt about mid-thigh."

Justine recalled Lydia coming inside to pick up Jana and remembered what she was wearing. "Oh yes, that's right, a sexy sundress. It was a short, blue-patterned sundress, a little on the low-cut side, and she was wearing sandals."

"It does sound like they were going out somewhere special. Please text us recent photos as soon as possible at (602) 484-2122. If you get any ideas, can check with their friends, or get any clues whatsoever text me. Please also provide me Sylvia's parent's information."

"Will do, Lieutenant Tatum. Thank you so much."

J: Sylvia, I just spoke to Lieutenant Tatum in Phoenix Missing Persons. I gave them a description of our girls and what they were wearing. Wasn't Lydia wearing a short blue sundress and sandals?

S: Yes, that's what she had on. That worries me now. These girls hardly keep anything hidden anymore. If you ask me, they're looking for trouble dressed like that. Glad you were able to report this to the police. Anything I need to do?"

J: "Yes, you need to send Lieutenant Tatum a photo of Lydia and your names and contact information as soon as possible to (602) 484-2122. That's his cell if you need to reach him."

S: "Will do that right now. Let me know if you hear anything back from any of her friends who haven't responded yet, and I'll do the same."

J: "Okay, I'm praying we'll hear something soon and hopefully this is something minor."

Justine and Sylvia sent in recent photos of their daughters and the lines of communication were set between the three. Lieutenant Tatum broadcast the missing status of the two young ladies to all of the officers on patrol and sent the images and full descriptions to their onboard computers. The eyes of Phoenix were now on high alert for the two missing teenagers.

At 3:45 a.m., Sylvia got a cryptic text from one of Lydia's friends, Chad Beaufort. Apparently her second text following the unanswered one she sent earlier had woken him up. He mentioned seeing them about eight o'clock when they were picking up something at his house. Sylvia texted him right back.

S: "Do you know where they were going? What was it that they had to pick up?"

C: "I'm sorry, Mrs. Cantu. I probably shouldn't tell you this, but they asked me to make them fake IDs. I did, and they picked them up."

S: "We can discuss the fake IDs later. I'm only concerned about finding our daughters, and you can be a big help. Do you know where they were going or what they planned to do? We just want our daughters back. Please help."

C: "Sorry, Mrs. Cantu. I didn't mean any harm. I was just trying to help some friends. I think they said they were going over to Central City to see if they could get into a club. That's all I know."

S: "Thank you so much, Chad. This helps a great deal and gives us a place to start."

S: "Justine, I just heard from one of the girls' friends, Chad. He made them a fake ID, of all things, and he said they came by to pick it up around eight and were probably headed to Central City to go clubbing."

J: "Oh my word. That's the last place I would have expected them to go. That really worries me. Are you planning to pass this along to Lieutenant Tatum?"

S: "Yes, calling him now."

Sylvia: "Lieutenant Tatum, this is Sylvia Cantu. You spoke to my friend earlier about our daughters who are missing."

Tatum: "Yes, Mrs. Cantu. Thanks for sending your daughter's photo. We have it circulated along with Jana's to all of our officers on duty and will let you know if we hear anything."

Sylvia: "Well, we just received some new information that should help our search. Apparently, one of their friends made them fake IDs so that they could go clubbing."

Tatum: "Did the person say where they planned to go?"

Sylvia: "No, just that it was probably Central City."

Tatum: "Okay, this does help. Although there's a lot of clubs in the village, it narrows the playing field a great deal. I'll pass this along to all of the on-duty officers, and if we don't hear anything by morning, we'll send investigators out to the various clubs and show them pictures, see if we can turn up anything."

Sylvia: "Thanks so much, Lieutenant Tatum. We really appreciate your help."

Tatum: "No problem. We'll be in touch if we hear anything."

S: "Justine, just talked with Tatum, gave him the info on Central City, he has the eyes of the police force looking for the girls. He said if we don't hear anything by morning, his investigators will begin canvassing the various clubs in the area, showing photos to see if anyone remembers seeing them."

J: "Thanks, Sylvia. We'll be waiting by the phone and praying in the meantime."

S: "Me too. Everything will be all right."

Three

Saturday, June 8, 2:30 a.m., Nogales

The van rocked back and forth as they traveled on I-10 an hour south of Tucson and began to approach Nogales. The city was in the southernmost part of Arizona, spanning the US border, and continued into Mexico under the name of Heroica Nogales.

As they closed in on their target location, Alex pulled out his phone. "Yeah, Manuel, put Raul on the phone."

"Yeah, boss?"

"Speak to me, my friend. What do you have for me tonight?"

"Sir, we have two of the best subjects we've seen in a long time."

"What you got?"

"These two are older, maybe eighteen, good bodies, real lookers."

"Where you get 'em?"

"In Phoenix, at Raining Nails. That's been our best spot, and it proved a winner again tonight. You'll love these two, real ladies, looks like they're from high-class families."

"Good, can't wait to see them. How long before you arrive?"

"We're about fifteen minutes away."

"We'll make ready for them. Remember, no touching the merchandise."

"Yeah, I've had to keep these two from drooling all over them. It hasn't been easy."

"Tell them hands off—you know how it works."

"Yes, sir. Will do. See you in a few."

The van entered Nogales, and the driver navigated the vehicle through the back roads, avoiding any cars that might be roaming the area late at night. They circled the house twice, checking for any traps or stray police making their rounds. Seeing none, they flipped off the headlights and parked in the rear of the large home that was only a few hundred yards north of the border. The mansion had a sprawling floor plan with six bedrooms, a pool, and an underground basement, which was rare in that part of the country.

As they arrived, a garage door opened. Three men stood at the doorway, and two were heavily armed. Inside the house, two more armed sentries were standing guard. The driver pulled into the expansive garage, and the door automatically shut behind them.

Raul Alvarez, a short, dark-skinned Mexican national strolled out to the van, greeted the driver, and met Alex in the back.

Alex opened both doors wide, illuminating the two young ladies unconscious on the floorboard. The other two henchmen stepped down from the van and excitedly shook their hands up and down.

Raul looked down at the two young ladies and noticed that Jana's underwear had been removed. He got into Alex's face, nose to nose, and said, "I thought I told you they were off-limits. What did you not understand about my orders?"

"Yeah, boss. We didn't touch them. I actually interrupted her and her boyfriend about to get it on in the back of his car. She didn't want what he was offering and asked him to stop, but he was persistent and ripped them off. I saw it all. I had to knock the guy out with a Corona to rescue her, and that's how we found her, honest."

Raul looked him in the eye for a few seconds with a steel glare and then backed off. "You better be straight with me, Alex. You know I can ask her what happened."

"Ask away—she'll confirm it."

The other two looked to the ground, avoiding Raul's stare and acting innocently uninterested.

Raul climbed into the back of the van and got a closer look at Jana and Lydia. He turned their heads to the side, checked their facial features, and raised each girl's shoulders to look at their breasts. He drank in a long gaze at Jana's exposed cheeks, admiring their shape and firmness, and then turned back to exit the van.

"You boys did good tonight; these two are perfect. We'll be able to demand a premium for talent this good. Congratulations, fellas. Come on inside, and we'll catch up.

Alex said, "Thanks, boss."

"Pedro, get a couple of men, bring the girls inside, and put them in the *Rojo* Room. You remember, no touching!"

The two men stationed at the door and two others in the garage parked their weapons. Two of them stepped inside the van and lifted Jana by the arms and legs and slowly lowered her to one of the others standing behind the van. The man took her from the two inside the van and folded her over his shoulder, once again exposing the better part of Jana's backside. The two picked up Lydia and repeated the process. The man waiting below held her limp body on his shoulders and followed the other man into the house. The two men brought them up to the Rojo Room and placed them gently on the bed. The two best friends were side by side and remained in a coma of drugs that would keep them incapacitated for hours. A guard was posted inside the room, and the doors were opened so Raul could monitor the situation and protect his latest prized acquisitions.

Raul's family were Mexican immigrants from the tiny village of Sinoquipe in Sonora. His father's small shop, operating out of his house, sold crackers, soda, Chamoy apples, and *elote* (fried corner on the cob on a stick). His older brother, Roberto, was twelve and sold the elote from a dilapidated, two-wheel cart pulled by a donkey, driving slowly through the village seeking buyers for the corn.

Raul would count the few pesos he made each week and somehow cobble together enough to keep the family just above water—until thugs began making periodic visits to the house, stealing food, and shaking his father down for whatever else they could confiscate. They stole his chickens, their eggs, or both, and one day, the donkey turned up missing. The final straw occurred when Raul was away. His only daughter, Susanna, age fifteen, was lured across the street by the same men. She was viciously raped and sodomized by the two gangsters and was discovered when little Raul, ten at the time, was sent by his mother to find Susanna. He stumbled on the men savagely abusing her, and when he saw the scene, he courageously, but feebly attacked the two until he was subdued. He was forced to watch the men continually attack Susanna as her mouth was bound and her hands were tied. Her dress was hiked up over her head, and she was bent over a wooden crate, flailing hysterically as the men had their way with her. The memory stole his slumber many a night. He would wake up in a cold sweat as the image burned an indelible scar on his impressionable mind.

His father couldn't take any more of the abuse and decided to immigrate illegally to the States, crossing the border at Nogales on a dark winter night. The border security wasn't as tight back then, and the five were able to cross with ease and establish a life that provided safety to his frazzled family. Poor Susanna got pregnant from the attack, and they raised the baby with the constant reminder of how the young child found her way into the family.

At age thirteen, Raul was a popular kid at school and was handsome and strapping. He took an early liking to girls at the school and would pursue them endlessly for kisses, even though deep down inside, he thought there was more.

One day, he found himself with a few older girls who thought he was cute. They took him into the janitor's closet outside the gymnasium and began teasing and kissing him. When the bell rang, two of the three went to class—but the other stayed and gave Raul an early education on the birds and bees.

After that moment, he was hooked. He craved attention, and he sought pleasure, and the only way he knew how to find it was through sex. He grew up too fast and became a man about town, chasing women and doing drugs. Raul and his friends would prowl the streets at night, looking for young girls to victimize, and they earned a reputation for violence and mischief.

While traveling back to Mexico one year, he visited a brothel. The owner introduced him around to the ladies for an evening romp and later put Raul in touch with one of his cousins who worked a prostitution ring on the US side of Nogales. It didn't take long for Raul to insert himself into the web of illegal activities that started his own enterprise twenty years ago. Raul was short and light-skinned with a head of hair that was full and thick. He was trim, muscular, and handsome, with a square chin and high cheekbones. His dark brown eyes captivated his prey, and he was a smooth talker, shrewd and manipulative.

With his illegal income, he built an empire and became sophisticated in his dress and acumen, giving him an air of confidence and refinement that was alluring to the opposite sex. After hundreds of sex partners, he developed a taste for young women and relished finding new talent to use or abuse. Raul was a dangerous man in many ways—physically, psychologically, and financially—and he knew how to use each quality to his advantage.

The cartel eventually sought out Raul and his enterprise, and they agreed to join forces and operate out of Nogales, establishing a network of sex trafficking that spanned several states. His primary income source was drugs, and he consistently smuggled narcotics through an expensive and elaborate tunnel system that took the cartel three years to construct, burrowing its way under the border between the two cities of Nogales.

Four

Saturday, June 8, 6:00 a.m., Phoenix: Missing Six Hours

Justine and Tom were sitting at the kitchen table. Tom had his head down on the table, arms flat and palms on either side of his face, as he struggled to stay awake.

Justine leaned forward with quivering hands on her face, tears seeping down around the edges of her fingers and trickling to her cheek. They hadn't heard anything from the police or the girls. They were now certain that Lydia and Jana had run into foul play. They prayed that it was something that could be rectified quickly, but the thought lingered that they were in some sort of danger—or worse.

Justine looked up at the clock as the second hand circled ever so slowly. Each tick reverberated in her ears. Their phones rested on the table between them, and Tom and Justine stared at the devices, expecting to hear them buzz any minute with news. Tom checked his emails and texts often, but there had been no notifications. Neither had eaten or slept since the night before, and they were emotionally spent.

Tom reached over and gently grasped Justine's hand. "It will be okay, honey. We'll find our little girl."

"Oh, Tom, I hope so. I'm not sure I could live without her. Why were we so lenient? I feel like it's our fault for not keeping closer tabs on Jana."

"It's nobody's fault. We don't know what happened yet, and those type of worries won't help get her back. We have to think positively and pray that she's unharmed. We'll get her back. I promise not to rest until we do. God is looking after Jana and will protect her."

"I hope so. I dearly hope so."

Sylvia and Art were in the den with their cell phones on the coffee table, which was strewn with empty coffee cups, wrappers from granola bars, and a writing pad with notes from the police. Sylvia had spent most of the night on the internet, writing down the names addresses, and phone numbers of all the clubs in Central City. She dug deeply into Google and identified every bar, dance hall, club, and concert venue in downtown Phoenix. She searched beyond Central City and created a second tier of clubs. There were more than forty bars and clubs on her list, and they planned to start contacting the clubs when the employees arrived. Since most of the clubs stayed open until two o'clock in the morning, it could be midday before anyone would be around to pick up the phone. They were losing precious time waiting for the establishments to open.

Justine popped up from the table and headed toward the study.

"Where are you going, honey?"

"I'm going to the study to print photos of our girls to circulate at the clubs. Maybe they'll allow us to post the missing person notices."

"Good idea—that will give us something to do until we hear word."

Tom texted Sylvia:

T: "Sylvia, sorry to text. I know you're waiting on pins and needles to hear something, like us. Justine is printing off missing person circulars with Lydia and Jana's photos so we can post them at the clubs in Central City. It will give us something productive to do, and this being so soon after their disappearance, the image of the girls might be fresher in the minds of club-goers."

S: "Yes, your text wasn't exactly what I was hoping for, but we appreciate the efforts on your end. That sounds good. I made an exhaustive list of every club, bar, and watering hole in downtown Phoenix that we can use. Once Justine finishes, Art and I can meet you to distribute the posters."

T: "Sounds good, how 'bout if we meet at the Starbucks on McKellips and Scottsdale around ten?"

S: "We'll be there."

Five

Saturday, June 8, 7:00 a.m., Nogales

The guard in the Rojo Room was nodding off, his head falling sideways, nearly nudging his shoulder, and then unconsciously moving it back up to its normal vertical position. A few seconds later, he repeated the motion. A moaning sound got his attention, and he perked up immediately. He listened intently, holding his military-grade automatic weapon. He peered over at Lydia and Jana, and the early-morning sunlight was illuminating the room and creeping over Jana's face. Jana's legs were open in a figure-four position, and her skirt was open, revealing everything she valued private, exposed for all to see who wandered by. Lydia's legs were uncoupled, and her sundress was fluffed open, drifting up to mid-thigh on one leg and nearly up to her waist on the other.

The guard glanced at the light blue panties underneath Lydia's disheveled dress, which covered her beautiful, olive, tanned body. The guard had the difficult task of watching the young ladies all morning long while they were unconscious, staring at their youthful, tightly drawn bodies displaying budding womanhood right in front of his face. There were many opportunities during this time when he was tempted to sneak over and explore their curvy physiques, which he was able to admire from his vantage point from across the room. Muscular and robust, wiry and fibrous, the two ladies with their shapely tanned figures were two of the finest females he had seen in many years, but the risk wasn't worth it. Raul would be infuriated and have him beaten or maybe killed. The temptation wasn't an option—but there was always the possibility he would have his shot at these two before long.

Jana let out a barely audible moan and moved her head slightly.

The guard had a radio in hand. "Raul, you up?"

A few seconds passed.

"No, what is it?"

"The two new ones … they're starting to come around."

"Okay, have Dr. Juel meet me over there in five minutes."

"Juel, it's Manuel. The boss needs you to come to Rojo Room. We have two new visitors. They came in last night, and we have them on your mixture of roofies."

"When were they given the injection?"

"About ten o'clock last night."

"Okay, be there in a few minutes."

The guard stood above the bed, watching for any sudden movements, but the young ladies were still unconscious.

A few minutes later, Raul entered the room with Juel.

Juel said, "For God's sake, cover the girls up."

Manuel walked over to Jana, pushed her legs together, and pulled down her skirt. He strolled around the bed to Lydia's side, pulled down the portion of her dress caught underneath, and pushed her legs together.

Juel said, “That’s better.”

Rubbing the sleep out of his eyes, Raul entered and took a long look at the two and smiled. “Doctor, give them the normal cocktail, but lighten it up a little bit so they’re somewhat coherent. I want them to be able to have the ability to communicate—even if it’s imperceptible.”

Jana’s eyes were still closed but shifted her head slowly from one side to the other and hummed a low muted moan.

Lydia remained comatose.

Raul said, “Manny, tie them up.”

Manuel went to the kitchen to get some zip ties and returned to the bed. He folded Jana’s hands on her lap, tied her wrists, and tightened it. He took a larger tie and put it around her ankles, securing the tie in place. Manuel replayed the scene with Lydia.

The doctor was preparing to administer his mysterious dose of narcotics. Juel had concocted a recipe of sedatives and opioids that kept their subjects incapacitated, but somewhat lucid so they could see and feel what was going on around them. The right combination immobilized their motor skills and the ability to physically resist, but it left them somewhat conscious, much like a person who is paralyzed from the neck down.

Dr. Edmund Juel was from Nicaragua and had studied medicine at the National Autonomous University of Nicaragua. He grew weary of his monotonous position as a family physician and met Raul while he was in town to arrange a drug deal. Raul suffered a snakebite while crossing the jungle to meet up with illegal drug farmers and was airlifted by his team to Juel’s hospital.

Through their conversation, Dr. Juel began to suspect Raul was involved in illegal narcotics and politely inquired about his occupation. One thing led to another, culminating in Raul inviting Dr. Juel to visit his operation in the United States.

Juel took him up on his offer a few weeks later, and he flew to Tucson, and they drove down to Nogales. After spending the day with Raul and hearing more about his enterprise, Dr. Juel considered an employment offer. That afternoon, he was fed a lavish dinner and treated to two young Hispanic ladies who spent the night entertaining him in a fashion he had never experienced. The final salvo Raul dispensed the following day was offering to pay the doctor $100,000 a year for his services with a promise if things worked out, a healthy bonus for each visitor he inoculated. His duties were to keep their subjects drugged, minimizing resistance, but providing for quality delivery of their services. Juel also provided general medical services to keep the clan healthy and was prepared to handle everything from cuts and gashes to bullet wounds.

Dr. Juel looked over to Jana, held up the syringe, tapped it lightly, and spewed a bit of serum into the air. Then he leaned over Jana and clenched her shoulder with his left hand and moved the needle close to her upper arm.

Jana was starting to come around and moaned slightly. Feeling the doctor's clench, she turned her head toward Juel and tried to open her eyes. The eyelids cracked ever so slightly, and her eyes tried to focus as Dr. Juel stuck the syringe into her arm, releasing the cocktail into Jana's system. Jana reacted to the jab of the needle by flinching slightly and released a troubled moan from the discomfort. Her eyes disappeared between the small eyelid separation, and they closed, returning Jana to an unconscious state.

Juel walked around the bed, followed the same routine with Lydia, and administered the identical recipe into her arm. She didn't move or seem to feel the injection.

"Doc, how long will they be out?"

"About six to eight hours. This afternoon, they should be lucid enough to be useful."

"Thanks, Doc. I'll have someone watch them closely to monitor their condition."

"I've got some errands to run in town. I'll be back before lunch and will check in on them."

"Doc, these are two special projects of mine. We don't see this high degree of talent very often, and I want these girls kept in good condition. Is that understood?"

"Yes Raul. I can tell they are special. I'll do everything possible to keep them in good shape."

Six

Saturday, June 8, 10:00 a.m., Phoenix: Missing Ten Hours

The Lincolns, the Cantus, and their children met at Starbucks promptly at ten. Justine made two hundred eight-by-eleven leaflets with the girls' images prominently displayed at the top with the word "MISSING" in large letters just below the photos. Their first names were centered below each photo, and a plea for help was written to anyone who could give them information on the girls' whereabouts. The two couples agreed to pitch in five thousand dollars each as a reward for anyone who could lead them to Jana and Lydia's safe return. They figured ten thousand dollars would get the attention of someone who had seen them and force to the surface information on the girls.

Sylvia carried her lists of the clubs and two maps of the area, dividing Central City into plots. The Cantu family would cover the north sector, and the Lincolns would cover the south. They would meet back at Starbucks when they were finished. They immediately went their separate ways and hit the streets. In one bar after another, they taped and stapled flyers on windows, doors, bulletin boards, and light poles. In clubs that were open, the couples asked to display the notices inside. Most club managers and employees permitted the notices to be posted with little resistance.

Seven

Saturday, June 8, 1:00 p.m., Phoenix: Missing Thirteen Hours

The Phoenix Police investigative team headed to Central City. The two detectives began canvasing the village bars, interviewing managers and employees, and showing recent photos of Jana and Lydia. As they suspected, some of the key players wouldn't be in until later; they were especially interested in the doormen, bartenders, servers, and bouncers. So, far, no one had seen or recognized the two young ladies.

Lieutenant Tatum texted Sylvia from his office at headquarters.

T: Mrs. Cantu, we haven't heard anything, but I wanted you to know our detectives are in Central City now talking to club and bar employees.

Sylvia heard a text buzzing in on her phone and quickly grabbed her cell. Her hopes rose as she saw it was from Lieutenant Tatum, and then she realized it might be bad news. She shakily opened the text.

Al and the children stood by intently, waiting to hear the contents of the message.

Sylvia read Lieutenant Tatum's text and had a mixture of feelings. She knew no news was good news, but it wasn't what Sylvia was hoping for. She felt a wave of disappointment flowing through her mind, but she didn't want to show her discouragement to Al. "It was Officer Tatum, no news, but they've got officers in the area, talking to employees of the bars."

Al said, "Well, I'm glad they're on top of this. We're doing everything possible, Sylvia. Not what I wanted to hear, but I find comfort that the police are behind us on finding Lydia and Jana."

Sylvia said, "You're right. They're being a big help."

Two men with sunglasses and short-sleeved dress shirts approached the Cantus.

"Hello, we're Detectives Sharp and Williams of the Phoenix Missing Persons Division. You must be who put up the notices. Are you the Cantus?"

"Yes, sir. This is my husband, Al. I'm Sylvia, and these are Jamie and Rosa."

"Nice to meet you. I'm Detective Sharp. You're doing a good job passing these out. We've seen them at every place we've been. We assure you we'll turn over every rock to find your daughter and won't stop till we do. I'll tell you though, the people we especially want to talk to at these clubs won't come to work till later this afternoon. We're doing some preliminary legwork now, but we will get a more comprehensive process underway later today and tonight. I have your cell and the Lincolns' so we'll relay any information we uncover later this evening."

Al said, "Call us anytime. It's never too late. We'll be up awaiting word."

Williams said, "Get some rest if you can. This may be a busy few days, and it's important for you and your wife to be fully alert and unfatigued. Even though it doesn't seem particularly productive, it will be in other ways that you'll understand later."

Al said, "Good advice, Detective Williams. We'll try to do that, although it may be difficult."

Sharp said, "I know it will, but try if possible."

Sylvia said, "We'll do the best we can. Thank you both for your help. As you may have seen, we've posted a reward for the girls' whereabouts— so feel free to mention that to whoever you speak with."

Sharp said, "Will do." The detectives headed to their next destination.

Sylvia and her family continued covering the area, hitting every establishment, including gentlemen's clubs, nude bars, restaurants, and dance halls.

The Lincolns were equally as dynamic, covering every possible place of business where Lydia and Jana may have been seen. They visited gelato and ice cream stores, doughnut and coffee shops, and all the bars and clubs in the southern sector of the search area. After the Lincolns had exhausted the list of targets on their list, Justine texted Sylvia.

S: J: "Sylvia, we've covered every inch of the southern part of Central City, even coffee shops and ice cream parlors. We'll be at Starbucks in about fifteen minutes."

J: S: "Okay, we have a few more places to hit then we'll be there, we're nearly finished too."

Eight

Saturday, June 8, 2:00 p.m., Phoenix: Missing Fourteen Hours

Twenty minutes later, the Cantus met the Lincolns at Starbucks. They were sipping stiff servings of expresso and trying to maintain their energy levels. Al and Sylvia flopped down exhausted, and the children pulled up chairs to the table. The Lincolns were spent from walking up and down the streets and the mental fatigue of worrying about their daughter. At least the physical exertion had a way of keeping the fears from dominating their perspective and helped them cope with the calamity that may have befallen their daughters.

The Cantus ordered coffee for themselves and hot chocolate for the kids. They rested for a while, hugged each other, and promised to keep in touch. Before they departed, they held hands as Al said a prayer.

"Dear Lord, help us find Lydia and Jana. Keep them safe and watch over them wherever they are until we can hold them in our arms again. Give us the strength to meet this challenge and give the police the power and insight to help us find our children. Amen."

Nine

Saturday, June 8, 2:00 p.m., Nogales

Lydia stirred from her unconscious state, but she was not yet awake. Jana remained limp, head tilted to the side, mouth open, breathing deeply. Lydia's eyelids began to show slight movement underneath, but her eyes didn't open. She moaned lightly, and her right hand twitched from the constraints of the zip tie.

Manuel grabbed his radio. "Boss, it looks like they're starting to wake up."

Raul said, "Okay, good. I'll be in there in a couple minutes after I finish what I'm doing. Have the doctor standing by."

"Ten-four."

A short while later, Raul and the doctor arrived and stood over the two girls.

Lydia was starting to move. Her hand twitched again, and her head turned toward the ceiling. The movement of her eyes below the lids continued, and she began to slowly crack open her eyes. She remained deeply sedated and was having difficulty aligning her faculties. She blinked a few times and stared at the ceiling, mesmerized by the fan rotating above her. Lydia couldn't comprehend where she was or what was happening.

Jana's left leg quivered slightly, and she whispered an uncomfortable moan. Her mouth closed, and she rocked her head slowly back and forth. Her eyes remained shut.

Lydia's eyes were fully open now, and she was becoming lucid. She tried to move her hands, but they were harnessed. She tried to sit up.

Doctor Juel sat on the bed next to Lydia, restrained her, and pushed her gently back onto the pillow. Her legs began moving, and feeling them tied, she struggled slightly.

Juel put his hands on her shoulder.

Juel said, "Now, now, young lady. Just relax—everything's good."

Lydia looked him in the eye and said, "Where ... am ... I? What's happening?"

"Your safe with us. Relax, and we'll tell you all you need to know."

"Where ... what is ... I can't feel my legs. Who are ... ...?"

Raul sat next to Lydia and asked Manuel if he knew their names.

Manuel said, "The one you're sitting next to is Lydia, and the other one is Jana."

Raul cupped Lydia's hands and whispered, "Lydia, you're doing good. Just relax—everything is going to be fine."

Her frightened brown eyes were blinking and trying to focus on his face. "Where ... who are you? Where is—"

Raul said, "You'll find out soon enough. Just rest, and we'll get you set up downstairs."

Jana's eyes opened halfway, and she slowly scanned the room.

She saw three unfamiliar men standing near the bed. "What's going … I can't see straight … what's the … …" *I think we've been kidnapped. Where are we? Oh, what are we going to do? We've got to find a way out of here. Last thing I remember was at Raining Nails barely avoiding being forced to have sex with that guy. Then this nice man helped me. He was trying to save me from Jeff, but what happened? I don't remember anything after leaving Jeff's car. It must have been him—had to be—he's the last face I remember. I want to go home. These men look mean and scary and might kill us. Oh, God, help us. This can't be true. What do they want from us? We're just teenagers. I'm so afraid.*

Dr. Juel sat down on the bed and tried to relax Jana by smoothing her forehead and tucking her hair behind her ears.

Jana blinked several times, but she couldn't think straight. It was like peering out of a cloudy bubble; she was confused and disoriented, and her mind was in a swamp.

Lydia saw Jana next to her and wanted to get up to figure out what was going on, but her arms and legs seemed to be cut off from the rest of her body. Lydia realized their hands were tied and started to panic, but her senses wouldn't fully engage. The instructions she gave her extremities were ignored.

Dr. Juel pulled out another syringe. This version of his unique concoction was meant to calm the subject and keep them fully cognizant. He injected Jana first, and she whimpered, closed her eyes, and slipped away. Juel walked over to Lydia, and she tried to move away from the needle. She looked at the doctor with trepidation and confusion. When the needle entered her arm, she let out a yelp, and tears began to form in her bloodshot eyes.

Juel said, "Give them about five minutes, and they'll be ready."

Raul said, "Manuel, go get Pedro. We'll be moving them to Sala De Agua."

Manuel said, "Yes, sir."

The girls opened their eyes, in complete passivity, but underneath the surface they were unhinged and trying to make sense of their predicament.

A few minutes later, Pedro arrived. He picked up Jana's shoulders, and Manuel lifted her feet. They carried Jana down the hallway and into a very large bathroom. In had a ten-by-ten open-air shower with a couple of chairs below and two handheld showerheads protruding from the ceiling. The two men put Jana on a cot and went to retrieve Lydia. They put her on the cot, and Raul motioned for the men to proceed.

Manuel cut and removed Jana's discolored white tank tarnished from the inside of the van. He removed her bra, unhooked the skirt, sliding it down over her hips, and pulled it from her legs. He put her clothes in the drawstring bag with the items from their purses and shoes along with the jewelry.

Jana's head was bobbing up and down in a meager attempt to see what was going on, but she couldn't really move. She was totally naked, and the tan lines circling her hips several inches below her navel drew the attention of the men who admired their latest haul. Her hands remained in front of her, waist high, secured by the zip ties.

While Manuel was undressing Jana, Pedro cut Lydia's dress off with a knife and lifted it up over her head. He unhooked her bra, freeing her ample breasts, and then cut away her blue panties. He tossed her clothes in the bag with the other belongings.

Lydia began to squirm as the three men looked at her. They glanced at each other and smiled, appreciating the two specimens and giving each other high fives.

Raul motioned for the men to move them into the shower. Manuel and Pedro lifted Jana and sat her in one of the chairs. Each chair had Velcro straps at the top to harness the doped-up subjects in a sitting position and keep them from falling. Pedro strapped the

Velcro just below Jana's breasts and tightened the belt. They followed suit with Lydia.

Manuel and Pedro grabbed a handheld showerhead and began washing and scrubbing the girls, spraying the stoutly streaming water over every part of their body. They shampooed their hair, shaved their legs and underarms, and washed their faces.

As they faced each other, the girls' eyes grew wide and realized their plight.

Pedro took the drawstring bag to the garage and laid it on the ground. He slipped on elbow-length gloves and gingerly removed the lid off of a vat, exposing a large volume of sulfuric acid. He carefully lowered the bag with the girls' possessions into the liquid. Within a few minutes, the only remnants left of Jana and Lydia's property was a black goo that swirled around in the bubbling corrosive. Any evidence of the girls' disappearance had now dematerialized.

After the girls were thoroughly cleansed, they were towel-dried and returned to the cots.

Raul said, "Doc, check them out."

"Will do." Juel bent down on one knee and probed Lydia with a flashlight, searching for any signs of disease or infection. He repeated the process with Jana and turned to Raul. "They're clean."

Raul said, "Good, I expected so."

Doc said, "I'll tell you though. It looks like they're both virgins."

Raul said, "You've gotta be kidding?"

Doc said, "No, sir. I don't think these girls have ever had intercourse."

Raul said, "Bingo!

Raul pointed to Jana and said, "Put this one back in Rojo. Put the other in Azul and strap her down. She looks kind of feisty. Doc, are they gonna go anywhere? Are we good?"

Doc said, "No, you're fine. It's okay to proceed."

Raul waved the three men out of the bathroom, and after they left, he shut the door. He took a hot shower and cleaned himself hurriedly. He was anxiously awaiting this moment since the girls arrived. He towel-dried his hair and body, wrapped a luxurious green towel around his waist, and slipped on his sandals. He went back to the Rojo Room and found Jana on the bed.

Jana was staring at the ceiling, conscious but confused and immobilized as Raul walked into the room.

He shut the door behind him, dropped his towel, and walked over to the bed. With horror in her eyes, Jana stared at Raul. His naked body flashed in front of her. She tried to move or talk, but she was totally powerless and didn't budge.

Raul picked up Jana's hands, cut the zip ties with a knife, and pushed her arms over to the side. He cut her ankle restraints, threw the knife on the floor, straddled Jana's hips, and it all began.

Raul was in the bedroom with Jana for more than two hours. His voracious sexual appetite was unparalleled. Raul was a blatant nymphomaniac who could go on indefinitely. The constant stream of new faces and bodies only fueled his obsessive nature, and he could never seem to get enough, especially with the younger ones. Even though these two were older, they were such exemplary subjects, and it excited him to new heights not yet experienced with other women or younger girls. He vigorously assaulted Jana, taking pleasure in being the man to steal her virginity.

Tears streamed down Jana's face as he pleasured himself. The pain was excruciating, but she could do nothing to ease the horror, agony, and guilt of being abused in this fashion. It was apparent to her now that she had been kidnapped and was someone's subject, powerless to defend herself or escape in her drugged condition. She also realized her virginity had been lost forever.

Raul took a long look at Jana, smiled, wrapped the towel around his waist, and left the room. "Pedro, go in and put the ties back on this one and clean her up."

"Will do, boss."

Pedro took more ties into the Rojo Room and secured her ankles and wrists.

Jana's tears were trickling down her cheeks as she cried silently. She was numb and achy, and her body was still anchored in neutral. She was unable to resist, and she flinched when Pedro bent over her. He took a towel and cleaned up the remnants of Raul's onslaught, a job he didn't savor. Her wounds were superficial, and he tended to her affected areas with great care. Pedro had seen so many bodies of young women that this became routine maintenance. It didn't do that much for him like it used to, but he still jumped at the chance when Raul offered up the young ladies for him to enjoy. He didn't like how they were mistreated, but he was afraid to mention anything to Raul. Once he finished cleaning Jana, he pulled a sheet over her, brought it up to her chin, and turned off the lights.

Raul made his way to the Azul bedroom. Three bedrooms in Raul's lair accommodated the cartel members, and three bedrooms were used for the girls, Azul, Blanco, and Rojo, for special occasions.

Lydia saw Raul enter in the corner of her eye and became silently hysterical, but she was unable to move. She quivered and quaked and tried to summon her limbs into use, to no avail.

Raul reached over to her ankles, snipped the tie, and then cut off the wrist cuffs. He moved her hands above her shoulders and planted them next to her head. He proceeded to lie with Lydia and noticed her legs were quivering.

After a few seconds, the shaking subsided, and he threw his towel on the floor next to the bed. He climbed onto Lydia, her eyes screaming in horror, and began attacking Lydia with the same fervor as Jana. Lydia was in much worse physical shape than Jana after he was finished; she really did something for Raul being Hispanic and displaying such a voluptuous figure. She seemed to be more aware of her surroundings, and he could sense reactions driven by fear and feel slight movements underneath. He rose from the bed and directed Pedro who was waiting outside to repeat the cleaning and mending process, which he did.

Raul said, "When you're finished, take her downstairs with the others. I'll send Doc down to take care of her."

"Okay."

Pedro and Manuel picked up Lydia by the shoulders and ankles, and they transported her down the hallway. They men arrived at a secured door, and Manuel pulled a key from his ring and opened the locked and bolted door. He unlatched the sturdy deadbolt, swung the door open, and bent down to pick up Lydia's ankles. The two men slowly carted her down the stairs and brought her to an unoccupied bed in the corner. They dressed her in a scruffy white shift, secured her hands and feet with metal handcuffs, and latched them onto the steel bed frame.

Four other young girls were shackled in their beds. Their heads turned momentarily to look at Pedro and Manuel and then turned back to continue their disinterested slumber.

Pedro and Manuel ascended the stairs and awaited further instructions from Raul. They noticed the door to Rojo was closed, and they heard their boss's audible grunts and groans from inside. He was having another go at Jana.

After half an hour, Raul emerged, draped in his towel, and said, "Hey man, do her over again. She's in need of straightening up."

"Will do, boss."

"I'm finished with her. You can take her downstairs now."

"Okay."

Pedro tended to Jana again. The cuts were more severe this time, and the corners of her lips were bleeding. He cleaned her and medicated her again and called Manuel to come in to help. They grabbed her ankles and shoulders and moved her down the hallway tracing the same steps they had taken with Lydia.

Jana was writhing in pain as they deposited her on an open bed next to Lydia. She was dressed and handcuffed to the bed.

Dr. Juel walked down the stairs with two syringes and proceeded to give each another injection.

They closed their eyes and silently slipped away.

Ten

Saturday, June 8, 8:00 P.M., Phoenix: Missing Twenty Hours

Detectives Sharp and Williams exited their nondescript police vehicle and made their way to the front door of Club Sopanga. They strolled into the bar, which was fairly quiet at that early hour, and showed pictures of Jana and Lydia to the bartender, the manager, a few servers, and some customers. None had seen the two girls, but they were aware of their disappearance because of the signs the two families had posted earlier that day.

Lieutenant Tatum and the Phoenix Police Department issued an Amber Alert, and the girls' information was broadcast nationwide and entered into the National Crime Information Center. The FBI was notified of the strong possibility of a kidnapping, and even though there was no evidence of interstate travel, they offered their assistance if it was needed, including use of their lab and forensics.

Because of the increased activity of international sex trafficking in the US—and the girls being in such close proximity to Mexico—the FBI took a strong interest in the case. They would shadow the PPD at this early stage of the investigation. Arizona, Texas, and California were the three hot spots that led the nation in missing young women suspected of being sex trafficked, and as time went on, their case would show earmarks of such an occurrence.

Before heading out that night, the two detectives checked internal sources to determine which clubs were the most likely places a younger crowd would frequent. Sopanga, Treasure Hunt, and Hotspot were identified as possibilities. The detectives' next stop was Treasure Hunt. Once again, they asked the employees and patrons if they recognized the two girls. Nothing surfaced, and they were coming up empty so far. This type of detective work was largely perfunctory and time-consuming work. It often felt as if they were looking for a drop of water in the ocean. Every once in a while, officers were able to pick up a clue or information that led to an advance in a case, which made the tedious effort essential.

The two men were skeptical of foul play at this early stage, given the girls' age and ability to drive. There were hundreds of documented cases involving young ladies who traveled out of town, enjoyed excessive partying, sleeping off a hangover, or maybe shacking up with friends for a few days. The only fact that affected their skepticism was how disciplined and responsible the parents claimed their daughters were and how unlikely any of those possibilities would apply to Jana and Lydia.

The detectives entered the Hotspot and questioned a few employees, again striking out. On their way to the exit, Sharp questioned a few customers and showed them the photos. As expected, none recognized the two attractive young ladies. As they turned to leave, one of the young men shown the photo threw out the name of a new club called Raining Nails in Central City.

The officers wrote down the name and returned to their car. Raining Nails was only a few blocks away, and they parked outside the front door. It was nearing ten o'clock, and the crowds were starting to filter in. As predicted, the new club was a cauldron of activity, mostly age-qualified teenagers and young professionals. The doorman was a large African American man in his thirties. They diverted his attention from screening the incoming club-goers, pulled him aside, and showed him the photos.

Sharp said, "Good evening. We're with the Phoenix Police Department." Badges flashed quickly. "We're looking for a couple of young ladies who are missing. Do you recognize either of them?"

Taking a long look at each of the girls, the doorman said, "Yeah, man. They were here last night, some really pretty young things. They came in alone. I would say it was about nine."

Williams was surprised they got a hit so early in the search. "Did you see them leave?"

The bouncer said, "I can't say for sure, this is a busy place and it's hard to keep up with everyone coming and going, but this one right here, I think she came out of the bar with a white dude maybe around ten thirty. I'm not real sure … could be someone that looked like her … we get a lot of hot young chicks like this one."

Williams said, "How 'bout the other one with the dark hair?"

The bouncer said, "I definitely remember her, man. No way I'd forget her. She came in with the other one, but I never saw her leave."

After getting a positive ID from the doorman, the two detectives questioned the bartender and several servers.

One of the servers was certain she recognized the girls. "Yes, I remember these two quite clearly. They were sitting in a booth in the corner over there and looked a bit out of sorts, possibly new to the club scene. They were young and had a deer in the headlights gaze. I wouldn't forget those two because the dress the brunette was wearing was way low-cut, and I kid you not, you could almost see her navel. The blonde had long, beautiful legs and a skirt that's hiked all the way up to here, barely covered her privates. I also recall they were by themselves at first, but later were joined by two young men who I served at the table. They were all drinking beer."

Sharp said, "Can you describe the two men with the young ladies?"

"All I can remember is that they were young like the girls, perhaps professionals who worked downtown. I don't remember what they looked like or any details of their appearance. Sorry."

"No, you've been a big help. Thank you so much. If we need to talk with you again, would it be all right if we contact you here? Here's one of my cards if you think of anything further that might be useful.

"Sure."

"And your name is?"

"Samantha, but most people call me Sam."

Williams said, "Thanks, Sam."

The detectives exited the club and handed the bouncer a card, thanked him, and advised him to call should he remember anything that could help them find the missing girls. He agreed and was glad to help.

Eleven

Saturday, June 8, 10:00 p.m., Phoenix: Missing Twenty-Two Hours

The Lincolns and Cantus were at home, on edge and cranky. They hadn't heard a word from anyone at the police department, and no one had called with any information or seen their daughters. The two couples texted each other occasionally to check in and see if any new ideas surfaced.

Around ten thirty, Sylvia Cantu got a call from Lieutenant Tatum at headquarters. He related the information about the two being seen at Raining Nails and being positively identified by the doorman and one of the servers. He was quick to say that there was no further information on their whereabouts, but it was a good start. The department would be issuing a subpoena in the next forty-eight hours to check the credit card receipts and security video with hopes of identifying customers who may have been in contact with Jana and Lydia. They were advised to stay calm and get some rest. They would be in touch the minute anything new was uncovered.

Al and Sylvia stood and hugged; this small morsel of hope buoyed their dispositions momentarily, but reality quickly sunk in. Merely locating their last known whereabouts was far from having their daughters back, and hearing they were with two young men alarmed the couple.

Sylvia immediately called Justine and relayed the information Lieutenant Tatum had provided. Muffled weeping followed over the phone and then a long silence. Both women were sobbing and promised to stay in touch until their cherished daughters were found. They wouldn't stop their efforts until their daughters were home.

Twelve

Sunday, June 9, 10:00 a.m., Nogales

Jana's eyes creased open, and she blinked several times. Everything was cloudy and surreal, and she was unable to focus. After the drug-induced slumber, her brain was foggy. She was trying to make sense of where she was, but nothing clicked. All at once, she felt sharp pains between her legs and then underneath on her haunches. She tried to reach down to feel the area, but her hand jerked to a stop as the handcuffs reined in her movement. She raised her head and became consumed with fright at seeing both wrists shackled by the cold steel cuffs. She thought, *What's going on? Where am I? Why am I here? Why the handcuffs?*

The questions came in rapid-fire succession, and she had no clue how to answer them. She sat up in the bed, still blinking, and tried to focus. At her feet, in another steel-framed bed, Lydia was conked out in a white gown. Several other girls in the same gowns were either sleeping or staring blankly at the ceiling. Jana violently jerked on the restraints, forcing a loud rattling sound, and the other girls looked over and watched her struggle. Jana realized her ankles were tied too. She released a frustrated guttural bark and continued to yank on the cuffs like a caged animal. A young girl from across the room was quick to give her advice.

Beth was from Albuquerque, New Mexico, and the daughter of a well-to-do insurance broker and a schoolteacher. She was kidnapped at the mall when she and her two friends were hanging out after school. Beth went to wash her hands in the restroom, and a female sex trafficker followed her a few steps behind.

Once inside, Beth was approached by Raul's lady and was drugged much the same way Jana and Lydia were. With the help of another abductor she was carried out to a van completely undetected by her two friends or anyone else in the mall. Beth was a spunky cheerleader who was chatty and energetic. She had boatloads of friends and was a good student. In her last year of junior high school, she took an interest in drama and writing for the school paper. With Beth's family's wherewithal, she had a promising future.

After arriving in Nogales, Beth was repeatedly raped and abused in any number of ways and was promptly put on the menu for Raul's customers to enjoy. She had been lost to her family for more than a year, and the search, for all practical purposes, had ended a long time ago. Her parents turned quiet and distanced themselves from social gatherings and seeing friends. They prayed and asked God for guidance to somehow get their daughter back. They felt forgotten and overlooked, but they continued to pray day and night for her safety and for her return. Beth's loss took a terrible toll on the family and shook the lives of good people who only wanted a happy life for their beautiful daughter. This was stolen all for the price of satisfying perverted pedophiles who preyed on helpless children.

Beth said, "Hey, don't knock yourself out. Those chains won't give. You're stuck—just like us. What's your name?"

"Jana."

"Hi, Jana. I'm Beth."

"What am I doing here? Where are we?"

"Hate to tell you this, but you're now a sex slave of the cartel. *El jefe* upstairs is Raul. He's the main man and someone you will learn to hate."

Beth thought, *Boy, these girls are in for a hard time. They're so beautiful. The men upstairs are going to really have at 'em.*

"What do you mean by sex slave?" *I don't want to have sex with anyone. Slave? Oh no, this has to be a dream. What are they going to make us do?*

"You were probably kidnapped by Raul's men and brought here for the sole purpose of performing sex acts for businessmen, important people, and his henchmen."

Another girl stirred and said, "Hi, Jana. I'm Tabitha."

Tabitha came from a middle-class family in Tucson and was another sad story. Her father was an accountant, and her mom stayed at home to watch Tabitha and her two siblings. The young girl was cleaning and tinkering with her bike on the family driveway early one Saturday morning when Raul's infantrymen spotted her as they were cruising the neighborhood. She was clad in a cute little pink bathing suit, and she was fairly well developed for her age, sporting a deep tan from sitting around her parents' pool.

The men stealthily approached and asked Tabitha for directions, and before she could point her hand in the direction of their destination, she was drugged and whisked away in broad daylight. No one saw her taken, and her parents were mystified when they began looking for her. Something was definitely amiss when they found the water still running from the hose, her flip-flops were by her bike, and her cheap cell phone was on the grass with water spraying all over it.

They frantically called the police, and a massive search was undertaken to find precious Tabitha. Since there was very little evidence and no eyewitnesses, the police had nothing to go on. Two long years had passed since her disappearance, and no trace of her whereabouts ever surfaced. Her missing persons file was still open, but it grew colder by the day. Tabitha's wonderful, innocent life was shunted, and she now lived within the soiled underbelly of a diabolical, cartel-trafficking ring only two hours from her home. Tabitha was short for her age, and she had thick, light brown hair and hazel eyes. Freckles dotted her pug nose. She was well liked and had served as a candle bearer at the nearby Catholic church. Unfortunately, her parents divorced under the strain and guilt of her loss and now led miserable, separated lives, blaming each other for losing their daughter.

Tabitha said, "I've been here the longest. What Beth is telling you is true. I know it's hard to believe that we went through the same thing you're going through right now. It's like life's worst nightmare. It's sad to say, but what you see is your new reality." *Glad I'm done with the preliminaries. It's the worst. Hope they can make it through.*

Jana fell back to the bed and began to weep loudly; her genitalia was burning and throbbing, and the crying only made it worse. She groaned, sobbed, wailed, and finally settled into a convulsed whimper. *Ouch, this really hurts. What's wrong with me? What did they do?*

Hearing the sounds of Jana's outburst, Lydia began to rouse. She felt the handcuffs and wrenched her hands wildly tried to free herself. Her head rose, and as she took in her surroundings, she screamed, "Help! Somebody help me!"

Jana said, "Lydia, it's me, Jana. I'm right behind you. We've been kidnapped. We're in Mexico or somewhere."

"What? Where are you, Jana? I can't see you. What are we doing here?" Lydia scanned the room, saw the other girls, and began to freak out. "No, no no. This can't be!"

"Lydia, I'm right here. You can't turn to see me, but I'm right behind you. We were kidnapped and brought here with these other girls. That's Beth over there. She said we were part of a sex-trafficking ring and that we were kidnapped."

Lydia sobbed and slammed her hands on the bed. *This just can't be, kidnapped? By who? Where are we? I want to leave.* "I want to get outta here. Someone get me outta here."

Beth said, "Lydia, no one will be coming for you. You're probably a long way from home, holed up here, God knows where. I've been here for over a year, and Tabitha has been here for two years. Emma and Charlotte just got here last week."

Charlotte said, "Hi. I'm sorry you guys are stuck here with us. This is a hellhole. *That's not the half of it. They're in for some tough days ahead.*

Charlotte was the apple of her mother's eye, and they had the same red hair and sparkling green eyes. Charlotte's dad passed away when she was thirteen and left a void in her life that her mother was unable to fill. Despite this, mother and daughter became the closest of the three children, and her mom spent countless hours with Charlotte since they were kindred spirits and thought so much alike.

Charlotte was in dance and had sculpted legs from the constant practicing, and her short hair was wavy and frizzy. Her friends called her Annie from the cartoon *Orphan Annie*, and she delighted everyone around with her spunk and off-the-wall sense of humor. Her face was covered with freckles, and her skin was as light as a blanket of snow, providing a unique backdrop for her striking emerald eyes.

Charlotte had been waiting for her mom to pick her up after dance class. She was outside talking with several of her friends. One by one, the rides picked them up, and she was left all alone in front.

The instructor was inside working with a student and didn't see the two men kidnap Charlotte. She made a good target, and her skintight black leggings displayed her shapely figure, which was barely covered by a tiny crop top.

As she was stretching out her muscular legs on the doorstep of the studio, several vehicles passed and one of them was a white van. Raul's men eased into the lot and parked behind the building. They left the van and circled back to the front of the studio from two directions. While one man got her attention, the other came up behind her and injected her with the narcotics. She fell limply and was carried away to the van, and they disappeared in the cruel night air, headed from Las Vegas to Nogales.

When her mom finally arrived at the studio, she was nowhere to be found, and after checking with the instructor, they assumed she had gotten a ride home. Mom quickly found out that wasn't the case and immediately contacted the police. She had been gone for a week, and her mother was distraught with guilt that she wasn't there to pick her up on time. She sat up most nights being comforted by her other two daughters, but after they retired, she cried through the darkness all alone and was unable to sleep.

The city rallied behind her mother's efforts to publicize Charlotte's disappearance, and the police actively worked the case with absolutely no clues. Charlotte was Raul's favorite before Jana and Lydia arrived because she was more cooperative and wasn't as abstinent as the others. Her red hair fascinated Raul, and he marveled at the fledgling crop of scarlet fuzz sprouting up between her muscular thighs. Charlotte was simply resigned to her fate and saw no reason to fight it; she just wanted to go home to her mother.

Emma said, "Yeah, hello. I'm Emma, ditto, this isn't a hallucination; it's real unfortunately. *Those poor girls, they're just now figuring this out. I remember how shameful and scary it was when I arrived.*

Emma's case was polar opposite from the others. She came from a broken home, lived with her father, and was unsupervised most of the time. She was allowed to run freely without boundaries. Her dad was an alcoholic and had a violent temper, which he sometimes took out on Emma. She grew up calloused and independent, basically going wherever she pleased and doing whatever she wanted.

A week before Jana and Lydia were kidnapped, she was taken from a park in her San Antonio neighborhood. She was alone on the swing set, smoking a cigarette and kicking her feet to the sky. Emma felt free as long as she wasn't at home and was most comfortable outdoors enjoying the sunshine, just being alone. The day was slowly ebbing away, and two of Raul's ruffians saw her from a distance and swung the van around, slowly parking out of her line of sight. The men quietly approached Emma from behind, caught the swing in midair as her momentum carried her back, and proceeded to drug her while she fought on the gravel underneath. She was subdued quickly and carried to their vehicle unseen, and they promptly drove away.

Emma was slight and undernourished, but she had piercing blue eyes and long dark hair that was tied in a knot behind her head. Her body was the least developed of the group and would more than likely become a pervert's favorite for those who wanted a tender young adolescent in her prepubescent years. Even appearing scrawny, Emma was rowdy and as tough as they came. When she woke up in Nogales and found herself being abused, she fought like a badger, biting and scratching her attackers even through the cloud of narcotics. Since Emma was skinny and undersized, the men who attacked her did significant damage to her immature private areas. It took her days to recover physically. Her dad noticed she didn't come home the night she was taken and cussed her existence, locking the door so she couldn't get in back in. When she never came around, he called the police. The search began, but he never distributed any flyers for his missing child.

Emma was fourteen, Charlotte was fifteen, and Beth and Tabitha were both sixteen. They were all brought to Nogales in the identical fashion that Lydia and Jana were: picked up in random places alone or somewhere they shouldn't have been. The girls were drugged and transported by van to cartel headquarters. Each young girl had been viciously raped, sodomized, and forced into unthinkable sex acts with all ages of men, mostly Mexican nationals who didn't speak any English. The girls' weekly routine evolved into their services being sold on sometimes daily or on an every other day basis so they could refresh and recover between clients. The cartel strongarms sometimes got use of their availability on their "off" days so it was difficult to know what any particular day would hold for the ladies. This rigorous schedule of constant abuse prevented the girls from healing. On top of these challenges, Raul would randomly call up one of the girls to satisfy his appetite, subjecting them to violent and harsh treatment that was much worse than his thugs and certainly worse than their frequent customers.

As Jana wept quietly, Lydia stared at the ceiling, which was just coming into clear view. *Where is this place? It looks like a dungeon. Where do they have us? I'm so scared.* Aged wooden joists crossed the top of the room, exposing the subfloor of the room above. Orbs of tangled spider webs hung in the corners between the sprawling beams attached to the underside of the flooring, harboring unwanted guests that were never disturbed or abused like the girls.

Scoping out the stale dungeon, Jana saw a large room, probably thirty feet long and twenty feet wide. In one corner, Lydia spotted a staircase that led up to a steel metal door, which she assumed was how they had entered the night before. Under the staircase was a heavy-duty double metal door. A hefty padlock hung conspicuously from the bolted entrance.

The other girls were all in restraints on industrial metal beds. Between Emma and Beth, a community toilet was out in the open and obviously hadn't been cleaned recently. Next to the toilet, there was an open-air shower. Its head snaked out of the ceiling, and the hose rested on a nail in the wall. There was a tiny, smudged window at the very top of the far wall where sunlight found an opening to eke its way in. The window was the girls' only source of light, and when darkness fell, the room followed suit and enveloped the ladies in a sea of gloom.

The ceiling was almost twenty feet high, and a ceiling fan in the center moved at a snail's pace, failing to even move the spider webs. The four walls were made of gray cinderblocks rising from the cold, cracked concrete floor to the dingy, worn ceiling. The stench caused by several young girls living together in close proximity, buried in the squalor of the cartel basement, pervaded Lydia and Jana's senses. A thick, sour odor hung in the air, a mixture of urine, perspiration, mold, and Lysol combined to sicken the stomachs of anyone who encountered the conditions.

Beth said, "Lydia and Jana, just so you know, the men usually come down here around ten thirty. They take the cuffs off, and we get to move around the room and use the toilet. Once a week, they'll take us outside to get some sun and exercise if we're able. They'll bring breakfast at that time too—never very good—but you need to eat it regardless of your appetite. We take turns showering, and there's no hot water. Be prepared, and we have a house rule, a maximum of ten minutes on the john. Raul and Alex, who you surely met last night, but may not remember, will put you on a schedule soon. You'll meet and entertain customers, mostly Mexicans, usually well-to-do with lots of money. Their manners aren't necessarily first-rate, and you'll be treated harshly, that's a given. They like Anglos, and that's why we were all brought here. Lydia, you're an exception, but it's understandable why you're here with Jana."

Jana thought, *I don't understand. How are we involved—and what do they want from us?* "Tabitha, what do we do with these customers?"

"You name it, some will want conventional sex, others may prefer something more kinky, and then there's those who are totally off the wall. You can't shirk your duties or give them a bad experience—or Raul will have you beaten within an inch of your life. I know from experience, so you have to give your all and make sure the customers get what they want. Unfortunately, they go overboard sometimes, and in certain cases, it takes days to recover. One thing I'll say though is that Raul doesn't tolerate the clients hitting us, especially in the face. He wants us to look pretty all the time once we leave this room.

Jana thought, *What are we gonna do? I don't want to be with these men. It's not right. I'm only a young girl. Why do they want me to have sex with older people who I don't know? I'm frightened. This shouldn't be happening. I want my mom and dad. Where am I? What Tabitha told us scares me. I don't want to be beaten, but I don't want to have sex either. What other choice do I have? I'm injured, and it hurts so bad down there. What did they do to me? I'm so scared. I don't want anyone taking advantage of me and touching my private areas anymore. That's so gross. I've had boyfriends, and we've made out a lot—I've even let them feel around—but nothing like this. I wanted to be a virgin for my husband, and now I've lost that. There was nothing I could do. Oh no. If they make me do more of these things, I'll just die. I just can't do it. If I don't do what they say, it may mean serious trouble for me. Raul may have one of those awful men hurt me. I'm so ashamed. I feel worthless and dirty. No one's gonna want me after I've been here. It's ruined my life. I wish we never stepped foot in that Raining Nails. Look where it's gotten us.*

If we would have only stayed at home last night, I'd be in my bed relaxing rather than bleeding down there and feeling like a tramp.

Tabitha said, "They have a room upstairs where we get dressed and put on our makeup, and they check us out before we're sent to our meetings."

Lydia sobbed loudly and tossed back and forth on her bed. *No, no, this can't be. I need to get out of this place. I can't do that sort of thing.*

Jana cried aloud and closed her eyes, wishing it would all go away.

Lydia's fears were justified. *Oh my God. What have we gotten into? This can't be happening. It's all a terrible dream. I want to wake up and be home. What are Mom and Dad gonna think after they hear what we've had to do? It's shameful and dirty. What are we supposed to do with these men? I don't know the first thing about pleasing an older adult. What they're doing is sick. I can't believe grown men would treat young teenagers like this. Why don't they want older women? We're just immature minors. If what Tabitha says is true, Jana and I may have to do these horrible things to avoid a serious beating. I don't know which is worse. I don't have the slightest idea what to do. How am I supposed to please these totally random men when I've never had sex with anyone? Now that I'm no longer a virgin, what are my parents and future boyfriends going to think of me? I'm no better than trash now. I just want to go home. I miss Mama and Dad so bad. I wish we could talk right now. They could tell me what to do.*

Emma said, "Did Raul have his way with you both last night? You may not remember much, but if you're real sore down there, you'll know the reason why. He can be very rough; the guy is an animal. He can go on all night long."

Jana said, "Oh no. I'm really hurting bad below. I do remember brief flashes of being with him last night. It's coming back to me now. Boo-hoo." *What did they do to me? I can barely move anything from my waist down. Ow, it stings. Ow, ow, ow. It hurts so bad. All this is so hazy.*

I sorta remember someone breathing in my face. He was heavy on top of me, and it began hurting between my legs.

Lydia said, "Me too. I'm rubbed raw and numb below my waist. I'm really hurting. Raul did this? I kinda remember this man on top of me, but I was all drugged up. I couldn't function or even attempt to make him stop."

Beth said, "Yeah, you probably met the doctor too. He's the dude who will give you your injections."

Lydia said, "Injections?"

Beth said, "Yep, they occasionally load us up, depending on our schedule, so we'll be less disagreeable. I've found it's better to go along with the program than be so doped up all the time. The doc meets with Raul, and they decide who gets how much, which depends on how cooperative we are."

Tabitha said, "I hate to be the person to tell you, but last night was the preliminaries. His gorillas are given free rein on the newbies whenever they first arrive as sort of a bonus for bringing in new faces. Raul takes his turn first, and then the second night, he lets his pigs have sloppy seconds. Just so you know, and you'll be ready mentally, they'll be coming down for you tonight—and you can expect a long evening.

Lydia said, "Oh God. I can't be here. I can't do this. Someone please help me." *My backside hurts and front too. They raped me hard. This is the worst pain I've ever had.*

Jana squealed in pain and bawled out loud, emptying any tears she had left inside.

The door at the top of the stairs was unbolted and opened, releasing the door to swing out.

Jana and Lydia flopped against the cuffs and were trembling and shuddering as they watched the two men start down the stairs. Pedro carried a large metal tray filled with a plastic bowl of scrambled eggs, a few slices of white bread, and some stale water in a plastic thermos. Dr. Juel was carrying a bag with the girls' solutions and mixtures.

An armed guard stood at the top of the stairs in case he was needed.

Pedro set the tray on the floor and went over to uncuff Tabitha, Emma, Charlotte, and Beth. They sat up and rubbed their wrists, feeling the first minute of freedom from the chains since the night before. They took turns going to the restroom and filled their plates with eggs and bread.

Jana said, "What about us? Let us out of these things."

Lydia said, "Yeah, let us loose, please."

Pedro didn't respond or even act like he had heard them. After a while, he unlocked Jana's cuffs from the bed, refastened one side, and put the open strand around her other wrist. He removed the ankle restraints and helped Jana up from the bed. Pedro walked her over to the toilet, shooed Tabitha away, and sat her down.

When Jana finished, she was escorted back to her bed, twisting and fighting all the way. Pedro struggled to keep her in check, but in her post-drug condition, she wasn't able to muster enough energy to challenge his strength. He lay her back down on the bed and cuffed her to the railing. He picked up a paper plate, shoveled on some eggs and a piece of bread, and walked it over to Jana as she flailed around in a delirium. He forked up some eggs and put it to her lips, but she spat it away. He tried again with the same result.

Beth said, "Jana, you gotta eat, girl. For your own good, take it. You'll need it to get through tonight."

Pedro tried to force it into her mouth, but she spat it back at him. He nonchalantly walked over to Lydia and offered to feed her Jana's food. Lydia opened her mouth slightly, and Pedro spooned in bites of egg and let her nibble on a piece of the bread. Lydia did what Beth suggested and finished the whole plate and then drank some water.

Lydia said, "Jana, you've got to eat. You'll get sick if you don't. Please ... for me?"

Jana remained quietly defiant. Pedro spooned up another plate of eggs and gave Jana a last run at eating. She held her lips firmly pursed, and when he tried to force it in, she spat it away again. Pedro dumped her food back in the bowl.

The doctor walked over to Jana, pulled some bottles from his bag, and conjured up a mixture for the ferocious teenager. She was hysterical, knowing what laid ahead, and she wanted to stay clear-headed. The drugs given to her the night before had frightened her, and she didn't want to repeat the feeling.

Pedro walked up behind Juel and held Jana to keep her from wiggling.

The doctor stuck the needle into her arm and released the narcotics into her pristine system. Within moments, she was motionless. Her eyes showed no emotion or movement.

Lydia was bouncing around on her bed, fighting the restraints, and yanking at the handcuffs.

Pedro looked over to Juel and said, "Remember the boss said he wanted this one less drugged."

Juel said, "Yeah, I got it. This is a watered-down version of what I gave the other one. Should be just about right for his purposes."

Lydia flopped to and fro, fighting her bonds and tearing the skin on her wrists and ankles.

"You better hurry, Doc."

Pedro put his full weight on Lydia's upper body so she couldn't move.

The doctor jabbed her with the syringe, pushed in the plunger, and released the purple serum into her bloodstream. Lydia calmed down immediately and stopped moving, but her eyes remained open.

Thirteen

Sunday, June 9, Noon, Phoenix: Missing Thirty-Six Hours

Justine and Tom were sitting at the dinner table and waited. Waiting is a powerful enemy; you can't touch it, move it along, trick it, steal it, or ignore it. It's right there in your face and rests comfortably, biding its time until an event happens that erases the plunderer from your life. They were sleep-deprived, malnourished, and agonized over the disappearance of their only daughter. Jana was their entire world, and the Lincolns had spent seventeen years grooming her for a life of her own. She had so much potential to succeed.

They reflected on the daughter they'd raised and how special she was. Jana epitomized the definition of competitive. If you were walking with her to the store, she'd sprint the last twenty yards to beat you to the door. She'd employ all of her resources to win at cards, ping-pong, or playing horse around the hoop in the backyard. If she couldn't beat you with straight-up skill, she'd rely on cunning, tactical maneuvers, psychological warfare, or just plain outworking her opponents. Jana's teachers declared that she was the most competitive person they'd ever met, and it didn't matter if it was the grade she earned or whether it was being first to give a presentation, she wanted to be number one.

It was no surprise that she was a 4.0 student and would be upset whenever she got a grade less than 100 percent. Jana did all this in a good-natured way where you admired and respected her effort. She never bragged or boasted and would help others achieve their goals by coaching, encouraging, or walking alongside them. She offered advice and insight to her friends and even those who were not. Jana was outgoing and gregarious and had never met anyone she couldn't eventually win over, if not a friendship, an appreciation.

Her sporting activities fed her full-tilt metabolism, creating a whirling dervish. She was someone who never found a dull moment. She liked and insisted being on the move and always doing something fun or challenging. Jana's sense of humor was dry and quick. If you were not paying attention, you'd miss her one-liners that flashed by you at sonic speed.

Jana's piercing blue eyes were positioned close together, and if you looked her in the eyes, it was as if you were standing in front of a jet taking off through a tunnel right at you. Her squared-off chin exuded confidence and power, but it was counterbalanced by the girlishly cute dimples that highlighted the edges of her lips. Dusty yellow eyebrows accentuated the light blue orbs that captivated anyone who caught her gaze.

You would think a young lady blessed with so many talents and desirable features would be deemed close to perfection, but Jana had her own vices and ghosts that plagued her every day. Her drive to succeed constantly led her to being afraid and worried that she would fail, and there was always a silent demon nipping at her feet and trying to trip her up. She succeeded many times because she ran from that very fear.

Jana's spontaneity and impulsiveness constantly put her in situations that required her to backtrack, rejigger, or reconstruct her actions. Many times, this caused her frustration, jumping into something before planning it out in advance. Her height and physical presence often intimidated those around her, including young men, and there were times when they were hesitant to approach Jana thinking she was far beyond their pay grade.

Being an only child, Jana was pampered and showered with constant attention, which at times was frustrating, and she'd seek shelter by hibernating in her room. Jana liked her alone time in her bedroom and would seek the quietness of a retreat away from outside distractions that attacked her conscience. Her room was appointed with women sports heroes, and larger-than-life posters gave her inspiration that conflicted with the daintily pink-painted room from her early childhood years. Her bedroom was an enigma of girlish femininity juxtaposed with signs of a young girl transitioning from a child to a mature young woman. Jana was the air her parents breathed, the water they drank, and the ground they walked. Jana was everything to Justine and Tom.

The lack of police activity was frustrating. To Jana's parents it didn't seem like things were moving fast enough. They were losing precious time, and they realized the more time that passed after a disappearance, the more recovery possibilities declined precipitously. The late opening of clubs cost them precious hours, and it was now the weekend, which only delayed legal proceedings to obtain the books from the club. Now a day and a half after the girls' abduction, it was evident that something was seriously wrong—and they were fearful of ever being able to see their astonishing daughters alive.

The couple tried to stay optimistic with each other, at least on the facade, but inside, the frightful reality of Jana never being returned haunted them every second of the day. Tom called his manager of the accounting firm and told him what had happened, and as of Monday, he was taking a leave of absence. Justine called all their relatives and many of their friends, announcing the girls' disappearance and asking for prayers and support. Naturally, any information that her friends could provide to help the case would always be appreciated, and they asked for this humbly.

The news traveled fast among their acquaintances, and word spread to many families across the Phoenix area. Jana's and Lydia's purported abduction had become headlines. The local and regional media were now involved and asked to interview the two sets of parents the next week. The four wanted to broadcast their plight liberally and sought national attention for the girls' disappearance. Tom and Justine resorted to prayer nearly on the hour. They were churchgoers and actively participated in the life of the congregation, as did Jana, each Sunday. The Lincolns firmly believed in prayer and had seen it change the lives of so many members of their congregation. At noon, they closed their eyes, hoping their appeal would be heard so they held hands and said a prayer.

"Dear Lord, please keep our daughter from harm, we fear for her safety and ask you for your shield of grace to protect her from evil. Please give us the strength to stay the course and do everything in our power to find Jana and bring her back to us. Please also look over Lydia and bring her back to Sylvia and Art unharmed. We pray these words in your name, Jesus Christ, Amen."

In their bed, Sylvia and Art stared blankly at a photo of Lydia and wept quietly. Their outstanding daughter who excelled in everything was swallowed up in a mysterious void that couldn't be defined, explained, or rationalized. Not knowing Lydia's fate kept their feelings in limbo. Most of the time, they found themselves captured in the depths of depression. A stroke of hope would yank them out of the doldrums, breaking through the surface of despair and elevating their spirts.

The Cantus were dragging bottom. The lack of information and updates from Lieutenant Tatum dulled their expectations for finding the girls, and their inability to do anything about it or help the police with the process discouraged them greatly. The hope they clung to was Lydia's unique ability to resolve problems. She had an uncanny gift of logic and reason. Her pragmatic approach to facing dilemmas set her apart from her peers. Lydia would face obstacles head-on, disassemble the issues one by one in her mind, and act promptly and wisely to resolve the challenge. The Cantus knew that Lydia was being sorely tested, and these instinctive qualities were probably at work. They prayed often, sincerely asking God to deliver their oldest child back to the fold unharmed and to look over and protect Jana until her safe return.

Lydia was as sensitive as she was strong. She was very sentimental and family oriented, cherishing her time with her mom and dad as well as her siblings. She and her younger siblings would hang out together and share all of their daily activities. Whether it was the ups and downs, the surprises, or the disappointments, they faced them as a family united. Her baby brother would sleep with her when heavy storms rolled in. When he was too scared to sleep by himself, they'd snuggle until he fell asleep. The three kids talked every night before retiring and were as close as brothers and sisters could be.

Lydia's mom was her idol, and she worshipped her very essence by going with her shopping or having late-night discussions about the challenges of growing up. She emulated her mother and had the same facial expressions, and you couldn't tell who was laughing when the two were together because they sounded so much alike. Whenever she had a tough day, she'd make a beeline to her mom for wise counsel.

Lydia had her father tightly wrapped around her finger, and he would sail to the moon for her—no questions asked. He protected her with strong parental guidance, and she respected her Dad for his sage wisdom. It would break Lydia's heart whenever he got mad at her, and she'd do anything to get back into his good graces. Her parents were everything to her.

Lydia attracted the opposite sex like flies on a watermelon. Her curvy figure and facial features melted the young boys into putty when they watched her walk down the halls at school. She was the perfect physical package wrapped in a tightly drawn frame. Her small ears were hidden by her thick black mane, silhouetting her perfectly copper skin and perfect pearly white teeth. Her smile could melt an iceberg, and her frown could bring tears. She was the most popular girl in the school and had more friends than the desert had sand. Everyone liked Lydia; she was smart, funny, and carried herself like a champion.

The Cantus communicated the girls' disappearance to family and friends, asking for support, information, and prayers. Sylvia undertook the task of coordinating the work they were doing with the media and spreading the word to all corners of Arizona and beyond so that whoever took Sylvia and Jana would know they were being sought.

A buzz on Sylvia's phone startled her to attention. Lieutenant Tatum texted the Lincolns and Cantus.

T: We're still chasing down leads from Raining Nails. So far, nothing to report, but we're working on a number of things. Should have subpoena tomorrow to get credit card receipts and make a list of names. The team here will try to contact everyone on the list. Will be in touch if anything turns up.

The two couples had a collective sigh. Dismal thoughts pervaded their consciousness. *Nothing new—again. We're losing too much time!*

Fourteen

Sunday, June 9, Noon, Nogales

Raul didn't rise until noon. He read the news online, checked his voice mails, and answered several texts to his cartel minions who were coordinating their next shipment of drugs, which were mostly cocaine and meth on its way to Nogales. He slowly got out of bed, showered, and dressed for the day. Memories of his foray with the two newcomers the day before were fresh on his mind, and thinking about the two, he began to get aroused. He exited the master bedroom and walked into the kitchen, grabbing an apple and a banana. Pedro brought him a plate of eggs with bacon and Mexican-style potatoes. He sat in the large breakfast area with his compatriots as they drank coffee and checked their cell phones. Raul inhaled his eggs and finished off his bacon and potatoes, and then he washed it down with a large glass of orange juice. He chomped into the apple, ate about half, and then wiped his mouth with a cloth napkin. "Okay, gents, here's the plan for today."

The men were anxiously awaiting this discussion to see who would be allowed to be with the new girls.

Raul enjoyed holding them in suspense, and he purposely built their expectations and flamed their pent-up appetite for pleasure. Alex, Pedro, Manuel, Juel, and Jorge were looking at each other with anticipation, trying to appear unemotional. Alex was second-in-command, and it was always expected that he would be first up. The others were silently competing in the remaining lineup. Juel typically bowed out, he was nearly sixty now, and he didn't seek the pleasures he once did.

Raul said, "The new girls, Jana and Lydia, are downstairs, and doc has them in la-la land, so they should be ready for us. Only one thing though—there's something about the Latino I really like and want her for myself tonight. Sorry. That leaves the four of you with the other one. Alex, you go first, and then Manuel, Pedro, and Jorge, you bring up the rear."

They all laughed at the reference to rear, and then a noticeable disappointment surfaced among the men who were looking forward to spending time with the young, voluptuous Mexican American girl. *Maybe another time,* they reasoned.

Raul said, "Pedro, you and Jorge go get Jana and put her in Azul. Alex, you and Manuel can bring Lydia up and put her in Rojo."

The men headed to the bolted door, descended to the basement, and looked at the girls. Beth was sitting peacefully on her bed, Charlotte was walking around the room, and Emma and Tabitha were talking on Emma's bed.

Pedro unlocked Jana's hands and feet, Jorge grabbed her legs, and Pedro grabbed her arms. They carried Jana upstairs and put her in Azul. She was completely underwater, barely conscious, and was only able to make slight movements. Her eyes snapped open halfway, and even though she was heavily sedated, a noticeable fright was trying to surface.

Alex and Manuel deposited Lydia in the Rojo Room, which was reserved for good customers and special occasions. Lydia was much more alert, and her body had some movement. Her eyes were gaping wide, and the white surrounding her tiny pupils broadcasted her fear and trepidation.

He shut the door behind him. He disrobed quickly and mounted Jana, not wasting any time getting started. Alex recalled the image of how hot Jana was in the back of Jeff's car with her skirt lifted to her waist. Watching the young man ripping off her panties had left him inflamed and kindled his thirst to have this classy Anglo chick. The moment had finally arrived for Alex. Now she was all his. He spent over an hour with Jana, and even though she was limp, he was able to enjoy himself throughout. He finished, got dressed, and walked out with a big smile on his face.

Manuel was waiting at the door; listening to Alex working on Jana had made him eager for his turn. Manuel removed his clothes and attacked Jana, hitting her callously with bottled-up, animalistic fervor. After his hour came and went, Jana was bleeding and virtually unconscious. She was only able to mumble indiscernible groans and was physically immobile.

Pedro was waiting in the den and got up when he saw Manuel departing and zipping up his pants. Pedro knew about her injuries from the previous night and was much easier on Jana than the others. He gently went about his business and left her sprawled across the bed, her head on one side and her eyes closed.

Jorge bounded in the room after Pedro left, undressed, hopped on the bed, and spent more than an hour with the prized white girl from Phoenix. The classy seventeen-year-old was now a mangled, disgraced, near cadaver of a woman. How lives can be turned upside down in such a short time.

After Jorge finished, Pedro once again did his duty. This time, it was a more difficult job since Jana hadn't healed from the night before. She was bleeding worse and in need of suturing so Doc gave her three stitches. Once cleaned and stitched, Pedro and Jorge took her back downstairs, put on her gown, lay her on the bed, and put on the cuffs.

Raul was with Lydia in the Rojo Room. He removed her smock, undressed himself, and crawled on top of Lydia, looking in her eyes. She stared back at him and didn't seem to have the fear that Raul was accustomed to seeing from the new girls they brought in. *She's just lucid enough,* he thought. *She's able to feel and respond, which is the goal.* He looked at her lips, and they mouthed something quietly. It was as if she was trying to communicate with him. He bent down and put his ear to her mouth and heard her saying lightly, "Be gentle … please be gentle … please be gentle."

Oh, I hope he goes easy on me, I can't take much of this.

Raul stopped suddenly, looked at her quizzically, and pondered her plea.

Lydia moved her arms closer to him and tried to embrace him. She repeated, "Please be gentle … please … please … please." *He's thinking about it. Oh, I hope he will.*

Raul knew she was pretty torn up yesterday, and hearing her plea—plus the physical touching—did something to him he hadn't felt before. It was unique and mysterious. So, he proceeded to have his time with Lydia, but he complied with her request and took it slowly and more gently.

Lydia closed her eyes and didn't struggle. It may have been Raul's imagination, but it seemed like the young Latino was actually trying to respond to what he was doing. After nearly two hours with this stunning young lady, Raul finally concluded his physical violation and got dressed.

She stared up directly at Raul.

The hint of a smile breaking on her lips surprised Raul. He instinctively bent over and kissed her on the lips.

She whispered, "Next time, show me … show me how."

Fifteen

Monday, June 10, 10:00 a.m., Phoenix: Missing Two Days Ten Hours

Phoenix Missing Persons obtained a subpoena to collect Raining Nail's credit card records for Friday night and early Saturday morning. When collected later in the day, there were more than one hundred receipts, and the team working with Sharp and Williams began to form a spreadsheet with names, amounts, and times of purchase. Since cards were typically closed out when patrons depart, they subtracted an average of three hours from the time of the charge to come up with a probable arrival time at the bar.

The list was disseminated among a group of four administrative employees to begin the process of locating the contact information for each. They called the credit card companies, checked internet sources, and queried all the department's central data bases for information. By three o'clock, they had 75 percent of the information they were seeking for the patrons. Two staff members continued the search for the remaining 25 percent, and the other two began making calls to the customers who were at Raining Nails that night. The security camera footage was obtained, and an operator scoured through seven hours of film, searching for the two missing girls. The camera was a good distance from the area described by the server, and it was tedious working with magnification software to target the booth in question. Lieutenant Tatum communicated these updates to the families, which gave them a renewed sense of hope.

Sixteen

Monday, June 10, 5:00 p.m., Phoenix: Missing Two Days Seventeen Hours

When the results of the analysis from the film operator came in, they located a grainy image of the two girls sitting in booth 12 at 9:29 p.m. They captured an image, although dusky, of the two girls sitting with two young men at 10:12 p.m. A thorough examination of the footage told the police that the two males in question were Anglo and approximately twenty-two to twenty-five years of age. They logged descriptions of their facial features, type and length of hair, what they were wearing, and body type.

The credit card spreadsheet was close to being finished, and the department team had reached a good number of the Raining Nails customers at the bar that night. So far, none of the people knew anything or remembered the girls. Once they had ascertained that there were two young males involved, they chose to eliminate female card charges. Another update was passed on to the Lincolns and the Cantus.

Seventeen

Monday, June 10, 7:00 p.m., Nogales

Emma and Beth were scheduled for customers at nine. Raul typically chose to use the bedrooms reserved at his headquarters for this activity and arranged the appointments for two wealthy Mexican nationals who met their criteria of price, house rules, and confidentiality. Beth was the more experienced of the two, and even though she abhorred what she did, the young lady carried out her duties flawlessly. A beating from Raul the first week she arrived had convinced her it was easier to go along with his wishes rather than buck the system. She refused to carry out her duties on her very first customer encounter, and the client complained and wanted his money back. Raul had Beth beaten with a stick on every inch of her body below the neck, and she couldn't walk for days. Beth was out of commission for over a week, but she learned an important lesson that night and eagerly shared it with all newcomers.

Emma was still shellshocked, having been in Nogales for only a little over a week, and she was still learning the ropes. Taking Beth's hard-learned advice, she complied with all customer requests and made sure they left satisfied. She was terrified of Raul, and after meeting her clients, she would return to her quarters and weep long into the night.

Raul's plan for the evening was to have Jana accompany Beth to meet with her customer. Beth was to be the primary "date," and Jana was to watch, learn, and participate if summoned. Since Jana was still recovering from the onslaught the night before, Raul gave her a pass on bodily contact, but he advised her that the customer may have other requests that she would be expected to comply with.

The girls were brought upstairs to the Sala De Agua, and they took a hot shower, shaved, put on makeup and jewelry, and were outfitted in suggestive attire. Jana was given a negligee. They spent the time preparing Jana for what was ahead and what she was supposed to do. Jana's legs trembled, and her pain below was excruciating. To be thrown into an appointment like this so soon after her encounter with the four men the day before kept her misty, and she had to reapply makeup twice. For the first night since she arrived, Jana wasn't given her dosage of drugs. She was clearheaded, and this only heightened her dread and fear.

Eighteen

Monday, June 10, 9:00 p.m., Nogales

The customers arrived promptly; one was directed to Rojo, and the other was directed to Blanco. Emma was led to the Rojo Room, introductions were made, and the door was closed. Jana and Beth were escorted to Blanco, and as they walked, Jana quivered all over. Her hands were visibly shaking.

Manuel had a tight grip on her arm, signaling she had better cooperate tonight or else, and he deposited the girls inside and stood at the doorway. Manuel spoke to the man in Spanish, telling him that Jana was a "trainee" and was there to watch, and if desired, she was available to participate.

Beth whispered to Jana to watch her and do what she did. "I'll get started with the customer, and you can partake if called upon."

The man undressed, climbed on the bed, put his hands behind

his neck, and looked at the beautiful young girls before him. He was extremely pleased to hear there would be two ladies for the price of one, and he waited with anticipation.

Beth undressed, approached the bed, and began pleasuring her customer. She'd look over at Jana from time to time as if to say, *See? This is how it's done.*

Jana covered her mouth, tears began to fall involuntarily, and her knees became weak. Jana was praying that it would be over soon and that she wouldn't be needed.

Beth proceeded until the man rolled away and motioned Jana over to the bed.

Jana froze momentarily and then slowly approached, full of dread. The young teenager wasn't sure she could do what was being asked of her, but she remembered Beth's warning about the beating she would receive if she didn't.

As Jana reached the bed, the man motioned for Jana to undress. Hands shaking, she took off her negligee, exposing her body as fear and alarm filled her countenance. The man's eyes lit up seeing Jana's body, and he patted the sheet next to him.

Jana was repulsed, but she complied out of fear, holding her nose and repeating the performance that Beth had showed her earlier. Afterward, Jana rose from the bed, held her hand over her mouth, gagged, and nearly threw up. She caught herself, put her clothes back on, and sat in the corner, quietly crying. *Ugh, oh my God. That was so gross. I can't believe I had to do that. Get me out of here. I'm gonna throw up. I don't understand how Beth can do that sort of thing and not get sick. I hate myself for doing that to him.*

Beth was continuing her routine with the client and worked relentlessly until he was exhausted. Beth tried her best to wear him out to protect Jana from having to join in again.

Jana watched from the corner and witnessed how Beth went about her business, and she had the feeling that she'd probably be needing those skills soon. After returning to her bed in the basement, Jana cried quietly. *Oh, Mom and Dad, I just want to go home. I miss you so much and pray that I can escape this nightmare and find my way back. I think about my room and the pink blanket on the bed. My soccer, listening to my music, and doodling on my sketch pad. I miss my kitty, Whiskers, sitting around the table with you guys, eating dinner, and talking about the day. Please, Mom and Dad, hurry up and find me before I go crazy. I love you.*

Nineteen

Monday, June 10, 10:00 P.M., Phoenix: Missing Two Days Twenty-Two Hours

Justine got a call from an unknown number. She jumped to her phone with anticipation, looked at the number, and lack of caller ID. Frightened, she put it to her ear. "Hello, this is Justine Lincoln."

"Yes, hi, Mrs. Lincoln … …"

"Yes, who is it?"

"Mrs. Lincoln … uh … my name is … uh … Jeff Bridgestone."

"Yes, yes?"

"I saw your notice on the bulletin board at Raining Nails … that Jana and Lydia are missing."

"Yes?"

"Well, I was with Jana for a little while Friday night."

"You saw her? Where were you?"

Tom bent his ear close to the phone and listened in. "We were at the club. My friend Ian and I met Jana and Lydia. We sat with them in a corner booth."

"What happened? Did they leave? Did you go somewhere with them?"

"No … uh, I mean, yes. Well, first I'd like to say I'm sorry."

"For what? Tell me what are you sorry for?"

"Well, Jana and I got along really well, and I asked her to go outside with me to smoke a joint."

"What?"

"Again, I'm really sorry. It was nighttime. We were all having a great time … had a lot to drink … we were all feeling pretty good."

"You must be mistaken. My daughter doesn't drink or smoke marijuana."

"Yes, I know. She said she'd never tried weed, but she decided to when I offered her some."

"Argh … go on."

"Lydia left us to be with my friend Ian, and they went over to his car and lit up a joint, standing in a dark area away from the club. Jana and I got into my car, and we smoked one too."

"Yes, yes, what then?"

"Well, Mrs. Lincoln, I feel really bad about this … and I hope you'll forgive me."

"What? Tell me … what … what?"

"Jana and I were pretty high and had a lot to drink. We started making out in my back seat, and I admit, I got a little carried away with your daughter. She is very beautiful. One thing led to another, you know, and I got overly aggressive and … well, I … tried to have sex with your daughter."

"You did what? How dare you! What do you mean *tried*?"

"Well, apparently I was moving too fast. Jana tried to stop me and opened the car to get out. I was reaching for her, and all of a sudden, I was hit over the head with a beer bottle, knocking me unconscious."

"Oh my God. Yes, yes, then what?"

"I don't remember much after that except that there was someone who came up to help her get out of the car … the man who hit me. The only thing I recall is that he was dressed in black … everything was black."

"Did you see her after she left the car?"

"No, not really, well, maybe."

"What do you mean?"

"I was hurting pretty bad and not seeing very well, but as I was comin' around, I looked up trying to make sense of what was going on. I noticed two men in the parking lot loading a girl into a van. She was out cold. I'm not 100 percent sure it was Jana, but it could have been."

"Are you able to describe the van?"

"No, not exactly, it was a full-size white van. That's about it. Mrs. Lincoln, I hesitated to call you, afraid that I would be implicated somehow in their disappearance, but I wanted you and Lydia's parents to know that my friends and I had nothing to do with them being taken. I was just trying to have a good time and got carried away, like I said, but I would never kidnap or abduct someone."

"Mr. Bridgestone, we'll forgive you for your advances on Jana … sounds like she was able to take care of herself. This information is extremely important, and we plan to give the police your contact information so they can question you, agreeable?

"Yes, Mrs. Bridgestone. I don't want any trouble, and I don't want this affecting my job or future, so I'll help in any way."

"Lieutenant Tatum at PPD will be calling, and you should be

familiar with the names of Detectives Sharp and Williams who are actively involved in the case. Thank you so much for stepping forward. This may lead to getting our daughters back, which is all that matters right now. Jeff, be assured we'll keep this confidential, and you should be okay with your job."

"Thanks, Mrs. Lincoln. I'll be ready to talk to the police any time they want."

"Thank you, Jeff. Please text me your information after we hang up."

"Okay, will do."

Moments later, Justine received a text with Jeff's and Ian's information.

Jeff called Ian to let him know that he'd talked to Mrs. Lincoln, and he was relieved that they were able to help in some small way. Ian volunteered to verify his story and talk to the police if needed.

As soon as she hung up, she called Sylvia and Art to relay Jeff's message. What Jeff related couldn't have come at a better time. A ray of hope broke through the dark clouds.

Justine dialed up Lieutenant Tatum and passed on all the information that Jeff had disclosed—along with his and Ian's contact info.

Tatum called Jeff and arranged a time for them to meet on Tuesday. Jeff was cooperative and wanted to do anything possible to help the case, and Tatum made the arrangements. Ian and Jeff agreed to go to the station together to give their statements.

Twenty

Tuesday, June 11, 10:00 a.m. Phoenix: Missing Three Days Ten Hours

The two young men arrived at police headquarters at the appointed time, and Lieutenant Tatum was summoned to the front desk. Detectives Sharp and Williams were already in the conference room when they arrived, and Tatum escorted the men to the meeting.

Jeff and Ian sat across the table from the two detectives, and Tatum sat at the head. Jeff started recounting the events exactly as he had described them to Mrs. Lincoln.

Tatum said, "Jeff, I can't say that your aggressive actions against Miss Lincoln will be overlooked by the law, especially since she's underage, but that will be up to the victim whenever we get a chance to talk with her. Furthermore, we don't condone the use of illegal narcotics, especially with a minor."

Jeff said, "Sir, I didn't know she was underage. She was in the bar, so I figured—"

Interrupting Jeff, Tatum said, "Fortunately for you, we're not here to discuss any of your actions prior to the girls' disappearance. So, let me ask you this. When Miss Lincoln was leaving your vehicle, did you see the man who approached the car and assaulted you?"

Jeff said, "No, sir, not really, all I can remember since I was knocked unconscious was that it *was* a man, and he was dressed in black. The rest is a blur."

Williams said, "Mr. Smith, let's hear your story."

Ian said, "Okay, Jana's friend, Lydia, and I walked over to my car, and we're smoking a joint outside my Camaro. We had a pretty good view of Jeff's car, and we watched the two of them smoke their weed and then began making out in the back seat. I could tell Lydia was a bit embarrassed and uncomfortable when they dropped out of sight behind the seats. I guess they were laying down. A few minutes later, I looked up and saw Jana struggling to get out of Jeff's car when this man came up with what looked like a beer bottle, and he whopped Jeff over the head. This part was pretty clear since the interior lights had come on when Jana opened the door, and I could see all of this goin' on. My view was partially blocked since Jana was between me and the man, but I could tell he was about her height and was wearing a black, kind of a western shirt with button snaps. He had dark hair, slicked back, and may have been Hispanic, I'm not totally sure. I wanted to go back inside and frankly get away from the ugly scene and left Lydia who ran over to Jana. The last thing I saw was Jana and Lydia hugging and the man in black standing nearby. Not sure what happened after that. Jeff came in later and explained what took place and how he was attacked."

Sharp said, "Do you remember any distinctive features of the man: tattoos, jewelry, facial hair?"

Ian said, "Not too much. I think he had a thin mustache though, and I seem to recall he was wearing boots, nice ones."

Sharp said, "What color were the boots?"

Ian said, "Hard to tell, but I think they were black."

Williams said, "Was there anyone with him at the time?"

Ian said, "No."

Williams said, "Did you hear the man speak?"

Ian said, "No, he didn't say anything that I heard."

Tatum said, "Did you see a white van in the parking lot?"

Ian said, "No, I didn't."

Tatum said, "Gentlemen, I guess that's all for now. We appreciate you giving us your statements. It's a tremendous help with the case, and we may be back in touch if we think of any other questions."

Jeff said, "We hope you find Jana and Lydia. They were nice girls, and we hate to know they may have been abducted."

Tatum said, "Thank you, Jeff and Ian. We'll be in touch. Let's kick the weed, huh?"

Jeff said, "Okay, Lieutenant Tatum."

After hearing Jeff's account about what happened that night, the task force redirected their attention to outside the bar. As part of the subpoena, they obtained the footage from the security camera in the parking lot. The administrative team closely examined the video and saw partial images of Jeff's car in the distance, but the figures standing outside the car were blurry and didn't reveal much. However, they did get an image of the two girls walking back to the front entrance at 10:58 p.m. They were being helped by the man described by Ian and Jeff. He was dressed in all dark clothing and was about Jana's height. He appeared to be Hispanic. The camera caught them walking between cars toward the entrance, but it lost sight of them as they neared. Another man briefly came into the picture: larger, muscular, and Hispanic. The two girls' images dropped out of sight, and there seemed to be some sort of struggle. The two men turned to leave and dragged Jana and Lydia to a light-colored van that was waiting. The camera angle didn't catch what occurred after they crossed behind a vehicle, but the assumption was the two girls were put in the back of the van. Due to the angle of the camera, they weren't able to get plates, but they were certain it was a newer model Chevrolet extended van.

Twenty-One

Tuesday, June 11, Noon, Phoenix: Missing Three Days Twelve Hours

After interviewing Jeff and Ian and speaking with the forensics team about what was captured on the video, Lieutenant Tatum called Sylvia. He talked to her briefly about the session with both witnesses and the evidence they had analyzed from the security camera. Tatum was careful not to disclose what happened with the girls over the phone at this point and explained that it would be better to meet in person. He made every attempt to make the meeting sound like it was a routine status update so they wouldn't be upset about what they would find out in the meeting. The Lincolns and Cantus agreed to meet at police headquarters at two o'clock. The couples suspected the department was prepared to share important news even though not much was said on the call from Lieutenant Tatum. The Cantus picked up the Lincolns and headed for the station. They were nervous and fretful about what was ahead, but they tried to stay positive and supportive.

Twenty-Two

Tuesday, June 11, 2:00 P.M., Phoenix: Missing Three Days Fourteen Hours

Upon arriving, they were directed to the same conference room. The four parents, the two detectives, and Tatum were present.

Tatum said, "We were able to speak with the two witnesses, Jeff Bridgestone and Ian Smith, plus we analyzed video footage from the bar's security cameras, both inside and outside showing the parking lot. Jeff's statement was virtually identical to what you told me on the phone, Mrs. Lincoln, and even though he didn't treat Jana in a very gentlemanly fashion, we feel his statement was convincing. Ian corroborated Jeff's version, and we feel his account was accurate and verifiable as well. The young men were able to provide a general description of the man who assaulted

Jeff, and we've catalogued his information for further analysis. We have reasonable evidence to think he's connected with the girls' disappearance."

Detective Sharp said, "Mr. and Mrs. Lincoln, once Jana exited Jeff's vehicle, according to Ian's statement, Lydia ran over to console Jana. She was distraught from the confrontation with Mr. Bridgestone. The unidentified male subject who came to help Jana was standing beside the two. The security footage showed Lydia and this individual helping Jana back to the club. Before reentering Raining Nails, there appeared to be a brief struggle, and the camera lost sight of both girls. Another man came into the picture briefly, and it appeared the two men took Jana and Lydia to a van. We're not certain, but we believe the girls were unconscious, given the fact it appeared they were dragging them to the van."

Sylvia and Justine broke down and began weeping. Al and Tom hung their heads, covered their eyes, and put an arm around their grieving wives.

Williams said, "We didn't get an image of the plates on the van, but we have a good description of the vehicle and model. The frames showing the two men were clear enough, and we feel like once of our forensic artists can put together a depiction of the suspects, we can circulate to all authorities involved. We'll be putting an APB out for this white van, and our administrative staff will be collecting data to determine how many vehicles of this description there are in the Phoenix metro area. This won't be an easy task, but in a day or two, we should have information to start tracing owners."

Tatum said, "We know this is difficult information to hear, but we wanted to be candid so you'll know as much of the information that we can share at this time. We feel reasonably certain that the two girls were kidnapped, which leaves two possible scenarios. I'm afraid neither are what you want to hear."

Tom said, "Tell us we need to know."

Tatum said, "Scenario number one is the girls were kidnapped and are being held for ransom. Given that it's been over three days since their disappearance, and you haven't been contacted, we're doubtful this is the case. The second and more likely scenario is that Jana and Lydia were kidnapped with plans to be used in trafficking."

Justine screamed, "Oh no, my sweet baby. Oh, Jana. Oh, Jana, this can't be."

Sylvia bawled out loud, and the men broke down and hugged their wives.

Tatum said, "It is imperative that this information stay between us in this room. We cannot have any information leaked to the press in any way or form. We'll call a news conference tomorrow and give an update on the investigation. We will keep the dialogue fresh with the media. The last thing we want to do is tip our hand to the kidnappers or create confusion among those working on the case. Can we all agree on that?"

"Yes sir."

Tatum said, "Please know that we're doing everything we can to return Jana and Lydia, and we won't stop until there's a resolution. In the meantime, pray, get some rest, and we'll be providing you with updates whenever we have additional information."

The couples walked out arm in arm, heads bent, weeping all the way to the car.

Twenty-Three

Tuesday, June 11, 11:00 p.m., Nogales

Raul had to leave town to visit some of his storage warehouses near Tucson and was away from the hacienda for two days. While he was gone, his thoughts continued to drift back to some of the words Lydia had whispered in his ear during their last encounter. He was skeptical that he understood her correctly, and if she was saying what he thought she was saying, it might be a feeble attempt at to escape the house. He'd seen it before and was wary of these girls' tricks, especially the gringos. They were manipulative and cunning, but Lydia appeared to be different. There seemed to be sincerity in both her gaze and her words.

Raul was distracted, and he had a hard time concentrating on the business at hand. He was looking forward to returning to Nogales so he could get Lydia in his bed again, and he would try to confirm what she said. Raul returned late Tuesday night, tired and weary, and he took a long, hot shower and put on his robe.

Dr. Juel was watching soccer on TV.

"Doc, how's it going?"

"Okay, Raul. How was your trip?"

"Very productive. We're expanding in all areas of the business and making lots of money—all music to my ears."

"That's good news. I'm glad to hear our business is doing well."

"How's Lydia?"

"She's getting better. A few days of rest has done her good. I haven't had to medicate her nearly as much as the other one. Jana's a feral beast, I tell you: unlimited energy, stubborn, and mean."

"That's funny. I like the feisty ones. Speaking of Lydia, if I wanted to bring her up, do you think she'd be ready?"

"I think so. She's not drugged, so she could be more combative and obstinate, just be ready to restrain her if she gets out of hand. Do you want me to slip her something before she comes up?"

"No, I want her alert and uninhibited. Do you think she'll put up a fight if you go get her now? If so, I can wake up Pedro to go with you."

"I don't think so. She's been surprisingly cooperative given the short amount of a time she's been here. I think she'll come with me peacefully. If I sense any problems, I'll call you."

Juel unlocked the basement door, slid open the bolt, and swung the door wide. All the girls were asleep, and he proceeded quietly down the stairs, shining his flashlight in front of his feet to keep from stumbling. He made his way over to Lydia and nudged her to see if she was awake. She had drifted off, but she awoke, startled, when she saw the doctor standing above her. She was worried that he was there to administer narcotics, but when he held his finger up to his mouth, Lydia complied and laid still. He whispered to her that he would be taking off her cuffs and that if she tried to do anything other than what he told her, he'd lock her back up. He bent over and whispered, "Raul wants to see you."

Lydia hadn't seen or heard from Raul since their last meeting in Rojo. He had taken it easy on her, which she really appreciated, and she was prepared to use the same tactics to protect her physical well-being if confronted again. Lydia felt that Raul may like her, more than just a call girl or a plaything, but something he valued, and she wanted to encourage this behavior. Lydia nodded her head to the doctor in agreement that she promised to be discreet.

Juel unlocked her cuffs and helped her out of bed. He held her by the elbow and escorted her to the stairs, and they quietly climbed the twenty steps so as not to wake the others. Juel locked the door while Lydia stood next to him, barefoot and dressed only in her white gown.

After securing the door, he led her to the Rojo Room. Lydia sat on the bed, awaiting Raul and not knowing what to expect. She sat with her legs crossed and worried about what Raul had in mind.

A few minutes later, he entered and shut the door behind him. Raul was wearing a yellow terry cloth bathrobe, apparently just having showered, and sat down on the bed next to Lydia.

"My little Lydia, how are you tonight?"

"Okay, … I guess."

"Last time we were together, you said some things that I didn't quite understand, and I want you to repeat them now."

"Not sure I know what you're talking about … you mean when I told you to be … gentle? You were gentle, and I really appreciated that."

"Yes, that, but also when we finished you said something else, do you remember?"

She knew exactly what he was talking about. She blushed and

looked down at the bed coyly. A long silence followed, and Lydia searched for the right words to say.

"Well, Raul, you were … you were … my first, the first I've gone … you know … gone all the way. I'm very inexperienced because of my youth, and I know you're someone who has been with many women and probably know more about having sex than anyone." She flushed again, more redly this time, and looked up at Raul for a moment then looked away. Unsure what to say next, she clumsily forced out the words. "What I said to you the other night was … well … I asked … for you to … to … you know … show me … show me how."

"What do you mean?"

"This is difficult to say … not sure you'll understand."

"Try me."

"Raul … you can probably tell … I really don't know what I'm doing, this is … all new to me. I was scared at first, but then … well after it was over, I was asking … I was asking you to, you know … show me … show me how. Show me … what to do and how you like it, and I'll do my best to make it good for you."

Raul was not sure he could trust her words. "You mean you want me to show you how to be with a man like me?"

Red faced, Lydia continued, "Yes, I guess so … I know this sounds kinda lame, but I've never experienced sex before, especially like this. I'm young and naïve and didn't quite know what to expect, so … after a while, I … sorta … didn't mind it. I know I shouldn't be saying such things being in my situation, but there's something going on inside me, … it's hard to explain … oh, what are the right words? I don't know what I'm saying. I'm just a dumb little teenager … disregard what I've said."

"No, no, child. I think I know what you're saying. So, I take it that you're starting to like it. Is that what you're trying to say?

"Well, sort of . . ."

"Last time, you had a look about you that led me to believe that's true. So, you want to be the student and me the teacher, huh?"

Looking down and embarrassed, she said, "I . . . I . . . I . . . guess . . . so."

"Well, this is a surprise, but I'm glad to comply and help you with your education. Would you like to start tonight?"

"Uh . . . I don't know, I guess so if you want to."

"All right, you will get your wish."

Raul spent a long time explaining what women can do to pleasure a man with their bodies and how she should learn what each man liked and perfect the process. He taught her things she had never dreamed of or wanted to know. Some of what he showed her at first was revolting, and Lydia had to bear up under the circumstances to show her interest. *Not sure I can do this, but I've got to fight my way through it. Maybe it will get easier once I get beyond this first go.*

Before the night was over, Lydia had overcome her fear and disgust and surrendered to Raul's training, impressing her teacher with her abilities. Fortunately, this night was gentler, and Lydia became embarrassed after some physical affection was shown on both sides. Lydia felt extremely guilty afterward—not because of her willingness to appease Raul but because she had experienced something unknown and unexpected.

Raul knew precisely how to compel Lydia's young body into uncharted territory, purposely directing her down the path of pleasure. It was a feeling she didn't know existed, and when it happened, it shocked her. She wasn't sure how it had happened.

Lydia proved to be a quick study, and once she understood what he wanted her to do, she would do it impeccably beyond what Raul could have imagined from a young girl. *So, he likes this huh? Okay, I can do that.* She'd concentrate intently on her role and responsibilities, and whenever she pinpointed something that seem to evoke a positive response, she would assert herself in that direction.

After that night, Raul was smitten with Lydia because he was able to teach his partner the exact ways to make love, and he was fascinated with her profound physique, her figure, and stamina, which was off the charts. Undrugged, Lydia could easily contend with Raul, and she never seemed to grow tired or breathe heavily.

He's not superhuman after all. I'm still feeling strong and vibrant.

Lydia impressed Raul for a number of reasons. She was inquisitive, willing to learn, and not afraid to explore or experiment, which left the boss intrigued and captivated.

From that night forward, Raul wouldn't allow her to be included in the customer rotation and gave strict orders for all of the crew who worked for him to keep a healthy distance from Lydia. He wanted her for his pleasure only, and in the upcoming nights, he would have her come up to Rojo where they constantly conquered new territory becoming even more intertwined within each other's spheres.

Twenty-Four

Wednesday, June 12, 6:00 P.M., Phoenix: Missing Four Days Eighteen Hours

The Phoenix Police Department called a press conference to provide the media the latest updates on Jana and Lydia's disappearance. It was important to keep the community informed so the city leaders and the residents would feel that the department was working diligently on the case and chasing every possible lead. Lieutenant Tatum conducted the presentation, and there were media from all the local stations in Phoenix, Tucson, Mesa, and other Arizona cities. Stations in California were present, and a gaggle of national news media attended as well.

When Tatum stepped up to the podium, there was a sea of microphones and continual clicks from cell phones and cameras snapping shots. The images of Jana and Lydia were prominently displayed on an easel, and it was announced that they had talked to several witnesses at the scene about their disappearance and were making progress on the investigation. He purposely avoided the mention of the security camera results since their team didn't want the kidnappers to know they had identified their vehicle. Tatum said they had a person of interest, but he didn't elaborate. Very few details were disclosed, and there were numerous questions following the short presentation. Tatum was evasive and told only pieces of what was known.

Afterward, Justine and Sylvia were asked to speak for a few moments, and they used the time to plead with anyone who had knowledge of the girls' whereabouts to come forward. They also mentioned the reward. Since their disappearance four days ago, contributions had begun to roll in, raising the reward total to over twenty thousand dollars. The Lincolns and the Cantus felt somewhat of a lift from the national attention, and there were so many people involved and supporting their ordeal.

Afterward, the parents returned quietly to their homes to continue the horrific waiting, fully aware that the next phone call could reveal their daughters' fates.

Twenty-Five

Wednesday, June 12, 7:00 P.M., Nogales

Wednesday rolled around, and Jana fell into the appointment book for her first solo gig. Her experience two nights ago repulsed her to no end, and she was dreading the night with all her spirit. She and Tabitha were scheduled to host customers: Jana in Rojo and Tabitha in Azul.

This time, Jana's customer was a wealthy businessman from Tijuana. She showered, dressed and put on makeup and jewelry. The nerves appeared in spades, and she became extremely frightened. Her hand shook while putting on the mascara.

Tabitha comforted Jana putting her hand on her shoulder and gave her verbal support.

Jana ran through her mind what she saw Beth do with the customer on Monday night and was building courage to try to emulate her techniques. She was still healing after the four-man gang rape by Raul's goons and could only hope the client wouldn't be too rough.

When the appointment time finally arrived, Manuel took her to the Rojo Room and whispered in her ear that Raul had a camera in the room. They'd be watching how she performed very closely. This made things worse for Jana, and the trepidation began to show in her disposition.

As she entered the room, she straightened up, put on her game face, and looked over at the man she would be with. Her customer was a middle-aged man dressed in a nice suit and tie. After taking off his jacket, he sat on the bed, removed his cuff links, and gave Jana a quick up and down. He greeted her and smiled with great anticipation of what the night would bring. He was impressed with what stood before him. He slowly undressed, pulled down the sheets, crawled under, and watched the beautiful young lady in front of him.

Jana thought he was somewhat sophisticated. *Perhaps this evening won't be as bad as I first feared. He doesn't look too bad, thank goodness, and maybe this won't be as gross as I thought. I'll do what they order me to and try to stay out of trouble with Raul and his maniacs.* Jana undressed slowly, reluctantly approached the man, and mimicked what Beth had taught her before. She carefully orchestrated her services, trying her best to deliver what was required—even if her vile duties brought about disgust. Jana worked hard and was diligent to make sure the man wouldn't complain to Raul. *Looks like it's going okay. I think he's getting his money's worth.*

The man was thoroughly enjoying himself and complimented her in English several times, which boosted her confidence. Jana's power and stamina left the man drained. Afterward, he could barely catch his breath and was drenched with sweat.

How's that, senor? I hope you're sore for a week. Jana knew she had accomplished her mission. She had a contented customer, and more importantly, she felt strangely victorious. She had conquered the demon, the demon she faced in her new life, and done it on her own terms. She would survive, and she started to understand how.

The nights Lydia was with Raul, Jana entertained her customers, and they began to understand more about what they were doing. Not by choice, but by necessity. When Tabitha didn't completely satisfy one of her customers, a complaint was lodged. Unbeknownst to the customers, but common knowledge to the young ladies, Raul had hidden cameras in each bedroom and recorded every session for three reasons: they had the men on video in case there was a need for blackmail, to monitor the girls' performance and make sure they were doing what they were being asked, and for Raul's men to entertain themselves.

After reviewing the footage, Tabitha was found to be merely going through the motions and failing to give the client what he expected. Pedro was told to punish Tabitha, and she was held down by Manuel. Pedro took a wire coat hanger and whipped her savagely. Up and down her legs were red whelps, abrasions, and bruises, and she could hardly stand. They didn't give her a night off either.

Tabitha was run back out the next night and told she better get good reviews—or they would repeat the whipping. This registered with Jana and Lydia, and they made sure to give their utmost to avoid the punishment. Since Jana didn't know that much about sex or pleasuring a man, the other girls would teach Jana during the daytime what men liked and describe their own personal approaches. The young girls told her that at first, they were repulsed by what they had to do, but over time, it became routine and wasn't as offensive and that Jana would adapt. They practiced with Jana in the basement by showing her positions and techniques and taught her all about G-spots and erogenous zones. The most important lesson they imparted was what they called "shrinks." Jana paid very close attention. The girls explained that it was their ultimate goal to refine the ability of inducing shrinks—or expediting the customer's satisfaction. This made the night shorter and less physically stressful. The quicker they finished, the easier it was on their bodies, so it was only natural they sought to perfect these skills in particular. So, they coached Jana on how to maximize shrinks so that she could become efficient yet effective.

Lydia however, was educated by Raul. Hearing it directly from him helped her quickly scale up the learning curve, and she became well versed after only a few meetings—except for the missing element of the shrink. Since Jana and Lydia were both quick studies, fast learners, and very teachable young ladies, within three days, they excelled at the art of pleasuring, and they both aimed to be the best in their own ways.

Twenty-Six

Thursday, June 13, 9:00 a.m. Nogales

The girls heard commotion upstairs early Thursday morning. The young ladies who had been there a while knew that Thursdays were typically the delivery date for narcotics and would arrive through the mysterious double doors under the stairway. Each week, four of Raul's henchmen would await the signal behind the door and were armed and ready for any surprises.

A password was spoken from outside the door, and Pedro unbolted and unlocked the steel doors, greeting two deliverymen who brought in large amounts of what appeared to be cocaine and some other substance. This was Jana and Lydia's first encounter with the ceremony, and they watched intently as the crew took the product from the delivery men, laid it down on the floor, said their goodbyes, and locked and bolted the door behind them. The four men took turns in an assembly line, passing the bags of narcotics up the stairs to the next man up. The whole process took only five minutes.

Lydia's bed was directly across from the double doors on the other side of the room, and she could see the scraggly and dirty men who brought in the drugs. They stole a glimpse of her and the other girls, which prompted Lydia to pull up her covers and look away. She did notice that just beyond the doors, the walls inside the tunnel were supported by large wooden beams holding up sand and rock in what looked like a pathway. When she questioned Tabitha about what was beyond the doors, she described a long tunnel, she believed was from Mexico and how they imported drugs on a regular basis right through their basement.

Twenty-Seven

Thursday, June 13, 10:30 a.m., Tucson

After the drugs were recorded, organized, and stored, Raul told them men it was time to round up some new blood for his stable. Alex, Pedro, and Manuel got the order to direct their search to Tucson. The Raining Nails kidnappings were causing too much heat, especially the attention generated by the press, and Raul pointed them to their target two hours north, far away from the scrutiny.

On Saturday around noon, their circuit included all the public swimming pools in the city. One by one, they circled the perimeter of each location in the white minivan and waited for a young girl to wander outside alone. The pools were busy this time of the summer, and the crowds that swarmed the entrance left no opportunities to pull off their hideous crime. They came up empty at five different pools, and it was getting late in the afternoon.

The three men assumed it would be a dry run that day. As they circled the last pool for the third time, they saw a mother holding an infant in a car seat with two other small children jostling at her feet. She sent her older daughter who looked to be about fifteen to open the minivan to and stow away their pool toys. After handing her daughter the keys, she turned, distracted by her two small boys who were fighting over a squirt gun, and the teenager walked away.

Mom put down the infant chair and went after the boys who were chasing each other along a fence in the opposite direction of the minivan. The teenager's long dark hair and bathing suit were still wet as she walked to the van, unaware of the men watching her. She was still wearing the swimsuit from two years ago and had outgrown the size meant for a preteen. Since Angela turned fifteen, her body had begun to flourish, and the small top intended for a younger girl was now trying to cover more than it was designed to. The bottom piece of her yellow bikini was also too small and drooped low enough that it barely covered the cleft of her backside.

The young girl's unintentional, yet revealing swimsuit got the men's attention as they caught a glimpse of her lugging the toys toward the van. It was parked on a side street a hundred yards from the entrance. While the mom was being diverted by her other children, they swung the van down the road, following Angela and checking around for witnesses.

As she opened the rear door of the minivan, Pedro and Alex jumped out and swiftly headed toward Angela. She dropped some of the toys, and when she bent down to pick them up, the two men moved in and grabbed the young teenager. She turned and screamed at the top of her lungs, causing Alex to fumble the syringe for a moment.

A man came running down the street and began shouting at the men.

Alex and Pedro bolted for the van, leaving a startled Angela shaking nervously as she watched the men flee the scene. The Good Samaritan comforted her until the mom ran around the corner, carrier in hand and her other kids trotting behind.

Angela was shaking and crying, unaware that her screaming had changed the horrible direction her life was headed. She was fortunate to be going home, frightened only by a near-miss attempt. Angela would be able to resume her typical teenage life rather than being tortured by grown men in an underground prison, who would rape and sodomize her and sell her blossoming body to brutal sex fiends.

The three men fled in a hurry and headed for the freeway. Reports of the near abduction would surely be made, and descriptions of the van would be disseminated across the area. As they neared the interstate, they spotted a late-model Acura on the side of the road with its flashers on. A college-aged female had her cell phone planted in one ear and was talking animatedly to someone on the other end. She disconnected with her caller as the van pulled over. Alex got out of the front seat and walked over to check on the young lady's plight. She cautiously greeted the soldier and tried to explain what was going on with her car. Being as smooth as ever, he disarmed her with a smile, took a look under the hood, and fiddled with a few wires, appearing to be making some adjustments. The young lady watched, but she kept her distance.

Alex pointed at something under the hood, and she leaned over the engine to see where he was pointing. When she did, Pedro came around from the back of the van and hit Marianne with the syringe. Seconds later, she fell into a heap. The two men carried her around the car. Marianne was twenty and was a sophomore at the University of Arizona. She was headed home for a long weekend with her parents and her boyfriend who wasn't able to come to her aid that afternoon.

Walking away from the disabled vehicle, the men looked down the entrance ramp for approaching cars. Seeing none, they carried Marianne to the back of the van, whisked open the doors, and lifted her inside. The men jumped in, and Manuel sped the Chevy toward Nogales.

Alex told Manuel to turn on the interior lights to give them a glimpse of their latest victim. The young woman was short, and her dirty blonde hair was braided in pigtails that framed her full, sunburned face. She wasn't as much of a prize as Jana and Lydia, but she would do. A bit on the older side, but Raul still might be able to make use of her with some of the customers. Marianne's cut-off blue jean shorts were slit up the side, barely falling below the cheeks of her buttocks, and frazzled strings dangled around the sides. She wore an old wrinkled red T-shirt with the arms cut just beyond the shoulders and pink flip-flops.

Alex called Raul and described Marianne's age and appearance and asked him what he thought.

Raul and his customers' tastes leaned toward the younger variety, and he wasn't sure that Marianne would fit with his cadre of young studs.

"Hey Raul, Alex. We struck out at the pools today, but we found one on the road that you might be interested in."

"Tell me about her."

"She's Anglo, probably nineteen or twenty. I think she's a college student. Short, light brown hair, figure's not bad. We've got her here in the van."

"That old huh? Not sure about her—we've had trouble with the older ones, and our customers seem to prefer under sixteen. Now that we have the two here that are seventeen, the older ages are pretty much covered. Good work hunting this one down though, but she's not right for our house."

"What do you want us to do with her?"

"She's all yours. Do whatever you boys want to do with her, but don't kill her."

"Got it. We'll take care of it. Thanks."

The three men were surprised at Raul's response and pulled into a secluded rest area.

Once parked, Manuel said, "So, Raul didn't need this one?"

Alex replied, "No, he doesn't want her, too old, said to do whatever we wanted."

"Hey, that's music to my ears."

"Yes, sir. This turned out better than I thought," Manuel added.

Alex reached under her blue jean shorts, unbuttoned the snaps, and slid them off—along with a pink thong.

Manuel said, "That's what I'm talking about—look at that body."

Pedro said, "Not bad, she's hot!"

"Be patient, fellas, and wait your turn."

Alex finished undressing Marianne and flipped her over on her back. She was unconscious, crashed out, and not feeling a thing. The men were surprised; they had underestimated her attributes that were displayed in front of them. Under the clothing, she looked even more impressive than dressed.

Alex began assaulting her and abused her harshly before giving way to Pedro.

Pedro continued the onslaught, laboring feverishly until he was spent.

Manuel finished off the gang rape, and they put Marianne's clothes back on.

"What do we do with her now?" Pedro inquired.

"Let's dump her in the ladies room over there." Alex pointing to a small building.

The men covertly carted her around the back of the women's

restroom at the end of the rest stop and carried her inside once it was clear. Manuel waited outside, running interference, and the other men left her on the floor, completely unconscious. Marianne was fortunate.

The three men sped away, heading south emptyhanded, but it had been a successful day in their minds. The close call at the swimming pool was sobering, but it quickly faded after they were entertained by the young coed. As they made their way back to Nogales, they stopped to get a burger, laughing about their latest conquest and what Marianne would be thinking and feeling when she finally woke up.

Twenty-Eight

Thursday, June 13, 11:00 a.m., Phoenix: Missing Five Days Eleven Hours

Calls flooded into the Missing Persons Division at police headquarters after the press conference. A task force was set up designed to handle incoming calls, take information, and follow up on any legitimate leads. So far, there was nothing of substance, and Tatum's team felt like they were fighting an uphill battle. They identified more than five hundred white Chevy vans matching the description of the assailants' vehicle, which proved to be a monumental task to begin whittling down and arriving at anything concrete.

The Lincolns and the Cantus remained optimistic, but as the hours and days passed, their energy levels were waning, and the lack of any calls from Tatum wore heavily on their minds. They tried to go about their days in some semblance of normal, but the girls' disappearance had caused a permanent wound in their minds that wouldn't heal.

Twenty-Nine

Friday, June 14, 10:00 a.m., Nogales

The four young women who were stuck in Raul's quarters before Jana and Lydia arrived were speaking quietly among themselves.

Beth said, "Why isn't Lydia being scheduled with any of the customers? We're over here working our tails off, including Jana now, and Lydia's over there galivanting with Raul every night. It's not fair; she should be holding up her part like us."

Tabitha said, "I wonder why Raul is only asking for Lydia. He used to bring us all up there from time to time—now nothing."

Emma said, "I know she's getting special treatment. She doesn't appear to be aching or sore like we are after a night's work, and I know she's been getting special meals."

Jana thought, *She's spending too much time that evil snake. She's enjoying comfortable nights, lounging around with Raul, while we're having to put up with these gross men, and what's more degrading is being forced to have relations with the other girls. That's so sick. She hasn't had to be with any man besides Raul. That's just not right.*

Lydia felt the animosity flowing from that side of the room. It didn't dawn on her that the time she spent with Raul would cause any friction with the others. Even Jana acted differently toward her, but she couldn't quite put her finger on it until now. The new ladies from Phoenix graduated from the restraints of handcuffs and were now able to move freely and talk, but Jana had been uncharacteristically quiet and avoided any discussion with her friend. Jana heard the others talking quietly among themselves and sensed they were upset about Lydia's privileges.

Jana thought, *What's up with Lydia? She's gone off the deep end being with that sex fiend. It's as if found something she likes and keeps going back for more. I can't understand how she can be with that man while we wallow in pain, meeting with these random dudes and doing such horrible things.*

Lydia decided to go to Jana's bed, sat down, and looked her in the eye.

Jana said, "So, what's the deal with Raul? You got something special going on with that gross maggot?"

Lydia said, "Just so you know he's not a maggot, and I can't help it if he calls me up every night."

"What do you guys do?"

"What do you think? Sex, sex, and more sex."

"So, for some reason, you seem happier than the rest of us. What's going on, Lydia?"

"I don't know. I just go up there, we spend time together, and he teaches me things. We do what y'all are doing with the customers, I suppose."

"What do you mean, teaches you things?"

"Never mind."

"No, not never mind, what's going on?

"Jana, he's treating me good, and I'm trying to get through this as best I can. We're stuck here, and I'm trying to figure a way out of this mess."

"Well, it doesn't look like you're in any hurry to solve the problem."

"I can't believe I'm hearing this from you." Lydia huffily stood, walked back to her bed, sat and stared at the bolted door.

Lydia thought, *What's wrong with her? She doesn't trust me. I feel so distant from her now. It's not my fault. I'm just trying to survive.*

Jana said, "He better start including you on the rotation. It's not fair what we have to do to all of these nasty men while you're playing house with Raul."

I can't believe Lydia's doing this. I hate her. She's thrown away our friendship for this joker. What has he done to her? It's like she's brainwashed. I'm not even sure Lydia wants to leave this place. I can't figure her out. I feel so alone without Lydia. I've lost her. She was the only thing I had left in this evil house.

The four girls interrupted their gossip and listened intently to the exchange between Lydia and Jana. They were pleased that Jana had joined their side, bolstering their reasons for objecting to Lydia's privilege.

Lydia thought, *Man, these girls really hate me. What have I done to them? If they knew why I'm doing this, they wouldn't be so bent out of shape. I can't help it if Raul likes me more than the others. He treats me good, and if I can avoid being with those other men by becoming Raul's girl, then why not? I guarantee they'd do it if they were in my shoes.*

Thirty

Friday, June 14, 7:00 p.m., Nogales

Jorge came down to the basement to announce the schedule for handling the evening's customers. "Charlotte in Blanco, Beth and Emma as a twosome in the Rojo Room, and Tabitha and Jana likewise in Azul."

The girls looked at each other with frustration and shot hateful looks at Lydia.

Lydia ignored their stares and picked at the blanket on her bed.

Jorge walked over to Lydia and whispered that Raul wanted to see her in the master bedroom in an hour. The five girls were led upstairs, and as they ascended, each one, including Jana, looked down at Lydia in consternation.

Later that night, Jana experienced her first ménage à trois and got to know Tabitha much more than she wanted to. It was obviously a first for her, and she was caught off guard when Tabitha began making love to her in front of the customer. *Oh my gosh. What is she doing to me? This is awkward, yucky, and so weird. What's she doing now? That feels really strange, oh my. What am I supposed to do? Repeat what she's doing to me? This is so gross. I can't believe I'm having to do these things. I'll admit it's much better than being with that toad who's watching us.*

Afterward, she felt the interlude was a welcome change from the appalling, sometimes gross men she had to entertain. Jana felt she would never become a lesbian, but she had to admit it was better than the alternative. Jana grew more experienced with each customer. She was quickly recognized by Raul and his men as the new star of the stable, and she worked hard to keep out of trouble. Each man Jana spent time with wanted to know her name and told Raul that she was their choice next time in town. Jana knew she was good at what she did and took some sort perverted pride in being able to drive men over the top.

After showering in the empty basement, Lydia dressed and was escorted to Raul's personal bedroom at eight o'clock. The two enjoyed another night of enchantment, and Lydia skillfully orchestrated the proceedings, much to Raul's delight.

Lydia thought, *What am I doing? A few days ago, I was holding onto my virtue, protecting it with everything I had. Then, after being with Raul, I've changed so dramatically. I've lost my virginity, but what's causing me to pursue my own satisfaction so recklessly? He's a hardened criminal who rapes and abuses young girls. I can't figure out why I keep going back to him for this. It's like a spell has come over me—something physical that's hard to explain. Where do I go from here? I want to stop, but I'm not sure how.*

That night, after the young women returned from their appointments, they made their way to their beds, exhausted. Jana found her place and noticed Lydia's bed was empty. Pedro handcuffed them and left. The others noticed too and were not at all pleased. Lydia didn't make it down to the basement that night because she was engrossed in a whirlwind night of pleasing Raul.

Thirty-One

Saturday, June 15, Noon Phoenix: Missing Seven Days Twelve Hours

Most of the leads gathered by the PPD task force turned out to be dead ends. The work on the list of vans proved to be useless, and they were unable to narrow the number down to any meaningful working figure. Since no contact had been made by any kidnappers, they officially closed the books on what could have been a kidnapping-for-ransom scenario.

Tatum and company began digging into suspected trafficking rings and identified several possibilities in the area, but they had no plan of action until they could gather more evidence.

Tom, Justine, Sylvia, and Art were deeply discouraged and were starting to realize they may never see their daughters again. The thought haunted them day and night, especially when they passed their daughter's bedroom or looked at her place at the dinner table. It dawned on them that it wasn't a dream. They feared for their daughters' safety and prayed around the clock for their girls' comfort and peace. They were slowly transitioning from the hope of their return to silently praying that they were still alive.

Thirty-Two

Saturday, June 15, Noon, Nogales

Jorge came down the stairs, gathered Lydia's few belongings, and took them upstairs. The girls had yet to hear a word from Lydia since Friday morning and suspected she'd been with Raul all night long. They talked among themselves and berated Lydia in vindictive fashion, jealous that she was continuing to get special treatment.

Jorge mentioned that they all had appointments that night and would be back to go over the schedules. That afternoon, the girls were allowed to go outside and mill around the pool. The swimming area was enclosed by a brick wall and tall trees that surrounded the entire outside area, keeping the pool completely secluded and private. The only person who was allowed in the area outside of Raul's team was the pool man, a drug customer who came every Wednesday.

After lunch, the group was escorted up to the pool area. Jorge,

Manuel, and Pedro stood watch outside, armed with automatic weapons. The girls were warned not to make any noise—or they would be beaten.

Tabitha walked around the pool, holding her head into the bright sunlight and trying to bolster her strength from the welcoming rays.

Emma and Tabitha sat on lounge chairs and tried to nap.

Beth shed her white gown and underwear and jumped into the pool for a swim.

Jana *took it all in, seeing the sunlight for the first time in a week and thought, Oh, it's so nice seeing the sunlight. I've missed this so much. The fresh air is beautiful. I can finally breathe.* Her thoughts lingered on her friend. *Lydia's not here with us. I wonder what's going on with her. I can't figure that girl out. She's acting really strange. It's like I don't know her anymore.* Lydia had, by all indications, disowned her and the other girls and taken up with a known criminal and rapist. She couldn't make sense of it. Perhaps Lydia wasn't the innocent person her best friend purported to be and had gone off the deep end with Raul. Whatever it was, she felt it was despicable that she and the others were being forced into selling their bodies and experiencing horrific sexual abuse, and she was upstairs enjoying her lustful flings with the criminal who orchestrated the very debasing acts. Jana was formulating a plan to escape, and in the next few days, she'd outline the undertaking for her bunkmates. She wasn't going to give in and live this kind of life; she wanted out.

Lydia slept in Saturday morning, and for the first time, she enjoyed the comfort of Raul's king-sized bed. They held each other throughout the night and awoke several times, spontaneously falling into ravishing moments of sex. Lydia could sense she was slowly taking control of their exchanges by aggressively pressing Raul to deliver more and more. In her short time with him, Lydia had honed her skills like a surgeon and operated on him with precision and strength, all with Raul's enthusiasm. *I can tell Raul is hooked. He's got it good with me. He won't get this from any of the others, but I feel like what I'm doing with Raul has made me his physical prisoner. The sexual feelings are addictive. I know it's wrong, but for some reason, I keep on doing it.*

Raul was still somewhat suspicious and constantly watched Lydia to see if what she was doing was an elaborate plan to somehow gain her release or perhaps escape. After what he'd experienced from her over the past week, and seeing her enjoyment, he was growing more confident that Lydia didn't want to go anywhere. Up to this time, he hadn't picked up on any indication to believe Lydia wasn't sincere in her appetite for sexual excess, and she did seem happy and content. It just might be that he had unlocked a demonic sex goddess turned nymphomaniac now at his disposal 24-7. Just in case, he had a plan to flush out his uncertainty about Lydia.

Thirty-Three

Saturday, June 15, 7:00 p.m., Nogales

Now and then, the girls would be asked to accompany men off premises to attend special events or occasions. Everyone except Lydia was told that they would be attending a bachelor party at a wealthy landowner's house ten miles outside of Nogales. They were given cocktail attire stored in the closet for just such use and were told in no uncertain terms that they were to look as elegant and classy as possible. So, the young ladies were given an extra half hour to prepare and donned evening dresses that best fit each girl. Lavish jewelry was passed around with expensive perfume and scented, glittered lotion. By the time the teenagers were ready, they looked like Hollywood screen beauties.

Lydia felt left out not being able to go with the group to the party, but she was more at ease being at home with Raul than a total stranger. *I wonder where they're going. It might be nice to get out for a change, but that's okay. At least I'm safe here with Raul and know what to expect.*

Raul called her up after the girls departed to spend another night tangled together in a steamy frolic and a whirlwind of adventure. It was apparent that his intentions were to keep Lydia all to himself.

At eight o'clock, a stretch limo picked them up at the front door.

Jana thought, *This is different. I wonder what the night holds for us. Gotta be better than staying around this prison cell and doing all of those dirty things with Raul's wormy clients.*

Alex and Pedro sat with the girls in the back, accompanying them to make sure they all returned safely and were on their best behavior. They were given stern warnings to be cooperative and provide anything their customers wanted. Furthermore, they were instructed to keep dealings at the Raul household confidential and to abstain from any personal discussions.

Pedro and Alex were dressed in suits and ties and looked pretty spiffy for two cartel hoods. As they pulled up in front of a gigantic mansion, they could hear the oohs and ahs from the back. It was secured by an iron security gate with a guard standing the front of entrance. They were waved through and proceeded to a long circular driveway in front of the estate. Parked around the drive were expensive vehicles, including a black Land Rover, a Mercedes, a few BMWs, and a Maserati.

The girls were greeted by a cultured doorman who opened the limo with grace and courtesy and politely welcomed the group. The striking young ladies straightened their dresses and hairdos and prepared to go inside.

Raul's henchmen cracked a smile, pleased with the talent they were bringing to the party.

The doorman escorted the five young women to the front door, and a manservant waved them inside. They slowly entered, taking in the grandeur of their palatial surroundings, looking up to the lofted ceilings, and admiring all the expensive furniture and artwork.

Tabitha thought, *Wow, this guy is loaded. Look at this place. It's huge—and get a load of all the fancy things.*

The girls were intrigued, being in such a drastic departure from their daily grind inside Raul's lair. They were escorted into a large sitting room that was filled with five young men in tuxes and an older man who was the owner of the house. Jana was curious about how this night would unfold.

A servant brought champagne and small finger food as they filtered into the room. Each one of the men greeted the teenagers politely and began striking up conversations with whomever they felt inclined. No one approached Jana. The young man talking to the elder statesman seemed to be the son getting married and the host of the bachelor party. *I'll bet he's my date. Thank goodness he's young, and he is quite handsome. Maybe he'll be easy on me.* She waited awkwardly all by herself while the others chitchatted, drank, and munched on the hors d'oeuvres.

The younger man walked over to Jana, smiled, and said, "You must be Jana."

"Er … yes … I'm Jana. How did you know my name?"

"Well, my father is a good friend of Raul's and asked for his advice on who should be with me tonight. You came highly recommended."

Blushing, she said, "Oh, I see."

"I'm getting married tomorrow, and this is my last fling before tying the knot."

"Fling?"

"You know, my last chance before …"

"Yes, I get it. You don't have to explain. And who are you?"

"My name is Alain, Alain Estrada. Welcome to our house."

"Thanks, I guess."

"Why so glum?"

Jana realized her place and Alex's instructions in the car. "Sorry, I didn't mean to be...it's just that ..."

"How's the drink? Can I get you something else?"

"No, this is fine." She took her last sip.

"Let me get you another."

"Well, okay."

Alain bought and sold quarter horses and trained them for racing in California. He was twenty-eight years old, and his wife-to-be was Anna. His father had lived in Nogales for fifty years and had made his fortune in the magazine business. Alain experienced an exciting life, hunting, playing golf, and traveling to distant locales in search of equine stock. He lived in LA, where he and his wife would call home after the wedding. He seemed sincere in asking Jana about her life and her interests, but she was plagued by Raul's rules and remained vague and evasive regarding her past. *Alain's pretty impressive. His wife hit the jackpot. It's a real shame he's having sex the day before he's getting married. If he's doing it now, how faithful will he be after they're married?*

After three glasses of champagne, Jana felt a little tipsy and began to loosen up. Her conversation with Alain was a pleasant distraction from her dismal situation at cartel headquarters, and he seemed very charming and sincere.

The other girls were starting to pair off and slowly making their way to different parts of the house, being escorted by the young men.

"Shall we?" Alain asked.

"I guess so." Jana was uncertain about what would happen next.

Alain held out the crook of his elbow for Jana to hold, and she slipped her hand through, holding onto his arm. *A gentleman, good start.* He led her up a spiral staircase to the third floor where all was quiet and peaceful. The other girls were on the floor below and scattered around the lavish abode. They entered a massive room that had a bed on one side, a kitchenette on the other, floor-to-ceiling windows, and luxurious decorations and furniture. He showed Jana to a room attached to the larger space and flipped on the light, revealing an immense jacuzzi with jets circulating foaming water scented with perfume. *Wow—look at this hot tub. It's unbelievable.*

Alain said he'd return in a moment and told Jana to get comfortable.

Jana looked at herself in the mirror and thought, *Who am I? This doesn't look like me.* She appeared five years older and more like a grownup woman than a teenager, but she was pleased with her appearance in the black, full-length, sequined dress. She looked classy and sleek.

Alain stuck his head around the corner and told Jana to make herself at home. "If you want to get in the hot tub, don't hesitate."

Jana was trapped in a quandary of indecision. She looked at herself in the mirror a second time and felt uneasy disrobing after looking so glamorous just to be used again by another strange man. *I wonder what he wants me to do now.*

Poking his head around the corner, Alain said, "Go ahead. Get in. I'll be back in a second."

Jana slowly undressed and hung her beautiful clothes on a hook behind the bathroom door. She closed it behind her, seeking some bit of privacy, tied her hair up, and slipped into the perfectly heated jacuzzi. The swirling jets caused the bubbles to multiply, and even though she was naked, she was completely covered up by the foam from the percolating water. *Oh, this feels so good. I could get used to this.*

A few minutes passed, and Alain came in wearing only his boxers.

Jana blushed and attempted to cover herself, but Alain couldn't see anything but her face through the mountain of bubbles. He threw a lush bathmat by the tub and knelt, taking a soft scrub brush and wetting it with perfumed soap. Then he leaned over to Jana—who had positioned herself as far away as possible—reached over, gently caressed her arm, and pulled her closer. "I won't bite." He lightly ran the brush it over Jana's back and shoulders, circling in mesmerizing strokes.

Oh my gosh, that feels fine. He's done this before. He asked for Jana to raise her legs, and he began the same motion on her legs. With the champagne's effects and this soft massage, Jana felt herself relaxing and falling into a stupor. *Aw, man, this is really great. He's making me limp.*

He continued on the other parts of her body, but he didn't linger in any one place or enter her more delicate areas, which Jana appreciated. She closed her eyes and let the motions of his stroke take her somewhere beyond her consciousness. Jana became very relaxed and appreciated the time to unwind and be pampered for a change.

Alain interrupted her trance when he stopped brushing and told Jana it was time to stand up.

Taking a few seconds to collect herself, she stood—with bubbles and water dripping off her body—and tried to cover herself as best she could. *This is embarrassing ... being so close with him staring at me.*

Alain offered her a hand, helped her step out of the hot tub, and began toweling her off in the same gentle manner. He handed her the towel so she could wrap it around her body and asked Jana to follow him into the main room.

A long padded table caught Jana's attention. *I wonder what that is. It looks like it might be a massage table.*

He asked Jana to lay down and helped her remove the towel.

Jana was very self-conscious and tried to cover herself as best she could, but Alain moved her hands away and softly placed her arms by her side. *This is so awkward. He's examining me so closely. I feel like I'm at his mercy.* Jana was nervous with her body completely exposed, and she stared up at the ceiling. She wasn't sure what to expect from the man she had met only minutes before, and she held her breath.

He instructed her to close her eyes, and he turned the lights down very low and put on a soft tune by Anugama. Peeking through the slits of her eyes, she watched Alain mix lotion with an oil of some kind. *That smells really good.* When he finished, she quickly closed her eyelids and felt his hands on her shoulders, gently massaging to and fro. He covered every inch of her body, and Jana slowly drifted into a dreamlike consciousness. The smell of the aromatic oil, the soft music, and the silky texture of the lotion lulled her into a trance.

Alain worked on Jana's front and turned her over to spend time on her back, taking equal amount of care to hit every inch of her body in an intoxicating elixir of pleasure.

Oh, this is so relaxing, and Alain's getting me really worked up. I've never felt this good.

He massaged her body up and down for over an hour, and Jana felt herself slipping into a comfortable sense of well-being.

As he finished and toweled off his hands, she said, "Alain, that was wonderful. Thank you so much. I've never felt that good. That was the first time I've ever had a massage."

"Glad you liked it. I thought I might lose you for a minute there—you were in some other sphere."

"Yes, I know. It was amazing."

He took Jana's hand and led her to the large bed. He removed his boxers and sat next to Jana. He looked into her beautiful blue eyes, smiled, and embraced her softly and gently.

I have a feeling this will be better than the other nights at Raul's.

Jana and Alain made love for quite some time that evening, and Jana became captured in a guilty emotional state, realizing she was enjoying Alain's tender lovemaking. After an extended pleasurable experience, Alain helped Jana up from the bed, walked her to the shower, and offered her an opportunity to clean up before leaving.

She showered and dressed, pulling the clothes from behind the bathroom door and slipping them on. Alain dressed in the other room. As they met outside the bathroom, Alain kissed her passionately and thanked her for the evening.

Jana whispered, "Alain, can you help me? I need out of this situation. Can you do anything?"

Alain pulled Jana back to look at her, smiled, and kissed her on the forehead. "I cannot get involved."

"But, Alain, I miss my home and my parents. I need to go home." Jana realized she'd stepped across the line and regretted asking Alain for help.

"I'm sorry, Jana. This is between you and Raul. I can't help you."

"Alain, forget I asked. I don't want to get in trouble. I shouldn't have put you in this position."

"Don't worry about it. I won't say anything. You're safe."

Why did I ask him for help? That was stupid. What have I done now?

Alain escorted Jana downstairs, and the four other girls were waiting. It was apparent that Jana's evening had been more comprehensive than their own. They smirked and cut glances at each other as the most handsome man in the room held Jana's hand on the way down the stairs.

The girls were loaded back into the limo for the quick ride home. When they were back in the basement, they talked about their evening. Everyone was dying to know about Alain and what Jana's evening was like.

Thirty-Four

Sunday, June 16, 8:00 P.M., Nogales

The girls hadn't seen Lydia in two days. They assumed she now lived upstairs, enjoying the conveniences bestowed on her by Raul, and their resentment grew by the hour.

Jana was flabbergasted and couldn't fathom Lydia falling into such an evil spider web, but her actions looked very much like that was the case.

Two more customers were coming in that evening, and Beth and Tabitha were summoned. Jana was a little surprised that her name wasn't called, but she was relieved that she had a night off to replenish her body.

As Beth and Tabitha were leaving, Jorge walked over to Jana and told her that Raul wanted her to come to the Rojo Room. Jana was floored. She hadn't been with Raul since the drugged-up night of her arrival, and with Lydia spending so much time with him, she never expected to deal with him again. Since whatever Lydia was doing was keeping him content and satisfied, it didn't make sense. Where was Lydia anyway?

Jana showered and was apprehensive as she made ready for the meeting with Raul. Jana purposely chose a seductively short dress to appeal to Raul's cravings. If she was to be forced into participating, Jana was determined to show up Lydia. Jana was uneasy as she nervously made her way out of the Sala De Agua. She walked down the hallway with Jorge, turned the corner, and spotted Lydia on the couch in the den, engrossed with something on TV.

Manuel and Pedro sat with her Lydia, munching on chips and hot sauce. Jana shot a hateful stare at Lydia who looked embarrassed to see Jana going to work when she was lounging on the sofa taking it easy. Jana looked away as she whisked by Lydia.

A few minutes later, Raul walked directly into the Rojo bedroom, ignoring Lydia. *Wait a minute. What's going on? Why is Raul going in there with Jana? Now, wait just a minute. This can't be happening.*

Jana walked into the empty room and sat in a chair by the bed, wondering why she was there and what was expected of her.

Raul walked into the Rojo Room, shut the door behind him and gave Jana a smile that caused shivers to run up and down her back. He was scary and alien, but Jana tried to conceal her loathing. Raul stood at the door behind him, pointed to the bed, and suggested that she lay down and make herself comfortable.

Jana hesitantly complied, still curious about his angle, and watched Raul's eyes as he walked across the room, hoping to get an idea of his designs. It became distinctly clear when Raul began taking off his clothes and sat at the foot of the bed. He put his hand on her leg, and she flinched. "Miss Jana, I've heard you are one spirited young woman."

Jana's face reddened, but she didn't smile. *If he only knew.*

"Every one of your customers said that you are the best they've ever had, and I've watched you on video. I must say you're very impressive."

Jana knew she was good, but this confirmed her own feelings about her capabilities. She remained silent and watched Raul closely. *He's asking for it.*

"You are very strong, I see, and very energetic. I like that. Would you like to show me your newly acquired talents?"

"Only if you make me, but if you do, you'll find out." *Payback.*

"Let us find out."

I'll show him exactly what I can do. He's been watching me on those hidden cameras and knows I've learned some things, and I'm good at this stuff. If I'm forced to do these disgusting things. I won't like it, but I'll call on my physical talents to go places where no others can. Lydia thinks she has Raul's number, but wait until I'm finished with him. He'll be begging me for more. Let's see if he can take it as well as he can dish it out.

In the den, Lydia's curiosity was killing her. She thought Raul was in the palm of her hand up until that evening, and now he and Jana were together? *I don't believe this. Jana's in there? What gives?*

Raul leaned over to Jana, slowly and deliberately removed her dress, and folded it neatly on a chair. He took an extended look and admired Jana's firm, sleek body and began caressing her gently.

Lydia assumed she had a monopoly on Raul. I could use some off nights from those dirty customers. If I show him what I'm capable of doing, maybe he'll show me some leniency too. Then I won't be so humiliated with the random customers who crawl in here. At least he's not that raunchy. He's gonna get something he hasn't seen from Lydia.

Raul coupled with Jana, and she immediately took the initiative by using all the skills she'd picked up from the other girls and the several men she'd been with lately. Raul was stunned at Jana's power and forcefulness and cried out loudly as they engaged.

Lydia heard Raul's groans and the huffing and puffing from inside the bedroom. She walked over to the bedroom, placed her ear against the door, and listened to the commotion.

Raul sounded as if he was totally enraptured, reveling in Jana's company. His groans grew louder. *If Lydia's hatching a hoax to get out of the house, then she shouldn't show any signs of jealousy. If she does show jealousy, that will indicate her sincere feelings toward staying here with me.* Raul thought to himself. That was his strategy. Jana and Raul were together for over two hours, and for one of the first times, Raul had expended every bit of energy he could muster.

Jana was still roaring like a freight train, and Raul finally had to call her off. Jana savored the opportunity to repay him for the roughness he dished out when she first arrived. As he anxiously tried to get out of bed, Jana pulled him back down and reversed the roles, attacking the cartel chief. Jana physically abused him until he was writhing in pain, but she wouldn't let him get up.

When they finally finished, Jana looked him in the eye with an expression of triumph.

Raul quickly got dressed and tried to catch his breath.

Lydia was growing more and more infuriated by the minute. The two soldiers on the couch looked at her periodically watching her frustration build. *Jana is doing this just to spite me. She doesn't understand. She always tries to outdo me at everything, and this isn't cool. Jana is purposely going overboard to impress Raul, and she's crossed the line this time. No matter what Jana does, he won't like her as much as me. I'm his girl, and he's just using her to make me jealous. I'm the only one who knows how he likes things done. He's taught me everything.*

Lydia felt a wave of jealousy sweeping over her like a green cloud. Her best friend was showing her up, and she realized Raul had never made the kind of noise he made with Jana. She came to the conclusion that Jana was threatening everything she had carefully constructed with Raul and could destroy her plan.

After a few minutes, Jana finally made her exit from Rojo, looking cocky and confident. She smirked at Lydia as she passed. *See how it feels, Lydia? I hope this shows you that two can play this game.* As she strutted her way past Lydia, she flipped her hair back to make her point and went downstairs with Manuel.

Raul walked out with a slight limp, but Lydia knew there was nothing wrong with his leg. He tossed her a glance, and she glared back at him with indignation and slowly shook her head visibly upset.

Raul sensed Lydia's raw jealousy, and his question about her feelings became pretty obvious.

Thirty-Five

Monday, June 17, 1:00 a.m., Nogales

Lydia was surprised she was sent down to the basement after Raul's rendezvous with Jana. He wanted to put her in her place and teach her that she could be back in the rotation if he sensed she was trying to pull one over on him. He believed Lydia was being authentic, but he wanted to drive the point home and make it clear to her who was in charge. She was dismayed and upset as Manuel led her down the stairs.

All the girls were asleep except Jana. In the darkness, she fumbled her way to the bed. She sensed that Jana was watching her and was awake.

Jana didn't say a word as Lydia crawled on top of the bed.

Lydia finally broke the silence, turned her head and whispered,

"Jana, what was that all about? You were berating me for being with Raul—and you go up there and try to outdo me?"

"Just doing what I'm told."

"You were doing more than that. I heard you two, and it didn't sound like you were just going through the motions."

"What's wrong, Lydia? Are you afraid that I'll take your place in Raul's bed?"

"Frankly, yes. Jana, I don't want that to happen."

"Why is that?"

"I've been wanting to speak with you in private for a few days now, and I can't seem to get any time alone with you without the others listening in." Lydia sat next to Jana on her bed.

Jana shrank away and crossed her arms.

Lydia leaned forward and whispered, "Jana, please don't tell anyone. Keep this quiet. Do you promise?"

"Maybe, depends. What is it?"

"I've been working on a plan from the day we got here. I've been trying to get into Raul's good graces so that I can find us a way out of here. The only thing he understands is sex, and my goal was to give him the best treatment possible so he'll let me circulate freely around the house, which so far, has been working. This will give me the ability to evaluate options and find ways to escape. I was making such good progress with Raul. He thinks I really like him, but tonight was a step backward in our relationship."

"Relationship? You gotta be kidding."

"By relationship, I mean encouraging the idea of me caring for him so he'll relax."

"Am I to believe you weren't enjoying his company having sex constantly?"

"Truly, Jana, I swear to you, all I've been doing is trying to get us out of here. I do admit that the sex has opened up my sensual awareness, and I can't say that I didn't enjoy some of it, but my head is fixed on our escape—not being with that man."

"So, what's your plan?"

"Well, I don't have anything specific yet. I was just trying to build his trust, which would lead me to options. That's why when he ordered you to Rojo, it threatened the progress I was making."

"Sorry to have spoiled your party. He may be calling on me in the future, and then I'll take my time trying to come up with a plan like you've been doing."

"Jana, that's not fair. I'm constantly thinking of you and what you're going through. You're my best friend, and I want to help you escape. We've gotta get out of this place."

"So, where do we go from here, best friend?" Jana said sarcastically.

"I'll try to rein Raul back in and continue to find a way out. I promise that I'll come up with something soon."

"Well, I have my own plan to escape. I've talked it over with the others, and they've bought in."

"What is it?"

"It's risky and dangerous, but it beats staying around here. I hate myself now and what I've become. I can't do this any longer. I need to get away."

"What's the plan?"

"You're probably not going to like it, but here it is. You know that pipe that runs across the top of the ceiling just above the stairs? That's a gas pipe. Once morning comes, look at how it droops on that side of the room? When you first came here, did it smell like gas?"

"Yes, now that you mention it."

"Well, it's obvious the gas line is in poor repair and has a slight leak, which tells me there's a loose connection somewhere."

"Okay, I'm following you."

"My plan, and this is the part you won't like, is to cause the pipe to rupture. We've talked about the danger, and the plan is to build a fortress out of our steel beds and set them up in the corner way over there. We'll shelter ourselves, wrap ourselves in mattresses, and be able to withstand the explosion."

"An explosion? That's crazy, Jana."

"I knew you'd say that, but think about it. The gas ignites, explodes, and opens a gaping hole in the ceiling. It probably burns the house down, and if we're lucky it, will kill the goons upstairs. We figure the force from the explosion will blow a hole in the walls or give us some avenue of escape. The men, whoever survives, would be confused and probably flee from the fire. We'll be ready though and escape in the madness."

"Jana, I'm not sure about this. It sounds insane—we'll never get out alive."

"I know it sounds risky, Lydia, but I think it's our only chance—unless you can think of something better."

"Well, I have nothing at this stage."

"So, do we have your support? Are you in?"

"Let me think about it. It's awfully risky. How do you plan to ignite the gas?"

"Well, that's where you can help us. If Raul still allows you to move freely around the house, see if you can find us a lighter or matches."

"You're kidding, right? Who's gonna be the one to light the match?"

"Well, we've talked about that, and we feel the only fair thing to do is to draw straws to see who ignites the gas line."

"No, no, no. That means that whoever draws the short straw will probably die."

"Yes, we've thought about that long and hard, but it's worth it to us if it means everyone else gets away. I'm perfectly willing to take my chances on the draw."

"Oh Jana, this is so far-fetched. I don't know. How are you going to rupture the pipe?"

"Since I'm the tallest, I'll try to reach it from the stairs. It'll require a pretty good jump, but I should be able to latch on to it. I'll grab the pipe, and my weight should pull it apart. The girls will form a cushion below in case I fall or miss the pipe on my jump."

"Jana, you are a brave soul. I hope you know this is a long shot. I guess I'm in, but I'll keep trying to think of other ways in case something goes wrong with this plan. Deal?"

"Deal."

The girls hugged tightly and enjoyed a sense of relief knowing where each other stood.

Thirty-Six

Monday, June 17, Noon, Phoenix: Missing Nine Days Twelve Hours

Lieutenant Tatum received a call from Jeff Bridgestone at his place of business.

"Lieutenant Tatum."

"Hi, Lieutenant Tatum. This is Jeff Bridgestone. I wanted to check to see if any progress had been made on locating Jana and Lydia."

"Jeff, we're not at liberty to discuss the case with you, but I can say we're tracking down all leads and following up on every possible angle."

"Okay, sure, sorry. I didn't mean to pry. I'm just interested. The reason I was calling besides getting an update on Jana and Lydia was that I may have something that could be helpful."

"Yes?"

"You know the man who hit me over the head and knocked me out?"

"Yes, go on."

"Well, after he hit me, I was vacillating in and out of consciousness. I'm not sure how accurate this is, but it just dawned on me yesterday. The vague recollection I had is that Lydia had come over to my car to check on Jana, and she thanked the man who helped her get free. He introduced himself to Jana and Lydia, and I don't know, this may be totally wrong, but I could swear he said his name was Alex, and that it was short for some other Spanish name that I can't remember. I hope this helps. I'm not sure if it's accurate, but you said to call if I thought of anything."

"Thank you so much, Jeff. This helps a lot. We'll add the information to our investigation, and it may open some doors for us. We can't tell you how much we appreciate your call. We'll be in touch if we need to talk further."

"Thanks, Lieutenant Tatum. Goodbye."

The national press was hovering in Arizona, chasing their own leads on the girls' disappearance. The heat on the governor's office grew, and concerned citizens were texting and calling his office daily, looking for answers. The governor placed a call to the Phoenix mayor and urged him to step up the effort and said he'd be authorizing state assistance to aid in the investigation.

The mayor called the police chief and gave him approval to add ten employees to aid the case. The chief called the two detectives and Tatum into his office and stressed how important it was to come up with some legitimate leads and show some progress. They were expecting additional manpower and funds to beef up the task force. He wanted results and put the pressure on the three to come up with something soon.

A few days before, Tatum had made notes on what he could do if he had unlimited resources, and now that the mandate was delivered, he started putting the plans into motion. Lieutenant Tatum arranged for undercover police officers to patrol all swimming pools, arcades, and bars across the city to monitor customers for suspicious activity. They put a plan in place that hired young and attractive female college students who were studying criminal justice. Their instructions were to hang out at locations that might attract sexual predators and establish a central point of contact to communicate anything they saw that was questionable.

Tatum had undercover police officers planted at Raining Nails and a half a dozen other bars that catered to the younger crowd and monitored the clientele closely. FBI agents volunteered to help run down the list of vehicles and were providing PPD valuable insight and data to weed out nonessential vehicles meeting the description of the white van.

With the name Jeff provided, they went back to the databases with one additional filter to apply, and it narrowed the list substantially. Detective Sharp came up with a list of Spanish names that started with an A, and there were seventy-five possibilities. They eliminated names that probably wouldn't produce a nickname of Alex, but included any name that started with "Al." That narrowed the field to twenty-two. Many of the twenty-two names didn't correlate very well with the nickname, and they chose the four names that made most sense: Alejo, Alex, Alexis, and Alejandro. Sketch artists produced renderings of the two men at Raining Nails, and these drawings were circulated to officers statewide.

Thirty-Seven

Monday, June 17, 2:00 p.m., Phoenix: Missing Nine Days Fourteen Hours

The Missing Persons Divisions got their first big break. The videographic investigator spent countless hours studying the two men captured by the parking lot security cameras. They never really noticed an important feature on the man in black. It was minuscule, but it was an important find. One of the operators noticed the man was wearing a prominent belt buckle, possibly three inches tall and four inches wide. It had two skulls and an eagle made of what appeared to be silver or some other metal surrounded by turquoise stones. It looked very expensive and may have been custom-made.

The investigators did some checking with local belt makers and aficionados and determined it was definitely a specially designed piece that could only have been made by a craftsman. They were hoping the person was local. The detectives searched for all custom belt makers in the state and found a list of six shops that had the wherewith-all to produce such professional artwork. Their next step in the investigation was to meet with the six shops and see if they recognized the image of the belt captured on video.

The Cantus and the Lincolns heard virtually nothing from the Phoenix police. They did receive a daily text from Lieutenant Tatum, stating that there were no new leads, but they were still working diligently on the case. He agreed to send a message if anything changed. The two sets of parents looked forward to the texts with guarded hope that one of the future communications would have some news about their daughters.

On Monday afternoon, Sylvia and Justine received a text from Tatum stating they had some new information to discuss with them and scheduled a conference call at four o'clock. They were eager to speak with the investigators, and a ray of hope shined on their improving dispositions.

Thirty-Eight

Monday, June 17, 4:00 p.m., Phoenix: Missing Nine Days Sixteen Hours

The conference call included the four parents and the three MP officers. They were pleased to inform the two couples that they had a possible first name of the unidentified man in the parking lot. Tatum told the couples that the man's name was provided by Jeff Bridgestone that morning after he remembered that moment outside of Raining Nails. With the help of the FBI, they were now cross-referencing white Chevy vans to owners using the four possible names.

The officers provided a general overview of what they were doing with the stakeouts and the statewide distribution of the sketches. They didn't elaborate on specifics, but they told the four parents that they had just discovered some valuable information from analyzing the video footage. This brought tears of joy to the parents, and they thanked them for their hard work.

Sylvia asked if they could say a prayer together, and the officers welcomed her request. "Dear heavenly Father, please guide our police force to help find our daughters. Give them the power and insight to seek out those that have done injustice to Lydia and Jana and shine a light on their operation from the darkness they dwell. Please provide us patience and guidance on how to cope with their absence, and most of all, protect Lydia and Jana from harm and return them safely to our home."

A round of amens resounded on the phone, and they ended the call.

Thirty-Nine

Monday, June 17, 7:00 p.m., Nogales

Monday was an off day for the girls, and no appointments were scheduled. Lydia however, got a message from Jorge that she was expected in Rojo at eight o'clock to meet with Raul. This gave her hope that she'd be able to reinstate herself after being temporarily derailed by Jana's intrusion. It would allow her to reestablish herself as his trainee and confidante. Lydia was determined to be in top form since Jana had set the bar so high the night before.

The fact that Raul was meeting her in the Rojo Room and not his master suite sent her a message that she wasn't back in his good graces quite yet. She began to question her feelings because she was actually jealous of Jana. She didn't know why, but it was there. It went beyond their ongoing personal competition of outdueling one another; it was something more profound. It was as if Jana was trespassing on her property. All the work and effort to mold and groom Raul into a facilitator for their escape may have been put in jeopardy, so it was essential for Lydia to restore her turf.

Lydia wanted to make sure she was still considered his number one, and she dressed in the most lavish, provocative attire available in the closet upstairs. She washed her hair, carefully shaved her legs and underarms, put on perfume and jewelry, and lathered down in lotion, trying to present herself as the irresistible temptress.

Manuel stood at the door, watching her thorough preparation and wondered why she was going to such an effort. Once satisfied with her appearance, she walked with Manuel to Rojo, as he looked her up and down admiring her beauty. The room was empty, and Lydia took her place on the bed and waited.

Raul purposely made her wait nearly half an hour, and when Raul finally entered, he gave her a sly grin to chide Lydia for the hateful stare he received the night before. "Did you miss me last night? You look ravishing tonight."

"Yes, I did." She stared harshly at Raul. "Why did you invite Jana up?"

"I wanted to make you jealous. Did it work?"

"Mm, yes, Raul, I was terribly jealous. It sounded like you two were having the time of your lives."

"I must admit it was very good. Jana is a fierce lioness and gave me a run for my money."

"Well, it was hard for me to sit outside and listen to you moan and groan."

"Precisely why I did it."

"Well, I was afraid I'd lose you ... to my best friend."

"Come here, Lydia. Who am I with right now?"

"Me."

They embraced and passionately engaged for half an hour. Lydia went overboard to impress Raul with new vigor and a more robust approach.

Without warning the door swung open and Jana stood in the doorway with Jorge. Lydia's best friend appeared wearing an equally seductive outfit. She was shoved into the room, and the door shut behind her. Jana stood in a state of shock. *What am I doing here? He's with Lydia. Why am I in the room? Oh my gosh. Look what she's doing. I don't want to see this.* Jana turned her head and looked away.

Hearing the door open startled Lydia. *Who? What?* She turned from her embrace with Raul and saw Jana in the doorway. *Oh no. What's Jana doing here? This has to be a mistake. Raul wanted me for himself. Jana doesn't belong here. Did he arrange for this to happen? He's crazy if he thinks I'm gonna keep this up if she's in the room. I don't want her seeing what I'm doing with him. It's embarrassing.* She moved away from Raul and glared at Jana.

Raul left Lydia on the bed, walked over to Jana, grabbed her by the arm, and led her back to Lydia.

Jana was petrified. *Oh no, he's bringing me over. No not this. I just can't—not with Lydia watching. We're friends for goodness' sake.*

Lydia quickly covered up.

Raul undressed Jana on the bed and crawled between the two young ladies.

Lydia was horrified, *No, what is he thinking? What is he trying to do? This can't be happening. I'm sorry. I just can't. How gross. I can't do this in front of another girl, especially not Jana. No, no, no. We just can't.*

Lydia thought, *This can't go on. Surely he doesn't want us to do this in front of one another. We have to stop this right now.*

Jana was horrified too. *No, not that. We can't! Gotta delay this. Maybe we can wait Raul out, and he'll tire. We have to think of something.*

Being with Tabitha the other night was bad enough, but this is unthinkable—not with Lydia. I don't want to touch her.

"I want you both tonight."

Lydia said, "Wait, no way." *No, absolutely not. Jana, and I can't. We're friends. We don't touch like that. I can't imagine being with a girl—much less with Jana. I can't handle her looking at me, touching me. Oh, God, get me out of this situation.*

Jana said, "I can't do this, Raul. No!" *Oh, no. Not with Lydia. This is so gross. I need to leave, but I'm afraid. I just can't face the punishment. What do I do? How can I touch her of all people? What will she think of me? I can't bear to think about it.*

"You will both cooperate or feel my wrath."

They looked at each other and were repelled at the thought of being with Raul together. Not so much being with him individually, but if they were forced to be with one another, that was unthinkable. Before they could consider much more about it, Raul pulled Lydia down to the bed and advanced on her.

Jana remained quiet and forced her eyes shut. She tried to tune out the sounds while he and Lydia were together, but it was agony being so close to their flurry.

Jana thought, *I can't take this. Please get me out of here.*

Lydia was cast aside and Raul grabbed Jana and continued his aggression, causing Lydia to become bitter and agitated.

Lydia sat up and thought, *I can't believe this guy. He's pitting the two of us against each other.*

Jana thought, *This is horrible. Right in front of Lydia? I've never felt so humiliated and awkward. Maybe if we can somehow exhaust Raul, we can avoid having to do anything with each other.*

Raul paused, sat up, and pushed Lydia toward Jana, motioning for them to embrace. They looked at each other aghast and at a loss for what to do. Raul clapped his hands and got angry. He ordered them to start immediately—or he'd have Manuel come in to administer punishment. The two young girls who grew up together and shared their most intimate secrets were now being forced to cross the line that neither wanted to breech. They never had a desire for this sort of thing and saw each other as sisters. It was atrocious for Raul to force them into this situation.

The cartel chief reached up and pushed their heads together, motioning for them to kiss. They fought the urge to leave the room for fear of the consequences and hesitantly commenced, bristling at the thought of kissing one another.

They kissed and then broke it off quickly and awkwardly, looking away and not wanting to meet the other's eyes.

Raul then motioned for them to lay down together, but Lydia and Jana paused, wavering from their uneasiness and doubt. They shuddered.

Raul forcefully guided them down to the bed, and they faced each other, averting their eyes downward. The moment had turned disturbing and shameful. Raul saw the hesitation and nudged Jana to get on with it.

Lydia retreated, and he leaned over, grabbed Lydia's neck, and pushed her toward Jana. The two were now forced into their worst fear, and both girls were trembling with dread. Raul was tired of waiting, and he threatened them again. The young women lightly engaged, which infuriated Raul. He yelled for Manuel to come in.

Jana and Lydia were quickly jarred into a more active exchange.

Manuel opened the door and looked inside, but Raul waved him off since the girls were finally cooperating. Manuel took a long look at Lydia and Jana as they embraced, smiled, and slowly retreated outside.

Raul persistently intimidated the two, pressuring the girls to continue.

Jana kept her eyes closed and tried to imagine it was someone other than Lydia, and she focused only on what was in front of her.

Lydia cooperated reluctantly, taking her mind elsewhere.

Jana recalled her night with Tabitha and began to emulate what she had learned, and Lydia cautiously accommodated her incursion.

It was inevitable that the teenagers would eventually fall into a deep well of physical pleasure instigated by the diabolical arrangement designed by Raul. He was delighted by the display of their affection and watching the two young women please each other in such compelling fashion. He could barely contain himself over the course of the evening. From that point forward, the threesome coalesced and gave Raul one of the most pleasurable nights he could remember.

As it turned out, the young ladies spent more time with each other than with Raul, but he didn't complain. He was taken aback when he witnessed Jana and Lydia actually preferring to be with one another as opposed to being with him. Jana and Lydia would spend a short stretch with Raul and then disengage and melt together in a steamy tangle of passion. Raul was amazed by Lydia and Jana's unique conditioning from their many years of playing soccer, which ushered in furious physical exertion that pushed one another to the boundaries.

After the emotional night was over, the two young ladies dressed, avoiding eye contact. They didn't speak, trying to convince themselves that it didn't happen. They silently made their way out of the room, heads down, ashamed, and humiliated, and were escorted back down into the dungeon. They remained quiet and extremely embarrassed at how intimately they shared their bodies and offered their womanly virtue to each other. The two friends were both filled with remorse. They couldn't wait to find their beds, crawl under the sheets, and hide from one another.

Before falling asleep, Lydia said to Jana, “We’re going with the plan you came up with—and soon.”

Forty

Tuesday, June 18, 2:00 p.m., Phoenix: Missing Ten Days Fourteen Hours

Detectives Sharp and Williams met with custom belt-makers across the state. They approached the first four and got four negative responses. The comment most of the artisans made was how finely it was crafted, and they wouldn't have the capabilities to make such a belt. However, the last man they spoke to said it looked like the work of a man from Kino Springs in southern Arizona. He produced a lot of belts with turquoise and was a silversmith as well. He suggested they talk with Jon Bratt, a native Indian who had been making jewelry for fifty years.

No other news surfaced to share with Jana and Lydia's parents, and Tatum's texts were starting to look like what they had seen before: empty and disappointing.

Forty-One

Tuesday, June 18, 7:00 P.M., Nogales

Jorge came down to the basement and announced the schedule for that night's patrons: Jana in Azul, Tabitha and Charlotte in Blanco, and Beth in the Rojo Room. Emma was given the night off.

Like other nights, Jorge walked over to Lydia and told her she would be meeting with Raul in the master bedroom. Lydia was elated. *The master bedroom!* She tried to mute her enthusiasm, and Lydia felt like she might be getting back in Raul's good graces. Lydia intended to ignore the previous evening's debacle with Jana and act like nothing had changed. She knew he would be watching her disposition closely. Lydia was determined to regain Raul's trust, so he'd once again allow her access to other parts of the house.

The four girls were taken to the Sala De Agua and prepared for the evening's assignments. Lydia showered in the basement and was retrieved by Jorge just before eight o'clock. The other girls went to their allotted bedrooms and began entertaining their customers.

Lydia was escorted by Jorge to the master bedroom, feeling a bit unsettled and not knowing what to expect from this man who had proven he was capable of doing just about anything.

Jana was in the Azul bedroom and drew a large beefy Hispanic man from Veracruz. He was probably three hundred pounds on a good day. Jana shuddered when she entered the room and saw what was ahead, but she kept an even demeanor and gave the man more than he bargained for, ending the night early when he was having palpitations. Jana was relieved and was able to return to her bunk early that night. She thought through the group's plan, which she hoped would be put into motion soon.

Raul was waiting for Lydia in his bed, and they proceeded to enjoy two hours of lovemaking. She went for broke by mirroring Jana's MO and strenuously besieged him with a physical assault.

"What's up with you tonight? You're great."

"I don't know. I just wanted to give you what you like. Hearing you and Jana the other night from the den made me reassess my techniques, and I wanted to show you I'm capable of doing it too."

"Well, whatever you're doing, I'm liking it."

The two relaxed, catching their breath, and wondered what the other was thinking. Raul was pondering Lydia's motives, and Lydia thought about the escape plan. The silence and her train of thought were interrupted.

"Hey, sugar. I'm thirsty. Could go into the kitchen and get me something to drink? I'll take a beer, a cold one, okay?"

"I guess so, Mr. Alvarez. I'll be right back."

Lydia slipped on her smock and walked barefoot to the kitchen. She got a Modelo out of the refrigerator and looked for a bottle opener. She searched through several drawers and finally found it. Right next to the opener, she spotted a lighter. Lydia flicked the wheel on top, and a flame popped up. She quickly turned it off, checked to see if anyone was looking, and slipped it in her pocket. She opened the beer and returned with Raul's drink.

They enjoyed each other's company for hour or so after he finished his beer, and Lydia was at her best. Raul was spent and told Lydia she could stay the night with him. After he fell asleep, Lydia couldn't get her mind off the plan and how it was to fall into place. She was still skeptical they could carry it out, but like the others, she was resolved to try to escape—even if it meant endangering their lives.

Forty-Two

Wednesday, June 19, 10:00 a.m., Phoenix: Missing Eleven Days Ten Hours

Detectives Williams and Sharp arranged an appointment to see Jon Bratt, the belt designer in Kino Springs. They made the long drive and found his shop on the edge of town. They showed him the photos of the belt from the security cameras, and he studied it closely from different angles.

Sharp asked, “Every seen anything like this before?”

“Yep. I made this belt.”

“You did? Are you certain?”

“Yes, I remember setting the stones and having a hard time getting them to line up properly. Solid silver, ten turquoise stones, lots of etchings, and an amethyst stone in the middle. Cost the buyer a pretty penny.”

"Can you tell us who the buyer was?"

"Well, I'm not sure I want to tell you."

"Why is that?"

"That is one mean hombre, and I think he works for the cartel. Not sure I want to get on his bad side. I may not be around to make any more belts."

"Mr. Pratt, we will not divulge the source of our information or disclose anything to do with you or your business. Is that understood?"

"Yes, but I'm still not sure—"

"Mr. Pratt, your information could save the lives of two innocent girls. We really need his name. This won't go any further than your shop."

Pratt went over to a simple file box and pulled out some receipts. He flipped through the invoices and said, "The belt was $450 and was sold to Alejandro Diaz."

"Do you know where Mr. Diaz is located?"

"No, sir. I don't. I'm sorry I can't help you with that."

The detectives thanked Mr. Pratt for the information and left his shop. On their way back to Phoenix, Williams called Tatum in the car and shared the information. The task force was alerted soon after.

Forty-Three

Wednesday, June 19, Noon, Phoenix: Missing Eleven Days Twelve Hours

The task force worked feverishly to find the suspected kidnapper and finally came across their suspect.

Alejandro Diaz lived in Nogales, Arizona, on West Crawford Street, a few blocks from the border. His name didn't appear on any register or official documents, but the team worked through local sources, including the FBI, which led them to Nogales. The police in Nogales were able to question residents and merchants to locate what was thought to be his residence.

Reliable sources told local police that Diaz was on the road constantly and spent little time in the area. Finding him at home would be iffy. He was a known criminal with a rap sheet in three states, and he was being sought by federal authorities for drug smuggling, attempted murder, rape, and sex trafficking. It was believed he worked for a high-ranking member of the Mexican cartel, and reports indicated that Alex Diaz was a midlevel hoodlum and part of the cartel's web in southern Arizona, employing hundreds of soldiers in Arizona, New Mexico, and Mexico.

Diaz probably worked for Raul Alvarez and had direct access to the top cartel chieftain in Mexico. With the suspect identified, Tatum scrambled to assemble his team to pursue Diaz. The coordination effort was complex and extensive, laden with red tape and bureaucracy. He called the FBI, AZDPS, the local ATF Bureau, and the Nogales Police Department to carefully plan a surprise visit to the house. The Missing Persons chief arranged for a PPD helicopter to transport the leaders of the task force team to Nogales after they were granted clearance from federal and state authorities to conduct the flight.

Forty-Four

Wednesday, June 19, 2:00 p.m., Phoenix: Missing Eleven Days Fourteen Hours

Before leaving for Nogales, Tatum called Sylvia, and she patched in Justine. He announced to the ladies that the task force had the name of a suspect and were in the process of running him down. They were urged not to divulge any of this information to any outside sources and to keep it confidential between the four parents. They agreed, and their roller-coaster ride lifted them from the depths and soared toward the sky, giving them hope that the police were narrowing the gap between the lost and the found.

Forty-Five

Wednesday, June 19, 2:00 P.M., Nogales

The girls were resting and very weary after an arduous night with their customers. Lydia was sent downstairs to get a breather, and it gave her the opportunity to pull Jana aside and secretly show her the lighter.

Jana called the girls together, and they moved to the far corner of the room. They stood in an area partially blocked by the shower walls to avoid the camera at the top of the stairs. They formed a circle, and Jana said the plan was now a go and that Lydia had generously provided them the means to ignite the gas line. Lydia cautiously looked over her shoulder, pulled out the lighter, and flicked it for everyone to see.

The eyes of all six girls widened as they realized that something profound, dangerous, and deadly would be happening soon. The girls rationalized that life as they knew it was no life at all and listened intently. They were determined to escape. Their plan was worth someone giving up their life to gain their freedom. There was no hesitation among the group to move ahead.

"Are we all ready for this?" Jana asked.

All the girls nodded.

Jana said, "Okay, here's the plan. I'm goin' up the stairs to try to reach the gas line. I've been measuring it in my mind, and I think I can reach the pipe if I can jump high enough. Once I latch onto it, my body weight should stress the pipe and hopefully break apart the ends where the line is weak and gas is seeping out. Since I'm jumping from the stairs, I'll need you guys to catch me if I miss the pipe or fall from the stairs. We've gotta to do this quickly because it's right in front of the camera, and if they see what's going on, we'll soon be out of luck. I figure we'll have a minute, maybe two, depending on how closely they monitor the room. That may give me a couple of tries."

More affirmative nods all around.

Lydia said, "Okay, let's do this. Now for the difficult part. Each person needs to draw a straw from Charlotte's hand, and the one who draws the short straw has to take the lighter, stand under the pipe, and ignite it. Unfortunately, the chance of survival may not be good, but someone has to do it. Are we all up for this?"

The realization entered their minds that one of them probably wouldn't be around after the blast. Fate would determine the outcome. Surprisingly, it didn't deter the girls a bit. They looked around at each other and bravely gave the thumbs-up to move forward with the plan.

Charlotte held out the straws taken from a broom in the basement, and each girl pulled one out of her hand. Tabitha received a long one, and Beth also got a long straw. Jana was next, and the straw she pulled out was an inch shorter than the rest. Charlotte opened her hand, and the rest of the straws were the same length as Tabitha's and Beth's. Jana had drawn the short straw.

Lydia broke down and began sobbing, but Jana stopped her and shook her by the shoulders. "Lydia, it had to be someone. I got it fair and square. I'm willing to do this so you five can have your lives back. It's that important to me. So, compose yourself—and let's get on with this." *I can't believe I drew the short straw. Why did it have to be me? Well, I got it. There's nothing I can do—so let's do this.*

Jana's bravery was commendable and certainly didn't surprise Lydia. She had seen her friend take life by the horns many times and dictate the end result. This time was no different.

Beth and Tabitha quickly began moving beds over to the far corner of the basement, turning them on their sides. The beds formed a V, and the girls stacked mattresses on the top and on each side of the beds, making a sturdy shelter to protect them from the blast.

While they were preparing the shelter, Jana scaled the stairs, stood as close to the gas line as possible, and waited for the girls to ready themselves below. Once in place, she leaped for the pipe, her long frame stretching to its full length and her arms extended, but she barely touched it. Jana dropped, but the girls next to the stairs caught her and cushioned the fall. Driven by her athletically toned body that was firing on all cylinders, she sprinted back up the stairs with little time wasted. She concentrated for a moment and made another leap from the stairs. She barely grazed the gas line on her second try. She fell into the grasp of the girls again, and now their hopes began to ebb.

If Jana can't reach it, no one could.

Jana wasn't giving up yet.

Charlotte said, "Come on, Jana. You can do this."

Tabitha said, "Yeah, we believe in you, Jana."

She bolted up the stairs for another try and focused on the pipe, staring at it with the intensity of an accomplished soccer player going for a goal. Jana leaped high in the air and this time she was able to get one hand on the pipe. She secured it with a tight grip, swinging on one arm. Jana tried to reach up and grasp the gas line with the other hand, but the pipe began creaking. The damaged seam buckled under her weight and separated. The smell of gas flooded the room, and Jana dropped into the girl's arms one final time. "Give me the lighter!"

"Here. Oh, Jana, do you have to?" Lydia handed Jana the lighter, and the others raced to their positions behind the beds. They quickly wrapped themselves in sheets and blankets and pulled the mattresses on top of the shelter.

The best friends since second grade gave each other an emotional hug, and tears streamed down their faces, knowing it might be the last time they would see each other. Lydia harbored painful guilt about Jana drawing the short straw and having had to endure all of the abuse over the past ten days with Raul's customers. Her despondency rendered her feet inoperable, and Lydia wasn't able to move toward the shelter.

Lydia realized that Jana's next bold shot at the goal may be her last. Lydia wiped the tears from her face, turned, and slowly headed to the makeshift refuge. Jana cherished one last look at her best friend and childhood companion and the other friends she made over the short stay at Raul's. Jana turned her back to the girls, focused on the pipe, and gathered the courage to ignite the gas. *Well, here goes. I'm not sure what's gonna happen, but I've gotta do it so the others can escape and go home.* She held the lighter in her left hand and started walking toward the stairs. Just when she took her first step, Emma darted from around the beds, ran up behind her, and snatched the lighter.

"Wait! Emma, no, don't. It's supposed to be me."

Before Jana could react, Emma ran up the stairs with the lighter.

Jana realized what had happened and that it was too late to convince Emma to change her mind.

"Come on, Jana. Hurry!" Lydia pleaded for her to get behind the shelter.

Jana dashed toward the beds and lunged onto the floor, trying to make it to the shelter in time.

Emma stood on the step closest to the pipe and heard someone inserting the key into the door. *Oh no! They're coming in.* Emma reached her hand above her head as far as it would extend, stood on her tiptoes, and flicked the lighter. A flame appeared, and a split second later the room exploded in a fiery combustion that rocked the foundation. The walls buffeted, flames burst up from the room, and the floor above collapsed, falling into a heap all around the girls. The door to the basement was obliterated, and the stairs were vaporized.

Pedro and Jorge were casually watching the security cameras as Jana ruptured the gas line. They were trying to open the door before Emma was able to carry out her mission. As they were opening the door, it was incinerated, blowing Pedro and Jorge all the way through the house and out into the front yard.

Manuel and Alex were in the den above the basement, and they were devoured by the detonation. They fell twenty feet below into the basement, aflame and charred. Tumbling down into the hole was furniture, the refrigerator, and all the appliances from the kitchen.

The blast jolted the girls' fortress all the way back to the cinder block wall, smashing them into the corner. The mattresses caught fire, and flaming ash was floating in the air as debris fell all around them. The blast didn't budge the sturdy basement walls since they were buttressed by the underground embankment. It only took out the ceiling above.

The girls' primary escape route would have been up the stairs, but they were obliterated in the blast and had disappeared. The initial concussion damaged their eardrums. All they could hear was a loud ringing, and blood was seeping out of their ears and trickling down their necks. The girls had blood splattered on their arms and legs from the cuts and gashes caused by shrapnel flying in all directions.

Jana was able to make it to the shelter at the last moment. After the blast, she stood and surveyed the room with pockets of fire crackling nearby. *No exit to the outside, and the stairs are gone now. What do we do?* Below the staircase, she spotted the double doors to the tunnel and looked to see if the passage could be accessed.

Lydia stood up and they peered over at the double doors.

Jana said, "Lydia, that's our only way out. Let's go."

"I'm right behind you, girl," Lydia replied.

Their path to the doors would take them past the fiery remains of Manuel and Alex. Their faces were unrecognizable. The girls stopped abruptly when they heard hysterical shouting from above and shots from Raul's automatic weapon strafed the floor around them. Projectiles slammed into the wall, throwing dust into the air and digging holes in a long, jagged pattern.

"Watch out!" Beth yelled.

The rounds sprayed around their feet, kicking up shards of wood and metal into their faces.

The girls ducked and shielded their heads, fright conspicuously coloring their faces. They stood like nervous statues, waiting for direction from Lydia and Jana.

Jana looked up and spotted Raul. He was enraged and intent on stopping their movement. He was resolved on keeping his harem intact and intended to prevent them from escaping through the basement.

Jana said, "Come on. He's not gonna kill us—we're too valuable."

Jana and Lydia sensed that Raul wasn't trying to kill them. They gambled and waved the girls forward to quickly follow them to the doors.

"Come on, get over here, hurry!" Lydia said.

Raul shot a half dozen more rounds above their heads, and they ricocheted off the cinderblock façade, sending sharp fragments of concrete in all directions.

Arriving at the double doors, they encountered a pile of damaged ceiling tiles, flooring from the den, and pieces of the staircase. One end of a massive floor joist had fallen onto the floor in front of the double doors and blocked their way. Lydia and Jana tried to remove the unwieldy truss, but the wooden beam was too heavy. They motioned for the other girls to help.

Lydia said, "Charlotte, you and Tabitha get that side with Jana. Beth and I will pull on this side."

The five tugged and shoved, their faces colored red with exertion, and Jana's and Lydia's biceps tightened with veins popping and their muscular frames bent as they tried to heave the wood from their path.

"Come on, y'all. Pull—we gotta get out of here! One, two, three, go!"

Finally, it budged as the two fierce competitors huffed and puffed, cheeks burning scarlet, until they were able to slowly move the impediment a few feet away.

"Get down!" Lydia hollered.

More shots rang out. Raul had reloaded and discharged the weapon again, this time closer to their heads. Unfazed, they cleared the path of the remaining ruins, revealing that one of the doors had blown off its hinges, leaning forward still blocking the exit. The other door was damaged, still firmly in place, and blocked by debris.

The girls put ten hands on the door and began pulling on it, but they were barely able to move the thick steel barricade. Jana picked up a long piece of steel pipe and tried to pry the door forward. The girls pulled and were aided by Jana's leverage, causing the door to finally careen off its hinges, barely missing Tabitha and Charlotte as they jumped out of the way.

Raul spat more lead, getting much closer, and Jana's forehead was cut by shards of cinderblock. With the door pulled out of the way, they crept into the pitch-black darkness of the tunnel, wondering where it led.

Lydia took a last look up at Raul, wondering how he was able to survive the blast. She assumed he was lucky and probably in his office on the far side of the house. That would be the only way he could have avoided the brunt of the explosion. Raul's survival flashed only briefly through Lydia's mind, and she joined the others at the entrance. They hesitated to see Raul's next move.

Raul shouldered his weapon for a moment, retrieved his cell phone, and quickly made two calls. One was to a squad of local soldiers, ordering reinforcements to meet at his house at once, saying that he and his men were under siege. Raul knew the fire department and local authorities would be flooding the neighborhood, and the soldiers would need to protect themselves until they could escape. He refused to surrender to the authorities and felt his men could hold them off until they could regroup and break away.

His second call was to one of his lieutenants in Mexico across the border in Heroica Nogales. After frantically explaining what happened at the safe house Raul gave the men strict instructions to warn his Mexican counterparts that his female inventory from Nogales was attempting to escape through the tunnel. He told them to be prepared to meet and intercept them at the Mexican entrance—if they made it that far. As he was hanging up, Raul ordered them to summon a cartel helicopter. The chopper was on standby for company emergencies and based in Agua Prieta, 180 kilometers away. He ordered the men to be in the air over Nogales as quickly as possible—locked and loaded.

Forty-Six

Wednesday, June 19, 3:00 p.m., Phoenix: Missing Eleven Days Fifteen Hours

After a hectic organizational firestorm, the law enforcement team was finally able to embark on the one-hour flight to Nogales. The helicopter ascended into the hot dry air of Phoenix and headed for Nogales. Upon arrival, they were to be picked up by a local ATF agent who would direct the men to their destination. They'd be also accompanied by Nogales police.

Forty-Seven

Wednesday, June 19, 3:00 P.M., Nogales

While Emma was clambering up the stairs with the lighter to ignite the gas line, Sonny Avila had just arrived at the home for his weekly maintenance on Raul's pool. Sonny was a trusted employee of Raul's, having serviced the large, rectangular pool for five years. Every so often, Raul would come out poolside while Sonny was adding chlorine or sweeping the pool for leaves, and they would sit on the deck after he was finished. They'd relax, kick back, have a drink, and talk about sports, food, and Sonny's appetite for the crazy white powder. Raul would trade him cocaine for his work on the pool and was very generous to the man he came to like because of his sense of humor and honesty. They became good friends, and Raul would share details with Sonny about some of the cartel's exploits and business ventures in Arizona.

Sonny was aware that Raul dealt in sex trafficking and had heard many stories of how they captured, drugged, and enslaved young women from all over the Southwest. Sonny earned Raul's trust because he never mentioned what he was told to anyone, mostly because of his loyalty, but the more punitive reason was that he would probably be killed if he did. Each Wednesday, he looked forward to hanging out with Raul if he wasn't busy—or if some of the young girls happened to be given recreational time to lounge around the pool. He'd watch as some of the young girls would slip off their white gowns revealing their young, supple bodies and dive into the pool to refresh themselves from the arduous nightly work. Most of the girls were between fourteen and sixteen, but occasionally he saw some, probably as young as twelve and on the older side, around twenty. Most times, they acted as though he wasn't there, and he seemed invisible at times. Sonny tried not to stare or look obvious when he drank in the beauty of the girls splashing around or sunbathing nude on the deck. It was difficult at times.

Raul knew of Sonny's fondness for the young girls and would compensate his dedicated friend by arranging an occasional meeting with a girl of his choice. His taste leaned more toward the older girls because they were more developed and mature. When he saw Jana at the pool, he couldn't take his eyes off of her and developed a feverish obsession for the tall, blonde gringo. He even fantasized about Jana at night and dreamed about being with her in Rojo. In his dreams, he would picture her long, sleek legs that were tanned around a tiny white area that was once covered by a bikini. Her distinct features, high cheekbones, and crystal blue eyes kept him up at night, desiring her body. After his duties were completed on the day he first saw Jana, Sonny made a point to find Raul and plead with him to arrange a rendezvous with her when she had a night off. Raul laughed, complimented him on his good taste, and said he hoped Sonny was man enough to handle her. Raul promised to set it up the next month.

Sonny was leaving his truck, pulling supplies out of the bed, when he remembered that his cell phone was left on the dashboard. As he went back for the phone, the blast knocked him back into the street, ten feet from his company vehicle. He sat in the road for a moment with his hand shielding his face and looked at the inferno billowing into the sky. His ears heard only a dull ringing, and his eyes burned, blurring his vision caused by the fumes of the blaze.

Remnants of the house blown into the air were falling all around him, and the intense heat forced him back. The roof caved in, and the brick chimney toppled lazily into the house cavity. Sonny's mouth fell open as he watched in shock, and realized that his routine visit, which he assumed would be another tranquil day at Raul's pool, had quickly turned into a horrendous search and rescue operation. He shuddered to think that if he had arrived five minutes earlier, he wouldn't be alive. Had Sonny not stopped for some cigarettes at the convenience store, his life would be all but over.

Sonny gathered himself and bravely ran into the house through the opening that was once the front door. Shielding his face from the heat with a folded arm, he hopped over debris and red-hot pieces of metal. Sonny entered the kitchen where what was left of the floor was sloping dangerously toward the open basement. The other half had been inhaled into the deep recesses taking the cabinets, appliances, and flooring with it.

Sonny carefully walked toward the ledge of what floor remained around the top of the basement and peered down into the smoldering crater. Raul suddenly appeared to his right, running from the other end of the house. Their eyes fixed, and Sonny saw Raul with a deranged look on his face as if he was in shock. Raul carried an automatic rifle and swung it back and forth past Sonny, causing him to jump back, wary of the weapon accidentally discharging. Raul's eyes darted to the basement and back to Sonny without acknowledging him and then squinted down in the burning pit and noticed two lifeless bodies on the floor. Inspecting them closer, Raul saw the two were the charred and dismembered torsos of Alex and Manuel. Raul was incensed.

"What's going on, Raul? What happened?"

No answer.

Raul noticed movement on the margins of the basement where the stairs once stood. He and Sonny looked over and saw the five young ladies rushing toward the double doors.

"Wait, Raul. Don't!"

Raul focused the barrel of the AR toward the five and fired above them with a burst of lead that scattered all around them. He didn't want to kill the stable of flesh that his team had worked so hard to collect, and he tried to dissuade the girls by spraying the walls behind them.

Sonny looked on horrified having seen the mutilated bodies of Raul's soldiers, the gun pointed at him, and Raul firing at the young women below. He saw the girls hurdling over piles of refuse, lumber, and twisted metal and snaking their way through the wreckage toward the double doors. He tried to remember the girls from his encounters at the pool and noticed a tall, lean girl sprinting ahead of the others with blonde hair fluttering around her shoulders. It was Jana.

Raul shoved in another clip and fired just above where the ladies stopped. Jana and Lydia's team stopped at the double doors and were attempting to move a large joist that had fallen in front of the doorway. While they were frantically digging their way to the door, Raul found his cell phone and made two quick calls, ordering backup from his Mexican counterparts. Then he focused the weapon down at the five frenetic females.

Sonny forgot his place, wanting to protect the girls, mostly caused by his interest in defending Jana. He didn't want harm to come to any of Raul's subjects, but he really wanted to protect the young woman of his dreams. So, he nimbly stepped behind Raul, grabbed the weapon that was pointed at the girls, and pulled his arm away. "I'm not gonna let you do that, don't kill them."

Raul looked back at Sonny like he'd lost his mind as he tried to yank the AR away. "Sonny, you've signed your death warrant. Get out of my way."

During the struggle, a piece of the flooring under Raul's feet snapped off and fell into the basement. Raul looked down, lost his balance, and toppled over the edge, his eyes screaming with terror on his way down. Sonny was horrified when Raul landed with a crash, snapping one leg on a pile of wood. His arm was contorted at an unusual angle, obviously broken. The AR had landed several feet from where Raul hit the floor.

Sonny scurried around the perimeter, seeking a way to reach the basement, but the drop was too far. He'd probably kill himself if he jumped.

The girls yanked at the door trying to get it open with a pry bar.

Raul was writhing in pain, but he was unable to move from his position. He thrashed and squirmed, and blood seeped from his leg.

Lydia moved toward him hesitantly, but Jana grabbed her arm. "Don't help him, Lydia. He's not worth it. Let's go!"

Lydia jerked her arm away from Jana and continued stepping toward Raul.

"Lydia, come on. Forget it. We've gotta leave before anyone else arrives!"

Lydia stepped over the piles of wreckage and approached Raul.

He looked up at her with anticipation in his eyes, raised his one good arm, and asked for mercy.

Lydia bent down, looked into his wild eyes, reared back, and spat in his face. *Take that, you pig.*

From the doorway, Jana smiled at Lydia and greeted her with a hug as she came back to the group. As they started to enter the tunnel, Jana broke away, ran over to Raul, and put an exclamation on Lydia's goodbye with a huge wad of spittle perfectly placed on his forehead. *From me too, pervert.*

Sonny watched the seminal moment from above. Seeing Jana disrespect Raul at her glorious best, he couldn't help but smile. He thought it best to try to get down to help Raul. As the thought registered, someone ran up behind him in a huff. Sonny wheeled around.

Simon Gutierrez was on his route delivering packages from his FedEx truck. When he heard the explosion down the street, he sped to the scene.

"What happened, man?" Simon asked.

"Not sure. The whole house just, like, exploded, nearly got me from outside. I ran in to see if I could help Raul, who owns the house, and he fell off the ledge as I was coming toward him. Raul's over there and looks hurt pretty bad. There's two others right over there, but it doesn't look like they made it." Sonny pointed to them in the basement.

Simon was shocked as he stared down at Alex and Manuel. Raul had finally passed out from the excruciating pain. "He needs help, man. Is there a rope or something we can drop down to help lower ourselves to the bottom?"

Sonny remembered the pool safety rope that he had taken out of a pool the day before. "Hang here. I'll be right back." Sonny weaved his way through the mess, went out to his truck, retrieved the rope, and hustled back in.

They examined the safety rope and the floats that were attached and started sliding them off one by one. The nylon rope appeared to be plenty strong, and Simon attached one end to a wall stud, pulled the knot taut, and threw the other end over the side toward the basement. The rope snaked down the wall and ended up being five or six feet short.

"We can work with that," Simon said.

"I'll go first." Sonny felt responsible for Raul's fall.

"Okay. I'll secure the line up here."

Sonny got a good two-handed grip on the rope, swung his feet over the ledge, and carefully started down the rope. Halfway to the bottom, Simon heard footsteps and another man ran into the house.

A mailman burst in with dread on his face. "Anybody hurt?"

"Yeah, man, there's like three guys down there. Two of them are goners. The other one's passed out and is hurt pretty bad. Hey, I'm Simon."

"David Jimenez."

"Help me hold the rope, Dave."

David held the stud where the rope was tied, and they both looked down as Sonny reached the end of the rope. He dropped down the rest of the way, landed on some drywall, and hopped to his feet. Sonny went over to Raul to comfort him.

Simon and David turned their heads when they heard sirens sounding in the distance.

Simon said, "Stay here and watch the rope. I'm going down."

"Will do," David responded.

Simon crawled over the side, holding the rope tightly, and slithered down to the end. He jumped toward the pile of drywall to avoid the sharp twisted metal and bounded over to Raul. He picked up AR from the rubble. "What's goin' on with this?"

Sonny pointed to Raul. "I don't know. I think it's his."

Sonny tried to bring Raul around, but he didn't respond. Simon slipped the weapon over his shoulder and looked at Raul's injured arm. Sonny tore off a piece of his shirt, made it into a makeshift bandage to stop the bleeding, and wrapped it tightly around Raul's shattered leg. He grimaced at its odd angle.

David watched from above, wondering what had happened to cause so much damage. The sirens grew closer.

Lydia, Jana, and company stood at the entrance of the cave and stared at the men trying to help Raul. It was obvious they weren't cartel since Simon had on his purple and black FedEx uniform, and the girls recognized the pool man. The five young women hesitated at the doorway before they went inside the mysterious dark hole and wondered whether the two men could help them escape.

Simon and Sonny worked on Raul, and he began moaning and coming to.

Everyone in the basement heard a commotion upstairs, and when they craned their heads upward, saw five of Raul's commandos armed and standing on the ledge. They came to help, after receiving Raul's order for assistance and barged in with guns brandished to aid their boss.

David was still holding the nylon pool rope as the gunmen stood on the ledge and stared down at Raul, then to Sonny and Simon.

Raul saw his men when he returned to consciousness and motioned frantically toward the girls in the doorway. "Get them before they get away!" Raul screeched.

With Sonny and the FedEx man standing near the door, the girls thought there might be an alternative to fleeing through the tunnel, but it dissolved when they saw Raul's men arrive. The split second it took his men to understand Raul's orders, gave Lydia time to quickly lead the girls through the door, and all five men began firing at the opening.

"Let's go! Watch out!" Jana screamed.

Shards of splintered wood and cinder block exploded into the cave, catching some of the young ladies on the back of their legs and buttocks.

It dawned on David that the cartel hoodlums were trying to kill the young women. He untied the rope and let it drop to the ground, hoping to keep the men from being able to reach the basement.

The goons didn't like his logic much, and they walked over and kicked him off the ledge.

David fell, and his arms fluttered as he tried to right himself on his way down. He fell backwards all the way to the ground and was impaled on a piece of twisted metal jutting up from the floor. He died instantly. The nerves in his foot continued to quiver, and his hands shook involuntarily for a few moments.

Sonny and Simon flinched and ducked from the firing when they heard the thud behind them.

David's body was limp, gored by a metal beam and blood was pumping profusely out of his chest.

The cartel members looked down at the two men, held their fire, and waited for instructions from their leader. Simon and Sonny did all they could for Raul and nonchalantly made their way toward the tunnel, acting like they were going to retrieve the rope and throw it back upstairs.

The tunnel was pitch-black. The blast had knocked out the lighting, and the only illumination filtered in from the basement, shining across the first few feet of the cave. After taking several steps in the tunnel, the girls were completely engulfed in the obscurity. The rocky floor was bumpy and unpredictable, and they had to measure their steps in order to move forward. Their urgency to get away from Raul and his henchmen pressed against their ability to move with any speed. They could no longer run or take hurried steps, and they inched their way along without a clue where they were going or what lay ahead. They found out soon after entering that there's no darkness worse than a cave. It was total, utter nothingness.

It didn't take long for the girls to understand the challenges of the darkness. It deceived their senses and confounded their rational thinking. Walking was treacherous, and the walls of the cave narrowed and widened without warning. The supports holding the earth above the tunnel and along the sides were made of rough cedar posts, and it was easy to pick up splinters as the girls felt their way down the tunnel. Progress was now measured in inches, and no one hurried—even though they knew pursuit would be close behind.

Jana and Lydia took the lead, reaching out with their feet to feel the contours of the floor and palming the walls like a blind man. It did no good to even have their eyes open; it was the same either way. The rest of the girls followed the two leaders in formation, one abreast. Each girl held onto their friend in front by grasping a handful their white dress, careful not to step on their legs or run up their backs.

Tabitha was bringing up the rear and was starting to fret and whimper. The stress of the explosion, the loss of her good friend Emma, the gunfire, and the insane darkness were wearing her down. All the girls, including Jana and Lydia, were emotionally spent. They were desperate, scared, and tired. Beth hadn't put on her shoes before the explosion, and she limped forward. Her feet were sore and bleeding from stepping over metal shards and glass scattered by the fiery blast. Not one complaint was heard from her, and she bravely stayed up with the rest, holding up the middle of the line.

Charlotte and Tabitha had small cuts on their legs and backsides from the shrapnel flying off the walls when they leaped inside the cave. Their gowns were soiled as they tumbled into the tunnel and scarlet from the dried blood of their wounds.

Raul's men were perched above, watching Sonny and Simon

closely as they neared the fallen pool rope. The gunmen weren't certain of their allegiance and whether they really planned to come back up the rope or had intentions to try to escape.

"Go, Sonny. I'll cover you," Simon whispered.

As the two men neared the rope, Sonny dove for the tunnel doors.

Simon swung Raul's AR up toward the men and sprayed several rounds at their feet.

The men jumped back behind the ledge, taking cover and allowing Sonny and Simon time to get inside the doorway.

Raul remained incapacitated, but he reminded himself that Sonny had caused him to fall into the basement so he ordered his sentries to fire. "Kill them. Shoot—now!" Raul roared.

Holding the rifles on their hips, they simultaneously emptied their clips in an impressive barrage, trying to stop the men from clearing the doors. The reverberation of automatic weapons echoed loudly throughout the home, and then all was silent. Smoke drifted up from the barrels into the open air. They had missed.

Simon and Sonny stood inside the tunnel, hidden behind the cave wall and just out of firing range, and heard sounds deep inside the tunnel of the girls trudging ahead. The two men quickly moved through the mouth of the tunnel. The absence of light became worse as they moved farther from the basement.

Sonny said, "Whoa. I can't see anything. It's pitch-black."

In the total darkness, Simon heard the men upstairs talking rapidly in Spanish. They were looking for a way down. Without the rope, it delayed their ability to reach the basement, which would give Sonny and Simon a head start.

Simon said, "They'll be coming down here soon, Sonny. We've gotta move."

Their pace slowed as the underground passage enveloped them

in an inky blur. The men couldn't see their hand in front of their faces or even their shoes as they stumbled ahead. Progress was slow, and the sounds from the young ladies didn't seem to be getting any closer. They pressed forward with a renewed pace, casting danger to the side in order to catch up to the girls. The men tripped and fell and bumped into walls. It was a virtual obstacle course, and it seemed like the cave was the opponent with Simon and Sonny were the challengers.

They discovered that crawling along the cave floor gave them a bit more control over their headway, and they walked for a while and then crawled at intervals. Creeping along the bottom of the cave was hard on their knees, but they were able to make better progress and avoid falling. They began gaining ground, and the girls' voices growing closer encouraged them to increase their speed.

Simon was following Sonny on his knees, and his AR-15 bounced around on his shoulder, making it a challenge to keep up. Sonny pawed his way forward, thinking about Jana and his desire to protect the girl of his fantasies. Ever since the explosion, he'd put away any thoughts of actually being *with* Jana. He was solely interested in her safety—and protecting the other girls. Once he saw Raul's deadly threat and the palpable fright in the girls' eyes as they fled, he felt guilty about his earlier passion for Jana. After all, they were very young girls, barely women, and for them to be caged like animals and treated like subhumans was too much for him to accept. With each step forward, he vowed to protect them and see that they were freed—regardless of the cost.

Back at the house, the gunmen were scrambling through the home's wreckage and trying to find something to help them reach the basement.

"*Encontrar algo para baja alli*!" a cartel gunman shouted.

Parts of the house were still intact, and they continued searching frantically. They found nothing that was long enough to reach the basement floor. Raul's soldiers became concerned when the sirens got closer and closer and two fire trucks pulled up outside.

Small fires were scattered around the home, and the roof over the west wing was starting to collapse as the firefighters hustled to their positions. The firemen hopped from their trucks and began pulling out hoses to connect to the hydrant and noticed two smoldering, mangled bodies in the front yard. One of the firemen ran over to the crumpled forms of Pedro and Jorge and knew with only one glance that they were dead. The rescue workers brought out plastic tarps to cover the two men, wrapped the bodies, and moved them from where the fireman were working onto the driveway.

The rescuers were unaware of the shooting inside and prepared to go in to aid any survivors. The men connecting the hose worked feverishly outside, and a few others trotted toward the house. Two of Raul's gunmen stepped out from behind the front door, leveled their weapons at the helmeted firefighters, and shot a few warning shots above their heads, which stopped them in their tracks. The firemen held their hands up and slowly began walking backward.

The delay caused the fire over the bedrooms to spread up to the roof. The men dragged the hoses over, cranked on the water, and began spraying the shingles with a strong stream.

Emilio, one of the cartel members, was guarding the front door. He peeked around the corner to the front yard. While he covered the front, it allowed his comrades to continue searching for a way down into the basement.

The fire started to rage, and the firemen were having a hard time keeping it under control. The men looked to the skies, seeking help from the rain clouds forming to the west, and hoping the monsoon storms would soon infuse moisture into the area.

The heat inside the house grew, and Raul's henchmen were sweating profusely. They became agitated and nervous with the fire raging so close, but they had to find a way downstairs. The possibility of the police arriving caused urgency to find a solution.

Two of Raul's men got spooked and ran outside, causing the rescue workers to move away. The two men got in their car and peeled off. The car's tires shuddered and swirled up circles of smoke as they backed out. The driver swung into the street, punched the pedal, and quickly scrambled away from the house. As they sped away from the scene, two Nogales police cruisers passed, driving at breakneck speed to Raul's house. The officers ignored the fleeing vehicle, more concerned with their briefing that morning where they discussed the raid on Raul's home and what to expect after being prepped on the specifics. They approached cautiously.

As the policemen screeched to a halt, they watched the fire department struggling with the inflamed structure. They looked around and tried to get a feel for what had transpired. It came as a surprise that the house they were targeting for the raid was on fire.

One of the officers called dispatch and asked to be put through to the captain. Officer Smith related the events unfolding at the house and how the fire department was battling the one-alarm blaze caused by a presumed explosion.

One of the rescue workers jogged over to Smith, put his head in the window, and shouted over the noise of the trucks and the fire.

Officer Smith put dispatch on standby to listen to the update from the fireman.

"We tried to enter the home, and shots were fired in our direction. So, we're not going back inside. We also found two bodies in the front yard, DOA, both men were burned pretty badly. We've got them covered over there on the driveway. Sorry we had to move them, but they were blocking our way in."

"Understand. We'll call the medical examiner and take care of the bodies. Who are the shooters?"

"Not sure. We didn't get a good look at 'em. They're just inside the door. Be careful—they've got automatic weapons."

"I see. Thanks. Stay out of harm's way. We'll call for backup." Smith reconnected to dispatch and reported that shots had been fired.

Captain Perez was put on the phone. "Yes, sir?"

"Officer Smith here, Captain."

"Did you say that shots have been fired at our West Crawford target?"

"Affirmative. We also have two deceased male subjects, found in the front yard, probably thrown from the house by an explosion."

"Explosion? I'll need a full report. We can talk more about it when I arrive. Can you describe the shooters and why they opened fire?"

"No description. They shot at the fire department when they tried to enter the house. Luckily, no one got hit, but it freaked them out. According to the water tossers, they have automatic weapons."

"Automatic weapons? Really? Okay. Is the fire contained?"

"No, sir. It's still active, and they're having difficulty getting it under control."

"This puts us in an awkward position. We have reason to believe that there may be underage hostages inside. From what you can see, would they be in any danger from the fire?"

"If the men who fired the shots don't let the fire department into the house, they certainly would be.

"For now, I want you to stand down. Do not enter the premises. Is that understood?"

"Yes, sir."

"I've got to make a quick call. I'll get back to you in five minutes."

"Ten-four."

Forty-Eight

Wednesday, June 19, 3:30 P.M. In Route to Nogales

Captain Adolfo Perez, of Nogales police was present at Raul's house and made an in-flight call to Lieutenant Tatum.

"Tatum."

"Hi, Lieutenant Tatum. This is Perez in Nogales."

"Yes, sir."

"We have a situation here at our target location."

"Oh really? What's going on?"

"Our target on West Crawford Street, which is the home of the suspected kidnapper, is engaged in a one-alarm fire. Our officers think it was caused by an explosion. The fire department is here and fighting it now. Rescue workers tried to enter the home to keep the fire from spreading, but as they approached the front door, they took fire from suspects inside. They have ARs."

"What? Oh God. What's going on?"

"Not sure, sir. We just know that we're on hold until you give us direction since this is your investigation. Is it accurate that there may be hostages inside?"

"Affirmative, possibly teenage girls. If the hostages are inside, are they in immediate risk from the fire?"

"Affirmative, the fire is spreading, and the smoke jumpers might not be able to stop it. If they can't get inside, we won't be able to rescue anyone.

"Oh, man. That is a problem."

"How many officers do you have on the scene?"

"Three with four more en route."

"When backup arrives, try to enter the house with all caution and see if the officers can find any hostages. If you or your officers aren't comfortable going in, that's another discussion."

"I'll tell you what I'll do. The backup should be here in a few minutes, and once they arrive, we'll try to go in and gauge how much resistance we get. If we can't get past the ARs, we'll reconsider our plan."

"Ten-four."

"Be careful, and if you see any sign of the girls, grab them. We have anxious parents waiting."

"Ten-four."

Forty-Nine

Wednesday, June 19, 4:00 P.M., Nogales

Perez hung up with Tatum and got back on the radio with Smith at the scene.

"Smith, what's the ETA on backup?"

"They're pulling up now."

"Good, here's the plan. I got confirmation that there may be hostages inside, young girls. They'd like for us to try to enter the home and measure the resistance, and if there's a way we can force our way inside without endangering you or your team, proceed. When and if you get inside, we want to search and rescue ASAP."

"Ten-four. We'll have someone on the radio for updates."

"Thanks, Smith."

Officer Smith hung up, and the four backup policemen joined the three on the scene and huddled behind one of the cruisers to plan how to approach the house. Three of the men—Gorman, Sanchez, and Estrada—were to start recon at each end of the home and work their way toward the front door, stopping just out of view. Rodriguez and Bates were to go to the rear of the house and assess any possible resistance from the suspects inside. Officer Janson was ordered to find a way inside by entering through the garage, and Martinez was assigned to stay on the radio to report any status changes. They were told to be ready to open fire if shots were discharged—or if they were faced with any threats.

¤ ¤ ¤

Sonny's idea to crawl was definitely paying dividends. The muffled voices of the girls grew louder and more distinct, and they could even make out what they were saying.

The girls stopped for a rest and sat on the floor of the cave, winded and distraught. Beth rubbed her feet and considered tearing part of her gown to wrap around her sore and bleeding toes.

Lydia heard Beth sighing and scooted over next to her to find out what was bothering her. "Girl, I can't believe you weren't wearing shoes. Oh my gosh, how are you able to walk on this floor?"

"It hasn't been easy, but I'll be okay," Beth replied.

Lydia handed her one of her shoes, which barely fit, and asked Jana for a shoe from the other foot so Beth could get some relief from the stress to her feet.

Jana said, "Okay, let's rotate the shoes so no one is without any. For now, Beth can use ours, and we'll walk with only one for a while. Then we'll switch out, and Tabitha and Charlotte will need to walk with one and give Beth your shoes."

Tabitha said, "Why do we have to give our shoes to her when she's the one who forgot 'em?"

Lydia said, "Because it's the right thing to do. We'd offer you the same option had it happened to you, Tabitha. We have to make it out of here, and we're not leaving anyone behind. It's not an option—so get it in your mind that we're going to be here for each other, no matter what. We're a team now. There are no individuals—so quit your complaining and let's get moving."

They heard a faint noise in the tunnel behind them. The group listened to the sound of shuffling and running behind them in the cave. It was getting closer by the second.

Tabitha said, "Listen. What's that? Someone's coming. Oh no. Let's hurry!"

The girls stood up and quickly tried to move forward on their route. The girls were fearful now that they were being pursued, and whoever it was seemed to be closing. They stepped up the pace. The shoes Beth was wearing were clunky—Jana's a size too big and Lydia's a size too small—but the minor discomfort wasn't nearly as painful as going without. She was thankful for their generosity and began to admire the leadership and character of Jana and Lydia.

¤ ¤ ¤

Simon and Sonny heard the girls in the distance.

"Listen, I hear them, they're not too far away," Sonny said.

The girls' voices were clear, and there was a sense of urgency in their tone. They slowly closed in on the young women, scrambling ahead and knowing the girls would soon become aware of their presence.

Simon yelled, "Jana, it's Simon. We're coming to help. We'll be there in a minute. We mean no harm."

The girls froze as the reverberation bounced off the walls, echoing through the cavity, indistinct and garbled.

Jana said, "What did he say?"

Tabitha said, "I don't know, but let's get out of here. I don't want to go back."

The girls began to panic and started moving faster than they should have. The fear drove them on, and they clumsily stumbled ahead.

Lydia desperately clawed her way along the walls, carefully picking places to put her feet to avoid falling. As she scuffed her hand along the wall, a large opening emerged. Lydia paused.

The girls were unable to see that she had stopped, and they ran into her.

Lydia said, "Shh, there's a passageway here. It looks like we've come to a fork, and I'm not sure which way to go."

Sonny and Simon were approaching, only twenty or thirty feet away.

The girls assembled at the mouth of the new entrance and decided to slip inside, perhaps giving them an opportunity to lose the men coming up from behind. The young ladies turned inside the passage and felt their way down the walls slowly and carefully. They heard the men nearing.

Lydia said, "Everybody, get down—and don't make a sound!"

They dropped to their knees in a tight huddle and stayed quiet, their hearts beating loudly, alarmed, and scared they were about to be recaptured. A hush enveloped the group as they waited and listened. Their pursuers were very close, and they could hear the men grunting and panting as they plowed forward.

As Simon and Sonny were groping their way down the tunnel, they came across the secondary passage and stopped. The girls held their breath in silence and listened.

The forked pathway caused the men to hesitate since the sound from the girls had stopped and was no longer guiding them.

"Jana, it's Sonny, the pool guy, and Simon. We're here to help you. Simon's with FedEx. We're trying to get you away from those guys. Where are you?"

The girls stayed silent. No one said a word. They all locked hands.

Is it a trick? Are they really who they say they are? Or is one of Raul's minions with them?

The cave was dead quiet.

Tabitha accidentally scuffed her shoe while adjusting her position, and the slight noise was amplified by the tunnel's acoustic trap. The men turned their attention to the fork where the girls were hidden.

"Jana, come on. We're here to help, honest. We've got to get you out of here. Raul's men will be in the cave soon, and we need to get moving. Come on. Let's go."

Jana realized they were trapped and were out of options, and she decided to take the risk. "Sonny, we're here."

Sonny and Simon crawled down the tunnel to where the girls were clustered together.

The young females held each other tightly and waited for the men to arrive. Unmistakable fear gnawed at their nerves, and the dread of facing punishment and going back into captivity caused them even more physical distress.

The men shuffled up to the band of escapees. Sonny sensed their close proximity, held out his hands and felt for someone in front of him. He ran into Jana.

"Sonny, it's me, Jana."

"Hi. You ladies are hard to follow. It's taken all we can do to catch up to you. Everybody all right?"

The ladies collectively exhaled a sigh of relief.

Jana thought, *Perhaps they are here to help after all.* "We didn't know who you were. We thought you might be Raul's goons. Are you sure you're here to help?"

Simon said, "Yes, we know you're in danger and not by choice—we are too. We need to get out of here and take you with us. We can all get out safely, but we need to move fast." *Aw, man, where's my cell phone when I need it most?* Following the explosion and chaos, Simon realized his cell phone was back in the truck.

Sonny said, "I have a feeling that the cartel gunmen will be tracking us. We need to get a move on."

¤ ¤ ¤

While the police officers huddled outside and planned their strategy, Chuy, one of Raul's soldiers, was searching for a way to access the basement. He emerged from the garage, opened the door, and carried an extension ladder to the kitchen. He lengthened the ladder, slid it as far as it would extend, locked it in place, and lowered it over the side. It was about seven or eight feet short.

Luis turned toward the front door and whistled to Emilio, the man guarding the front, for help.

Emilio said, "Hey, man. There's police out there."

Luis said, "Don't worry about them right now. We need to get down the ladder to Raul. He wants us to stop the girls."

Luis and Emilio kneeled and braced themselves on a nearby stud. They held onto the top rung of the ladder as Chuy climbed around them and stepped on second rung to see if they could hold his weight. The men struggled, but they were able to hold him up. Chuy put his weapon on the ledge, nimbly climbed down the ladder, and jumped the last several feet down to the bottom. He turned his ankle on a pile of clutter, and limped over to catch his weapon when Luis dropped it. Chuy went over to check on Raul who was racked with pain.

Raul pointed toward the tunnel. "Chuy, forget about me. Go get the girls. Don't let them get away. Someone will help me later."

"You got it, boss," Chuy replied.

Emilio was able to secure the top of the ladder by hanging it over a floor joist, which would help him hold it up while Luis went down the ladder. Luis set down his weapon and climbed onto the second rung to see if it would hold.

Emilio strained to hold it in place as Luis moved down the rungs, stepping lightly. As Luis neared the end of the ladder, Emilio lost his grip and let the ladder fall. Luis landed on a soft pile of damaged dry wall and dodged the ladder as it crashed down beside him. Once in the basement, Chuy gave Luis a hand up, and Emilio pitched down his automatic weapon. Luis caught it cleanly, and they headed to the tunnel.

Officers Gorman, Sanchez, and Estrada divided up at the entrance of the house and approached the front door. They didn't see any resistance and poked their heads around the splintered doorjamb. It appeared clear.

Officer Janson entered through the garage and hesitated just outside the entrance to the kitchen. He slowly turned the knob and quietly made his way inside.

Rodriguez and Bates were assigned to the back of the house and entered from the pool area. The officers carefully and quietly slid open the glass door. Peeking inside, Rodriguez and Bates stepped into the damaged perimeter of the den, and they spotted Gorman with the two other officers tiptoeing into the front entryway. Rodriguez and Bates met up with Janson as he came in from the garage near the kitchen, and they crouched, poised to fire. As the lawmen converged, they spotted Emilio leaning over the ledge and looking down into the large recess. Emilio's automatic rifle was clutched in his left hand.

Gorman and his team snuck up behind Emilio, came within ten feet of the cartel gunman, and stopped.

Sanchez said, "Nogales Police, let's see your hands!"

The policemen ordered Emilio to drop his weapon. Emilio was

caught off guard and turned around, instinctively aiming his firearm at the three men kneeling by the front door.

Janson was crouched on the other side of Emilio, and he discharged three shells into the suspect's chest. Emilio convulsed, teetered, and fell backward into the basement.

The seven police officers spread out to check the front rooms and weren't concerned with the rest of the house, which was engulfed in the raging fire. They determined there were no other suspects inside and then scanned the basement. The men saw five bodies scattered in the debris and the torso of a small-framed female with her legs dismembered. They surveyed the wreckage below but were unable to locate the rest of the body. Two other bodies were badly burned and appeared to be male. Another corpse was an unfortunate postal worker who had impaled himself on a piece of wreckage. All three were obviously deceased.

They also spotted Emilio, the man they just took out.

Raul saw the police officers looking down and cursed under his breath that his day was not going very well. With his broken limbs, he was unable to move the rest of his body. Raul squirmed uncomfortably, but he was unarmed and not an immediate threat.

Bates kept an eye on Raul.

The other police officers fanned out and tried to find any sign of the girls. If the young ladies were in the far reaches of the house, which was engulfed in flames, they stood very little chance of survival. There was no way the police officers could get near the hallway, stymied by the punishing heat.

Fearing the fire was growing out of control, Officer Janson scampered outside and told the firemen to proceed inside to fight the inferno. Janson trotted out to Martinez's cruiser and gave him a status update so he could pass it on to dispatch. Two firemen dragged their hoses through the front door, and the water pressure started to fill the hose. They doused the hallway and the ceiling, trying to contain the fire over the bedrooms. The firefighters were aggressively pouring water on the roof and starting to extinguish the flames. It looked like the firemen would succeed in extinguishing the fire.

Fifty

Wednesday, June 19, 4:00 p.m., Nogales

Chuy and Luis burst through the tunnel door and trotted into the darkness. The complete lack of light slowed them to a creep. They cursed the darkness and agilely stepped forward, showing nimble moves, and abandoned all fear for what lay ahead.

"*Vamos, vamos por ellas*!" Chuy said.

The henchmen were on a mission and wanted to save the cartel's assets and assist Raul in recovering his lost sheep. Furthermore, they knew the police would soon be on the scene and would probably chase them down the tunnel to capture anyone suspected of working with Raul. They had to move fast, catch the girls, and make it safely to the other side. Once in Mexico, the authorities would be helpless to pursue them.

Raul had phoned earlier, asking for support and instructed his counterparts in Mexico to capture the girls if they exited the tunnel. By pursuing the girls, they were essentially trapping the runaways between two cartel bookends, ensuring their seizure.

Chuy and Luis were determined to kill the two men who had fired on them and fled after the girls. They were probably innocently involved, but they were witnesses and stood in the way of capturing their prey. Chuy and Luis had a distinct advantage besides knowing about the trap that was set. They were very familiar with the tunnel and were able to use their cell phones to illuminate the passage. The young ladies had no way of knowing that the tunnel was over a mile long.

¤ ¤ ¤

An EMS truck arrived just after the police. Billy and Thomas, the two attendants, rushed in and look for injuries.

"Over here, guys!" Officer Bates waved them over and pointed down to Raul.

Officer Sanchez said, "Guys, I've got a rope in the car. I'll be right back." He ran out, grabbed the rope from his trunk, and hustled back inside.

They met to determine the best way to get down to the basement. They noticed an exposed load-bearing beam above where they stood and threw the rope over the wooden truss protruding from the ceiling. Sanchez pulled it over the beam and secured the rope.

They tied the other end to the body harness and prepared to lower Billy down to assist Raul with his injuries. Bates and Rodriguez leaned against the stud holding up the rafter, giving it extra support, and Sanchez carefully lowered Billy down as he rappelled his way down the cinderblock wall. Once Billy arrived in the basement, Rodriguez carefully dropped him his supplies and equipment.

Thomas, the second paramedic, ran outside and returned with a rescue basket.

Bates pointed down and said, "Look, he's right down there. Your buddy's working on someone."

The policemen guided Thomas to where he could see his partner working on Raul.

Billy untied the rope, and Sanchez pulled the harness back up to where Tommy and the police were gathered. They secured the rope to the basket and lowered it down to Billy. He untied it and threw the rope back up to Sanchez. Thomas was harnessed, and the officers lowered him down to help Billy get Raul into the carrier.

Officer Martinez was manning the radio outside and reported to Captain Perez.

Perez connected to Tatum in the helicopter as he neared Nogales.

"Tatum here."

"Perez in Nogales."

"Yes, how's it going there? Any updates?"

"Yes, sir. Our backup arrived at the house, and the two squads were able to make it into the house without any complications."

"Thank God."

"They had limited resistance. Two of the cartel footmen left the scene before we arrived, and there was only one in the house who wasn't injured. He was armed, and when our guys confronted him, he wouldn't stand down. We were forced to take him out. We have multiple casualties that were here before we arrived. There were two deceased in the front yard that we assume were thrown clear of the house by an explosion. There were three more bodies, presumably members of the cartel inside. Two were probably killed in the blast given their appearance and physical condition. The other was the man we confronted and eliminated. Unfortunately, there was also a civilian who probably came in to help. It looks like a postal worker. We found him in the basement. He had fallen to his death, pretty gruesome I might add. The last body is a mystery for now. We only found parts of what looked like a young female."

"Could you repeat? Parts?"

"Yes, we found an unidentified female's remains: a partial torso and legs. So far, we haven't had access to the basement to search the rubble for the head or upper torso. Once we get our team down there, which right now has limited accessibility, we'll scour the debris to see if we can find he rest of her body."

"Perez, if you find the upper torso before I arrive, could you shoot me a photo of her face? I don't care about the condition. We need to compare it to the images of the two missing girls we're seeking. Maybe we can determine if it's one of the young women we're searching for."

"Yes, sir. Will do. One more thing. We have paramedics on the scene. They're attending to a male subject who was severely injured in the explosion. There's indications that he's the owner of the house—so he's presumably cartel too."

"Ten-four. Thanks, Perez. We're within minutes of landing. Our ETA is about half an hour. We'll see you there."

¤ ¤ ¤

Officer Rodriguez went out to meet with the firemen to see if they could assist in getting the police officers down into the basement. "Say, do you guys have a ladder? We've got injuries and casualties in the basement, but we can't get to them. You got anything we can drop down about twenty feet?"

The firefighters returned with a tall extension ladder that had plenty of length to allow access below. Rodriguez and a fireman extended and locked the ladder and swung it over the side of the basement wall.

Billy helped make sure it was on secure footing and then waved the officers down.

Bates and Janson stayed on the first floor, and Rodriguez and the other men descended the ladder. The paramedics strapped Raul to a spinal board and lifted him gently into the basket.

Bates, Janson, and the firemen raised Raul from below, and the paramedics guided it up the wall. Once Raul was raised over the top, they set the basket down safely away from the overhang and took photos of Raul, not much to his liking.

The paramedics clicked up the ladder, took charge of Raul, and carried him out to the EMS vehicle.

The police officers fanned out and began combing through the basement rubble. They photographed the deceased men, Emilio, Alex, and Manuel, and the unfortunate mailman who had been in the wrong place at the wrong time.

Officer Rodriguez slowly approached Emma's lower midsection and legs. He scanned the area around the piles of refuse and looked for her remains. The other officers joined the search. They stepped over splintered lumber, gnarled metal, appliances, carpet, shards of metal, and disintegrated drywall. They lifted piles of rubbish and scraps as they looked for any sign of Emma's body.

When the officers had just about covered the entire floor, Sanchez saw a hand protruding from under a dishwasher. "Guys, come over here. I've got something."

The other officers gently lifted the dishwasher, set it aside, and knelt beside Emma. They uncovered her forearm and then her shoulder, which was still attached to her torso. Her right arm was blown away, but her head was still intact. The police officers continued the grisly task and pulled her head free of a pile of refuse and turned her head at an angle to see Emma's face. She was obviously a young white female with brown hair. Her face was darkened from the explosion and somewhat disfigured, but it was surprisingly in good enough shape for a possible ID. A photo was texted to Captain Perez back at the station.

Perez texted the image to Lieutenant Tatum as he landed in an open field about five minutes away from Raul's house.

¤ ¤ ¤

"*Vamos, hombre*!" Luis commanded.

The two cartel underlings dashed through the tunnel like trained bloodhounds, making much better time than the group fleeing in front of them. Chuy and Luis knew the terrain as well as anyone because they were part of the team that transported narcotics down the tunnel each week. They could probably make it through the tunnel with their eyes closed, but they chose to take advantage of their cell phones in order to catch up. The phones were invaluable to illuminate the path and gave the two men a distinct edge. Their pace was incredible. They dodged potholes, level changes, and juts protruding from the wall. Fully aware of their speed and abilities, they bored down on their quarry. In the minds of the two henchmen, their prey would be easy marks. They passed the fork in the main tunnel, making unbelievable headway only a hundred yards from the seven flight victims.

Since Simon had the only weapon, he was bringing up the rear. He heard obscure noises behind him and stopped to listen.

"*Oir algo?*" Chuy asked.

"*Si las eschuche. Ellas no estan lejos.*"

It was true. There was someone else in the tunnel, and by all indications, Simon could tell they were moving fast. Simon got Sonny's attention and told him and the girls that they had heat on their tails.

"What is it, Simon?"

Simon shouted, "There's noise behind us. Someone's coming up fast. My guess is that they're not friendly."

Lydia yelled, "Let's get moving, girls. We have company. Let's push it."

"What is it?" Tabitha questioned.

"Someone's behind us, and they're gaining on us," Lydia replied.

The seven moved into overdrive, but they stumbled and tripped as they proceeded. Sonny began crawling, and a few of the girls tried to follow, but their bare legs under the gowns made it difficult. They tried to keep up as best they could. Tabitha was lagging behind and trying to keep up with the group.

Charlotte and Tabitha were walking with one shoe, and it slowed their progress. The sounds came closer and closer and closer.

Jana felt her way down the dark passage with her fingertips, unexpectedly finding a handful of air. "There's something here … or I should say, not here. Come look."

Sonny said, "We don't have much time. What is it?"

"It's some sort an opening. Come back for a second."

Sonny felt his way into what seemed like a cutout in the main tunnel about six feet wide. Feeling around, he stumbled onto a couple of large plastic barrels. He moved his hand up the side of the barrel and tried to make sense of what it was.

Lydia clasped the rim of the barrel, reached over the top, and recognized the feel of cold metal shovels and other tools. "Tools!"

Sonny said, "Yeah, these might come in handy. Any kind of weapons will help."

Lydia pulled out a few shovels and passed them around to Tabitha, Jana, and Beth.

The sounds that had been a few hundred yards behind them were suddenly on top of them. The group was silent, and Jana whispered, "Everyone in here. Maybe we can surprise them when they go by. For this to work, we have to remain completely silent and let them pass."

The seven refugees scrunched into the small rectangle and pushed up against the barrels to inch as far away from the tunnel as possible. Beth, Lydia, and Jana stood at the front, and Tabitha and Charlotte stood behind them. Sonny was at the far end, and Simon with his AR-15 stood closest to the oncoming pursuers. They stood in the pitch-black murk, silently waiting for the men to approach.

Jana whispered, "Shh, everyone. Don't make a sound."

The girls were hushed and frozen in the darkness. They measured their breathing and didn't make a sound. The two cartel men were scurrying along at an unbelievable rate and made them wonder how they could move so fast. They were coming closer and closer as the group heard the scuffing of shoes, labored breathing, and clawing along the walls. Everyone remained as still as a corpse, and the girls primed themselves for battle with their new weapons. After the two cartel members bore down on the group, their hands began to quiver, and pulses were pounding loudly inside their heads.

In the quietness, a trickle was heard. Tabitha had lost control and urine seeped down her leg.

No one said a word. The men were very close, and the seven could hear their breathing as if they were right next to them.

All of a sudden, it stopped. The men shut down their engines, stopped, and listened.

"*Donde estan ellas?*" Chuy whispered.

When Chuy and Luis didn't hear any sounds, they mumbled something in Spanish and proceeded quietly one step at a time. They were within feet of where Simon was hidden. The FedEx employee leaned back behind the wall and inched away from the main tunnel.

The group began to see the light of the cartel phone approaching. The two hoodlums stopped and became suspicious of the silence. Luis walked forward quietly, and Chuy followed a few feet behind. Both had their ears pinned back, listening for any clue where the escapees might be hiding. Chuy moved beyond Simon and was directly across from Lydia when he turned his head and shined the light of his cell on the group cowering in the recess.

Before Luis could react, Jana swung her shovel as hard as she could and hit Chuy upside the head. "A-ya, take that."

Chuy grunted and fell in pain.

Luis wheeled around and tried to decide where to aim his weapon with seven bodies moving in all directions. In the midst of the confusion, Luis dropped his cell phone, which cracked on a rock, and he hurriedly fired a few rounds in the air that whizzed right by Lydia's head. The bullets slammed into a support beam just above where Simon was standing, and it knocked out large chunks of wood.

The discharge from Luis's weapon blinded everyone momentarily, but it gave him a backdrop to make out the seven bodies who scattered in the tunnel.

Simon stepped forward and squeezed off three quick rounds. He heard Luis fall. "Did I get him?"

"Yeah, I think so. He's down here," Beth replied.

He writhed on the rocky floor of the cave and moaned in pain.

They heard a rumble overhead. The noise became more prominent, and the walls of the tunnel began to tremble.

The seven stopped to listen for the source of the shaking.

Dust began cascading down from the ceiling, and the damaged beam cracked and dropped loads of soil and rocks on the path. The avalanche of sand and rock began piling on top of Luis's cell phone.

Chuy was dazed and tried to get to his feet. He scrambled backward, and another beam gave way. Even more sand and silt fell on him, and as the soil accumulated, it began rolling forward.

The seven escapees ran from the falling earth and moved several yards down the tunnel. It streamed down onto Simon and Tabitha before they had time to react and piled on top of them. Simon lunged forward to avoid the cave-in, but he was covered in the rubble up to his waist.

Tabitha wasn't as nimble. The tons of sand and rock consumed her before she was able to move. She fell down, and the rubble piled on top of her. All was quiet as the final dust settled on the mound.

Lydia said, "Is everyone okay?"

Simon freed himself from the pile. And said, "Not sure. Where's Tabitha?"

No sound and no reply.

"Tabitha was right here with me when everything started to fall. She has to be here somewhere."

The girls rushed to Simon's voice and encountered a large mountain of sand.

Jana said, "Where was she? Where was she standing when it fell?"

Simon said, "Right behind me, right here."

Jana said, "Everyone get over here, quick."

Sonny and the girls rushed over to the pile and began digging furiously to find Tabitha.

Simon was flailing away at the dirt pile.

A horrible thought materialized in Jana's mind, *If she hasn't suffocated by now, the weight may have crushed her.* They dug like desperate animals, flipping sand behind them and moving the earth away as quickly as possible. They located strands of her hair and then dug around her head. They were able to clear the sand and silt from her face. They found her arms, uncovered her chest, and tugged her out from under the avalanche. They tried to revive her. She had been under the pile for at least a minute and was unconscious.

Simon opened her mouth, cleared it of dirt as best he could, and then started CPR.

Lydia said, "Give her some air, Simon. Let's revive her. She's gotta still be alive."

He worked on her for several minutes, and she finally began to twitch and move her head.

After a few moments, Tabitha moaned and coughed up a wad of sand. She gasped for air and hacked up more grit until her lungs were finally clear. "Oh, I don't feel good. What happened?"

The girls let loose a shout and crowded around Tabitha, giving her hugs and patting her on the back.

Beth said, "Tabitha, you gave us a scare. I'm so glad you're okay. We were really worried."

Charlotte said, "Yeah, we're lucky we got to you in time."

Tabitha replied, "Thank y'all. I owe you my life. It looked like it was all over."

Jana said, "We'd never leave you Tabitha—no matter what. Just glad you're not injured."

They assumed Chuy was overwhelmed and covered by the landslide. The tunnel was mostly blocked from the rear, and if Chuy somehow had survived, he would be on the other side of the mass of sand. Without regret, they left Luis's body where it was and moved down the tunnel to gather their composure. They stopped to sit and were fatigued and frazzled. There was enough adrenaline between the two men and five women to light the whole tunnel—if they could only make a connection.

¤ ¤ ¤

Tatum and team landed their helicopter a mile from Raul's house. Perez and one of the ATF officers met them at the landing area and picked them up. Detectives Williams and Sharp crammed in the back seat.

On the short drive to Raul's house, Perez said, "We removed the injured male suspect from the house—who we suspect is cartel—and he's being taken to the emergency room with multiple fractures, body trauma, and a lot of cuts and bruises. He'll live, but it'll take him a while to recover. We'll question him as soon as he's well enough to give us a statement. Did you get a chance to look at the photo I sent?"

"Yes, we compared the photo to the missing girls, and there was no match. The girl in the photo had light brown hair, which didn't correspond with Jana's blonde hair or Lydia's dark brown hair. Since the girl who died in the blast was Anglo, it automatically eliminated Lydia since she's Hispanic."

Tatum was relieved that it wasn't Jana or Lydia, but he felt sympathy for the girl whose life had ended so violently at such a young age. As his thoughts loitered, he was interrupted when Perez got a call and put it on speaker.

"Perez here."

"This is Martinez Captain. We've found something unusual."

"Oh yeah? What's that?"

"We didn't really notice it at first, but there's a swimming pool rope that looked like someone used to drop into the basement. We also found an extension ladder."

"Where are you going with this?"

"The only person we found in the basement was the injured subject, and he was unable to move. We looked around and noticed a set of double doors leading to a tunnel. Not quite sure where it goes. We concluded there's been other people down here, and since no one's around, they must have escaped through the tunnel."

"Are you pursuing the subjects?"

"Negative. We were waiting for further orders."

"Okay. We'll be there in a few minutes. Stand by."

Perez got on the phone to dispatch and said, "Shirley, get one of our canines over to 500 West Crawford Street, pronto."

"Yes, sir."

As he hung up, the captain's car pulled in front of Raul's residence. The scene was surreal. The house looked like someone had dropped a huge bomb on one end of the house, and the other side was on fire. The firemen were stubbornly battling the persistent blaze. Black smoke spiraled to the sky, and the smell of burnt wood hung in the air. The firemen covered the premises like ants and were scattered across the lot at various stations. Two more police cruisers arrived as Perez and the throng of officers met on the front lawn to assess their tactical alternatives.

¤ ¤ ¤

The seven runaways rested after their arduous rush through the cave and the confrontation with Chuy and Luis. The danger had been avoided, and Raul's two men were subdued. They tried to recharge and prepare for the next phase of their journey. They were confident they were close to the end of the tunnel and would soon be able to escape Raul's nightmare. The thought of what they had gone through in the house of humiliation kept them frozen in a warped capsule of shame.

The discussion shifted from their present predicament to where they thought the tunnel might end. The girls assumed that it probably opened up somewhere across the Mexican border, and they talked through alternatives about how they planned to get back to the US.

Sonny said, "Guys, what are we gonna do when we get to the

other side? We'll be in Mexico, and none of us has any papers. The authorities might detain us—or we might be thrown in jail."

Jana replied, "We'll figure something out, Sonny."

Charlotte spoke quietly, "Tabitha, what are you gonna do when you get home?"

Tabitha said, "Sleep in my own bed for a week! Get some of my mom's home cooking and rest. Hibernate. I just want to be left alone. I feel so ashamed about what I've been doing. It's been two years of being abused and sexually tormented. I want to crawl in a hole and lay low. Maybe I'll feel better once I see my parents. One thing I know for sure is that I won't come close to a boy. I want nothing to do with sex. I've seen enough for a lifetime, and I just want to get away from it all."

Charlotte said, "Yeah, me too. Don't know how you've done this for so long. It must be hard being away from home for as long as you have."

Tabitha said, "I hope my parents can remember who I am. Do you think they'll still want me in my condition?"

Charlotte said, "Of course. They love you very much and will be so happy when you return."

"I hope so. I just want to get out of here. How much longer do you think we'll be in this tunnel?"

"We've been under here for so long. It's gotta be close."

"I pray you're right. I'm not sure how much I have left."

Simon was upset that he had left his cell in his work truck. If he had only brought his cell phone into the house, they'd be able to see in the tunnel and call for help. He vowed he'd never be more than three feet from his cell ever again. Sonny mused at the thought of surfacing in Mexico and how he and Simon would look a bit suspicious escorting five young maidens in grungy gowns back across the border.

The girls wondered how their ordeal would play out, which led them to yearn that much more for their homes and families.

Jana thought about her parents and how they were probably beside themselves since her disappearance. Jana wished that she could somehow call and assure them she was all right, but at the moment, a call wouldn't be that reassuring. They were stuck underground in a dark, dingy tunnel, going no telling where in Mexico. The last thing she needed to do was to worry them even more, so the thought evaporated.

Lydia's mind wandered in a different direction, first to their plight over the last eleven days and how they were terribly abused the first night. Then all the sexual encounters they were forced to participate in. Lydia harbored a fair amount of guilt, which was understandable given the fact she voluntarily entertained Raul to find a way out. Lydia knew she had gotten carried away and took it too far with the cartel kingpin. Somehow, he inflated her ego to a point where she continually wanted to prove she could rise above the level of his other sexual exploits and satisfy Raul's expectations.

And there were times when she was genuinely fired by the flame of lust, and that's what really bothered her. If that wasn't enough to conjure sufficient guilt, then a stronger wave of regret crept across her mind thinking about her exploits with Jana, her best friend. Lydia shuddered to think of that night and quickly tried to move her mind somewhere else to rid herself of the memory when they shared such bliss.

Sonny couldn't help but think of Jana as they walked closely together, and her mere presence lifted his mood. He knew there would never be anything between them, and he was extra cautious to conceal the feelings he had toward Jana. He dared not show his hand and kept the passion to himself, especially with a person of Jana's age.

Simon, on the other hand, continued to wonder how he got into such a mess. One minute, he was delivering a package on West

Crawford, and the next, he was running from cartel hitmen who want to kill him. It made him wonder if future opportunities arose whether he'd ever help someone again or choose not to get involved. There was some consolation, at least he was helping these poor girls to freedom, he surmised.

Sonny said, "Okay, everyone. We need to get going."

The drained group of deserters slowly began to stir and forced themselves to rise and start moving ahead. They were sore, tired, and mentally exhausted, but they had to go on. With their conditioning, Lydia and Jana were still fresh and had plenty of energy in reserve—the others not so much. Jana and Lydia switched shoes with Tabitha and Charlotte, and Beth gratefully accepted their generosity. Her feet were feeling better, and she was thankful for the others allowing her to borrow their shoes. She was upset at herself for not thinking ahead and how she put everyone else in such an uncomfortable situation due to her oversight.

Following closely behind Beth, Tabitha was embarrassed from her little incident in the cutout and being smothered under the pile of rubble, so she walked in silence, still bringing up the rear and occasionally being prodded by Simon to keep up. Jana and Lydia lugged the two cartel AR-15s they had confiscated from Luis and Chuy. It made them feel keenly powerful and dangerous to carry around a real weapon, and they were fully prepared to use them if needed. Simon gave them some quick lessons on how to use the firearms in case it was necessary, and the girls picked it up quickly.

"Think you can use that thing?" Lydia said.

Jana said, "What the rifle? If I have to, sure—it's either them or us."

"Just don't shoot me!"

"Ha ha ha. If I do, I'll try to nick you in the leg," Lydia quipped.

"You're all heart, *mi amiga*." Jana laughed.

They hoped it wouldn't come down to using the firepower, but they were prepared just the same.

The group walked with less urgency now. They had been in the tunnel for more than two hours and had made good progress, notwithstanding the assault from Chuy and Luis. They continued to feel their way through the corridor, and Jana startled those following her when she fell headlong down a steep drop-off. The floor of the cave plummeted into a hole six feet down. When she planted her foot on a cushion of air rather than the cave floor, she was unable to prevent herself from falling down the embankment.

Sonny cautiously felt his way down the hill and came to Jana's aid to check on her and give her a hand up.

Jana was sore, but fortunately, she didn't injure herself seriously.

He hoisted Jana to her feet, and the touch of her hand stole his breath. Jana expressed her thanks to Sonny, and they continued on, walking side by side and leading the entourage. Those behind Jana carefully stepped down into the depression and helped each other climb up the other side.

Once on level ground again, Simon and Tabitha carried on a conversation about how he accidentally ended up with the group. He answered Tabitha's queries about how he had gotten involved.

She was inspired by his courage and chivalry, and she clumsily tried to locate his face and surprised him with a kiss on his cheek. "Simon, you're the best. I can't thank you enough for looking out for me. It makes me feel good to be with someone like you."

"I'm good at delivering stuff, and I want to deliver you home, young lady."

"I'll let you. That sounds good to me!"

The compliment didn't soothe his fear much, and he was still having second thoughts about rushing into the house to help the girls. However, once Simon became familiar with their plight, got to know the girls, and saw how young they were with the horrid tales of their abuse, he was glad he did.

The air in the cave gradually became musty and damp, the temperature had risen slightly, and the walking became more labored. The walls of the tunnel were made of cedar timbers and were constructed vertically along the side of the wall supporting the beams of the canopy above. The wood smelled of rot, and the muggy air and lack of ventilation created an atmosphere that made it difficult to breathe.

The floor was sandy, and the dust kicked up by their feet began to cake on their shoes, their faces, legs, and clothes. The grit was abrasive on their toes and behind their knees, and they had inhaled a fair amount as well. Those who brought up the rear were covered from the dust kicked up by the others ahead, causing smudges of sand to collect around their noses and mouths. The trail began a slight incline, which caused the walkway to become more demanding, and more rubble appeared scattered on the path. Stepping around the obstacles was unwieldy in the dark, and the team of escapees began to stumble more often and stub their toes on the unseen impediments.

As the girls continued down the tunnel a distinctive odor pervaded the stale air. It became more and more rancid with every step.

Beth said, "Ew, what's that smell? It's awful."

"Don't know—and I'm afraid to find out," Jana replied.

It was so stifling that they girls had to cover their noses with their robes. The smell got worse as they progressed, and it was apparent something was decomposed and rotting in the tunnel ahead. They walked ever more carefully, cupping their hands over their noses and expecting something hideous.

As the stench grew worse, they came to an area sliced out of the main tunnel where the air reeked with a putrid odor. Jana cautiously stepped into the recess, using her dress to cover her nose, and the others waited behind. Feeling along the walls, she stumbled upon something on the ground. She poked around in the sand with her foot, and two small rats jumped past her and ran into the main tunnel. The other girls screeched and jumped out of the way.

Jana creeped forward and tripped on a boot. Feeling around, she touched the partially buried cowboy boot and felt a foot inside that had been dug up by the four-legged rodents. The rats had gnawed through the boot and were feasting on the foot of some poor soul who had been buried by the cartel. Jana screamed, jumped to her feet, gagged, and then threw up, disgorging what little fluid she had left in her body. She hurried out to the main tunnel, moving away from the half-buried body.

"What was that all about, Jana?" Sonny asked.

"You don't want to know. It was a *who*—not a *that*. It was a body. That was the rats' main course. How gross! Let's get out of here."

A few hundred yards back, Chuy was trying to pull himself out from under the pile of rubble that had collapsed over his body. When it began to fall, he had tried to scramble out of the way and was just able to avoid being consumed. He dragged his hips and legs out from under the mound and sat dazed from being hit by the shovel and the mass of falling sand. Chuy was dizzy and bleeding from his right ear, and it was caked with a dried, grainy mush from Jana's strike.

After pulling himself free, he reached up to feel if there was any room for passage. The pile of rocks and silt towered to the top of the tunnel, but a small opening was left uncovered where the crumbling had subsided. He considered going back to the house; it certainly wasn't that far, but it meant certain arrest and possible jail time for any number of charges. His status with the cartel would undoubtedly be discovered, and he could spend a majority of what was left of his life in prison. The other option would be to somehow get through the small opening above the mound to see what happened to his best friend, Luis, and track down the girls.

Chuy recalled Luis firing his weapon and maybe he was able to wound or kill one of the captives. He bristled at the thought of being clouted by a lady, and revenge inflamed rage in his mind. Chuy considered the possibility that there might be a weapon left behind that he could use to pursue the women and their accomplices. He planned to track them down and deliver the girls back to his boss.

Chuy knew that if he could track them to the end of the tunnel, his compadres in Mexico would capture the fugitives—and he'd more than likely be restored to his position within the company. There might even be a bonus for him somewhere—either cash or enjoying evenings with the girls. These ideas streaked through his consciousness, and he decided to make an attempt to dig his way to the other side. He sat on top of the sandy hill and began clawing away, moving rocks and earthen silt. What began as a small passageway slowly began to expose more and more space, and he continued to work feverishly to dig out a hole large enough to crawl through.

Fifty-One

Wednesday, June 19, 5:00 p.m., Nogales

The girls were slowly becoming dehydrated from exerting themselves on their flight from the cartel, the dust in the tunnel parched their throats, and their bodies began to cramp. They needed to rest more frequently and chose an opportunity to sit quietly, hearing only the sound of their labored breathing. The foul odor persisted as the group traveled down the passageway. It smelled like the banks of a hot, muddy swamp.

They sat with their legs extended, holding their noses from the horrible odor of the body that Jana discovered. After fifteen minutes of rest, the group decided to rise and continue down the dark hallway.

While standing, they began to hear the sound of shallow scratching and squeaking. Before they knew it the group was surrounded by a mob of large rats scuttling forward in the tunnel. The girls jumped back in fright and screamed, and the men hopped out of the way to avoid the rodents as they scurried past. There seemed to be hundreds of them passing the cluster of young girls and men, and they cringed and cowered while the little creatures scrambled past. The rats showed no sign of fear of the human visitors being secure in their own domain.

¤ ¤ ¤

Perez, Tatum, and the two detectives exited their vehicle and began surveying the smoldering home. The sprawling mansion must have been seven thousand square feet and ran parallel to West Crawford Street with a lavish sea of green Bermuda turf. The entire wing to the right, comprising more than half of the home, had been gutted by the blaze and was slowly being extinguished by the persistent group of firefighters. They were aided by the on and off rainfall. The left half of the home was missing its roof and had a gaping hole in its core.

While searching inside the property, the police discovered large quantities of acid stored in vats that were lined up inside the garage with protective coverings to prevent leakage. Also confiscated were thousands of rounds of ammunition and various illegal weapons, including RPGs, grenades, land mines, and Kevlar jackets. They discovered kilos of marijuana and several pounds of cocaine in the garage. The police reported this to Tatum's team and notified the ATF who were en route to the scene.

The FBI was notified and planned to send over a team to make a report. As the police officers were waiting for Perez and his team to arrive, they scoured the basement for evidence and found combs, hairbrushes, women's gowns and shoes, feminine hygiene products, and several sets of handcuffs scattered across the room. It was becoming more evident by the minute that the house they planned to raid that night was a sex trafficking lair. The house was a way station for key cartel operatives and housed subjects who were imprisoned for their trade.

Perez instructed Officer Martinez to call dispatch and give instructions to make sure Raul was closely guarded at the hospital since he was either in charge or closely tied to the cartel's activities there. Lieutenant Tatum, Captain Perez, and the two detectives stepped through the home's entrance and maneuvered through piles of debris and furniture. They made a beeline to the basement and wanted to inspect the tunnel and evidence that might lead them to the girls' whereabouts.

The men scaled down the firemen's ladder into the field of scattered refuse and damaged materials and appliances. They scanned the large room, and the detectives began to formulate an idea of what had occurred.

The Nogales police on the scene reported to Tatum and the detectives that they had discovered the large quantities of female articles in the basement. Emma's body was found in the rubble, and the shackles on the beds made it obvious that female hostages had been imprisoned there. Perez and the Tatum team slowly came to the realization that there had to be several young prisoners detained in the dungeon, and they were hopeful that two of them were Jana and Lydia. This information was based on the number of beds, the handcuffs, and the other accouterments in the rubble.

Detective Sharp said, "Lieutenant, they had a lot of girls down here. Look at all the handcuffs. There's at least six beds that looked like they had sheets on them, and we found numerous items used by the girls—way more than what two or three would need."

Tatum said, "I agree. There must have been five or six girls living here. God help them."

Their primary interest focused on the cave and whether it was used for an escape route by the hostages.

Sharp and Williams analyzed multiple sets of footprints by the mouth of the cave and judging by the size of the prints determined that a group of adolescents had sought refuge in the tunnel. They factored in the swimming pool rope, the fallen extension ladder, and sets of larger footprints alongside the girls' prints. Tatum concluded the hostages were in the tunnel and more than likely were being pursued. The tunnel would probably lead to the border and empty out on Mexican soil. The girls may have already made it to the other end or suffered a more drastic fate if whoever was chasing them caught up. It was imperative that they undertake a trek inside the tunnel to try to extricate the hostages from harm's way before they crossed over into sovereign Mexican territory.

Nobody knew how they'd be able to determine where the US border stopped and the Mexican border began in the underground maze.

Two heavily armed policemen with spotlights were to accompany Tatum and the detectives into the tunnel. Perez would remain at Raul's home to coordinate the investigation. The canine from headquarters arrived, and the officers harnessed the German shepherd and lowered her down to the basement to the waiting men. The police let her smell the rope, the ladder, and some of the remnants of Raul's clothing ripped away when he fell. They discussed the plan, and the five men entered the cave with Betsy, their four-legged companion tethered on a strong leash. They solemnly embarked on their mission into the darkness. Besides the powerful lights, the men were fully equipped with weapons, first aid kits, and water.

¤ ¤ ¤

Chuy dug and dug, throwing rock and soil in all directions. His hard work had slowly created a niche for him to slip over the knoll. His efforts started to pay off, and he began to feel a weak draft of air floating above his head, which hastened his labors. When he heard screaming in the tunnel, he wondered if Luis had squared off against them. If so, he was on his way to help.

When the swarm of rats finally passed, the rush of dread eased among the bunched men and young women. They left their positions on the sides of the cave to distance themselves from the intruding vermin and continued their walk, unnerved by the invasion of the long-tailed scavengers. The rats' presence caused an uncomfortable feeling about how so many of these animals lived underground.

As they moved forward in the cave, moisture seemed to be hanging in front of their faces like an invisible curtain. It thickened as they inched forward. Jana scuffed through the sand, and her foot unexpectedly stuck to the damp floor. She slowed down and asked Sonny to accompany her as she moved forward.

Sonny held her arm, and they walked carefully and slackened their stride. The dry ground phased into soggy sand that seemed to get wetter as they moved ahead. It made their progress much more laborious having to lift their feet from the muck that was starting to accumulate on their feet and shoes.

A good distance behind, Chuy finally wiggled his way through the hole, over the top of the dune, and slid down the other side of the mound. His phone illuminated the dark hallway, and he scanned the area around the cave-in to see if he could find Luis. It didn't take him long to discover his friend at his feet.

Luis was facedown on the rocky floor of the cavern just a few yards past the pile of dirt.

Chuy searched for a pulse, and finding none, he sat down and cried. Luis was his running buddy. They had completed hundreds of missions together and had each other's back 24-7. They lived in the same house, cooked for each other, and didn't travel unless the other man went along. They were a stellar team and had passed on countless experiences to the incoming young soldiers. They were the senior-ranking hit men of the Nogales cartel operation and were counted on because of their dedication, tireless work, and savage brutality. He felt like he had let down Luis and had failed to come to his aid when he needed it most.

After sitting for a few minutes and looking into the open eyes of his deceased brother, his anger slowly turned to fury. He stood and hurried forward with revenge in his heart. The memory of the blow to his head fueled his anger, and he vowed to avenge his friend's death and his own injury in the harshest way possible. Chuy searched for their weapons, but he came up empty.

Fifty-Two

Wednesday, June 19, 6:00 p.m., Nogales

Sonny, Simon, and the young women were completely unaware of the environment outside. Being trapped indoors every day, the ladies were unable to communicate or hear any news reports. They were isolated and uniformed. Every day seemed the same, and their routine was planned and executed without their input. They had to adapt to Raul's whims. They involuntarily became recluses and human moles and were trapped in the tunnel below the surface unaware of the world outside.

The girls didn't know that Arizona was steeped in the clutches of one of the most oppressive monsoon seasons in the state's history. Severe, periodic rainfall befell the dry, barren land, causing flooding and washes that sculpted the terrain in the southern parts of the state. Torrential rains unleashed slashing winds and caused a horizontal deluge of unprecedented proportions.

In the past week, Sonny and Simon had to work through the heavy rainfall. Simon had to shield himself from the precipitation on the streets and defend the important packages he delivered. Sonny's pool business was turned upside down by the weather, disrupting his schedule to service his customers' pools. The wind caused him more work by blowing sand, trash, and leaves into the water and turning the normally sparkling clean eddies into murky lagoons. His appointment schedule had dwindled to about half of the normal customer visits due to the unpredictability of the weather, and there was no end in sight.

When the group mucked its way through a fifty-yard stretch of the gooey sand, the two men clued in on their situation and how it could be tied to the weather outside. The humidity began to rise, indicating that the cave's atmosphere was changing, and the ground was beginning to feel saturated. As their hands pawed their way along the walls, they felt moisture and drops of water slowing trickling down the walls. The flow created small puddles, and before long, their feet were sloshing through a syrupy sludge that slowed their progress even further.

Up ahead, they heard the familiar sounds of the furry cave dwellers. It sounded like they were congregating; apparently something had stopped their forward movement. The group came to a stop and heard the small beasts chattering. The rats seemed to be stymied as the water continually descended around the fleeing team and collected in ruts and low areas. They considered the possibility that there was some sort of obstruction ahead.

Jana, as adventuresome as always, carefully crept forward and told the others to hold their positions.

Sonny instinctively followed behind her, and they inched ahead, measuring their steps down the path. The squishy, muddy mire seeped between Jana's bare toes, and she had difficulty lifting her feet to move forward. She was heading directly toward the rodents that had gathered in a swarm of chaos. Jana approached slowly and could hear the creatures squealing and sloshing around, apparently uncomfortable and out of their element. Her hearing had become more acute, and she was relying on sound rather than the ability to see her surroundings. She picked up the sound of the rats sloshing around in the water. The little animals, unaccustomed to being in deluged in water, were trying to cross a wide pool that had accumulated from the rain, and they couldn't ascend the slippery bank of mud on the opposite side of the depression. It sounded like they were trying to claw their way up the bank of the far end, but they weren't able to get traction and fell back in.

The rats were becoming agitated, and they tried even harder, which exacerbated their plight and continued the cycle, causing it to become even more slippery. The hordes of rats became animated and were vocally expressing their frustration as the humans were approaching.

Jana bravely inched her toe into the pool where the rats were swarming and tried to gauge the depth so she could try to cross.

The panicky rats were sloshing around, squirming, and circling Jana's leg, which was submerged to the knee. The little pests tried to latch on to her leg, hoping for a way over the water, and Jana yelped and knocked them off with her hand. Standing in the pool, she fought to keep her balance and then backed off, turned around, and tried to decide how to cross the small depression.

The water had accumulated into a pool and covered the cave floor from wall to wall. It seemed to be about three feet deep. As they paused to think of their options, the men and young women heard the water in front of them receding into the pool, causing the scope of the puddle to widen.

Jana explained that the pool was only a few feet deep and could be crossed fairly easily, but they needed to move quickly to avoid the rats.

The girls shuddered and debated whether or not they wanted to cross. Without any warning, Jana decided to plow forward. She quickly sloshed through the puddle, carrying a couple of rats with her, and then swatted them off in disgust as she successfully made it to the other side. "Come on. It's not that bad. It's not deep at all. If any rats grab on, just knock them off."

None of the girls moved forward until Sonny decided to cross, and he did so without incident. He urged the next person to move forward, and Beth stepped up. She retraced Jana's and Sonny's steps, treading through the tepid water in total darkness as dozens of rodents nipped at her legs. Sonny held out his hand to pull her over. She proved how fast a person can move when they're frightened. Beth's foot barely touched the bottom of the pond before she hopped up on the other side. She carried a few stragglers, cursed the little demons, and knocked them away.

Lydia made it over easily, plowing through the water without incident.

Charlotte started slowly, lost her footing, and stumbled, but the girls on the other side pulled her over with a quick yank as they swatted away the rodents milling around her feet.

Tabitha was petrified and shaking from head to toe. She had an aversion to rats, and being in such close proximity to the mass of squealing rodents had her in a tizzy. She reluctantly waded into the water, and one of the swimmers latched onto her leg. She shouted and withdrew back to safety behind the pool.

Simon urged her forward and held his hands around her waist.

Young, frail Tabitha was becoming his rescue project, and he felt inclined to help her get through this ordeal as he had with the landslide earlier. He pushed her forward, and the others grabbed for her hand, but they missed her in the darkness, and she lost her balance and fell headlong into the pool. She popped up, gasping for air, and the rats begin crawling on her back and hair. She screamed at the top of her lungs, and Sonny stepped back into the pool, grabbed her arm, and pulled her forward, knocking off the pests.

Simon jumped into the pool, grasped her from behind, and helped Sonny lift her up to the other side, knocking off the scruffy little demons.

Once on the other side, Tabitha stood drenched and shivering from the cold and the dread of having crossed the pond. The others consoled her as Simon quickly treaded across the pool, kicking stowaways back into the water. The girls' legs had minor scratches and a few bite marks, but everyone made it safely across.

¤ ¤ ¤

Chuy heard the screams and plowed forward in the faint light of his phone. His battery was running low, but based on the sounds carrying clearly through the tunnel, he didn't think the girls were that far away. His progress began to slow as he ran into the same quagmire as his prey. He slogged and sloshed through the thick mud that had grown worse since Jana and her team were there. His head was pounding, and he was having problems with his balance and equilibrium because of the concussion. The pain and confusion didn't stop his cumbersome pursuit by any means because of the wrath he harbored in his heart.

¤ ¤ ¤

Tatum and his team were making quick progress with the two large beacons lighting their way and covered a lot of ground fast. The shepherd was pulling Officer Baez at a pace that a human could barely maintain. Betsy had the scent and was proceeding full tilt, tugging her master forward and coughing from the restraint around her neck. The ground was shifty, and they experienced the dives and dips as well as the chuckholes and narrowing walls as had their predecessors.

The men wondered where they were and how far they could go in the tunnel before finding themselves under Mexican soil. For now, it didn't matter. They just wanted to catch up with the girls, and they pressed on. Their main concern was finding the missing young women—and it was obvious there were several—and the possibility of finding Jana and Lydia. Tatum thought about the Lincolns and Cantus and the other parents of the girls who had been waiting for news on their daughters. *We have to find them and return them to their homes. This evil must stop. We can't quit now.*

Officer Stephens and Officer Baez, the policeman handling Betsy, carried fifteen-round Glocks with plenty of ammo, and Baez also had a sawed-off shotgun slung over his shoulder. The detectives were armed, but not accustomed to being thrust into battle with such dangerous felons. Their lights illuminated the walls of the cavern, and the men were amazed at the sophistication of the construction and the massive amount of materials used to build the cartel tunnel. It must have taken years to excavate and remove the volume of earth required to dig the tunnel. It was a monumental task to haul away the soil and truck in the quantity of wood required to support the lengthy underground channel. They wondered how it could go undetected by the Mexican officials, and the men assumed they were paid to look the other way. The cartel's money and influence evidently made a significant undertaking fairly simple by eliminating any red tape or restrictions. Raul's forces had been free to work around the clock to burrow the nearly one-mile subterranean passage.

Baez was leading with the floodlight, searching the passage walls, and Betsy tugged hard on the leash. They saw numerous footprints on the sandy floor, and some of the smaller impressions were from bare feet, which they found odd. They came across a piece of Jana's smock on the pathway and stopped to inspect the material. The ragged, off-white piece of cotton fabric looked like it had been dropped recently.

As the lawmen neared the cave-in, Betsy pulled Baez even harder than before. Betsy approached the hill of sand and rock and bounded up to the top, sniffing the hole that Chuy had dug out. She began yelping and acting erratically.

The men shined their lights to the top of the cave, saw what caused the roof to collapse, and gauged the danger of continuing their pursuit.

Tatum had a fearful, queasy vision and wondered if the girls had been engulfed in the landslide. He prayed they weren't buried by the gravel and silt in the passage. After scanning the aftermath of the rockslide, the lieutenant didn't see any evidence to indicate they had been caught in the slide, which brought him relief.

The policemen inspected the ceiling and scratched around the pile of rubble, looking for any signs of the bodies, but found none. They saw imprints along the top of the mound where Betsy was sniffing; someone apparently had crawled on top, probably trying to find a way through. If the prints were the stalkers, they may still be in pursuit.

Betsy kept sniffing at the top and was pulling Baez through the opening Chuy had created. Baez leaned over, got on his stomach, and slid through without much effort as Betsy pulled him forward. He slid down the back of the mound and stood up, showering the dark cavern with a bright light. Luis's body was sprawled out in front of him. "Hey, guys, there's something you need to see over here."

"What is it?" Sharp queried.

"I think it's one of the cartel soldiers. Come look."

One by one, the men scaled the slope, crawled through the opening, and slid down on their bellies. Their eyes were riveted toward the passage roof, watching for any signs of another collapse.

Baez shined his light on Luis, and they saw him facedown in a pool of blood. After inspecting his lifeless body, the men determined that Chuy had been shot multiple times by a large-caliber weapon and probably died in seconds. Betsy sniffed around his body and pawed at him before whimpering and jerking the leash like she wanted to continue.

They shined the lights up at the girders and saw where the rounds of the AR-15 had splintered the support, and they found the expended shells scattered below.

So, that's what caused the tunnel to cave, Tatum thought.

This gave the law enforcement team optimism now that one of the pursuers was downed, and they were intrigued by the girls' fighting spirt to continue their escape.

I wonder how many more are chasing them, Tatum thought.

This question hung in the air like a cloud. The sight of the downed cartel footman inspired the lawmen to hurry down the tunnel, leaving Luis's body behind.

¤ ¤ ¤

Chuy slugged along in the thick mud, trying to gain on the gang of wayward cartel assets. He began to hear sounds in front of him, closer than before, but his cell phone died and the light went out. He was pitched into darkness and lost the advantage that had gotten him that far; he was now on equal footing with his adversaries.

His eyes had a difficult time adjusting to the severity of the darkness, and he began to stumble and trip. *Gotta keep up the pace.*

They're near. Chuy heard splashing and commotion in front of him and tried to walk quietly through the mud so as not to arouse alarm. He flinched when a rat ran across his foot, and then he heard several others rushing by. He froze and listened to the sounds of the cave. He heard tiny little footsteps scratching in the sand, chattering among themselves, squeaking, and calling to one another. He also heard the sounds of two girls urging one another along, splashing, a startled scream, and the rustling of hands and legs. He also heard men's voices and the sound of what could have been a weapon. He drew his knife from the scabbard and positioned it in front of him, ready to strike.

Chuy slowed his approach and quietly pulled his feet out of the mire. He moved forward and crossed the pool of water teeming with rats, continuing to be as discreet as possible. Chuy tried to minimize the mud's sucking sounds as he pulled his feet free with each step. The noise of the group just ahead masked his advance somewhat, and he crept unnoticed, growing ever nearer.

Chuy brandished his razor-sharp blade and sensed someone very close. He was prepared for the thrust with only a few more steps to go. As he slinked past the pool of water, his foot got caught in the thick mud. He tried to pull it out from the mire silently, but the sound gave his presence away.

Simon pointed his weapon toward the sound, but Chuy remained motionless, disguising his proximity. Not hearing any more noise gave Simon a false sense of security, and he relaxed for a moment. He turned back toward the girls, and Chuy leaped forward. His boots broke free from the quagmire, and he lunged toward Simon. Raul's hardened soldier waved his knife in a wide arc, trying to slash anyone that stood in front of him. The tip of his blade caught Simon's shirt as he tried to move away, but it did little damage.

The FedEx driver sprung backward, trying to dodge the assassin's thrust, and slipped sideways in the dark, just out of reach. Simon grabbed Chuy's arm as it flailed back and forth, and they wrestled for a moment. Chuy dropped his knife, and they fell to the floor in a tangle.

The girls had no idea what was happening, but they heard the struggle and rushed to Simon's aid. Jana clumsily fired her weapon at the ceiling of the shaft to discourage the attacker, but it didn't seem to faze Chuy. It did give them a glimpse of the two struggling on the ground in a life-or-death struggle in the pitch-black expanse.

Chuy's experience as a street urchin taught him the skills of fighting at an early age, and he quickly gained the advantage by flipping on top Simon as they squirmed in the mud. He found where his knife had fallen, picked it up, and was poised to strike. As the two men were fighting on the ground, they heard a rushing sound advancing behind them.

With a growl and a leap, Betsy was all over Chuy, digging her teeth into his arm, violently snarling, and growling as she took him to the ground. He tried to fight off the angry canine, but Betsy had him reeling, snapping, and grabbing his arm and biting and hissing with frightful strength.

Chuy was able to struggle to his feet, and Betsy grabbed his leg and gnawed on it relentlessly. He became unnerved by the shepherd's violent attack and swung his knife back and forth, trying to free himself from her jaws. He finally got a clean shot on Betsy and dug the shiv into her thick, muscular neck, bringing her down with a whimper. Betsy lay motionless.

Chuy immediately ripped his knife out of Betsy's neck and swung it to and fro, trying to connect with someone nearby. Without warning, an AR-15 spat lead in his direction, shredding his midsection with several rounds. He gasped, dropped the knife, and fell face-first into the mud.

Lydia lowered her weapon and heard the sounds of his life ebbing from his body. Blood gurgled and oozed onto the wet ground, and the air escaped from his lungs. She made her way over to Simon and put out an arm to help him up. He was still in shock from the knife attack and was confused and disoriented.

Betsy's body was next to Chuy on the cave floor. They were confused as to where the German shepherd had come from, who could have sent her to their aid, and why the dog attacked only Chuy.

In the distance, sounds began reverberating toward them. Someone was yelling, and they strained to hear the words that echoed through the chamber, but they were too distorted to understand. The water dripping down the walls caused a vacuum of sound that garbled the shouts of the sender.

Sonny thought, *Probably more cartel soldiers, but why would the dog attack their own man trying to kill us?*

Lydia decided to yell back, asking the men to identify themselves, and the reply came back more distinctly: "We're the police, and we're coming to get you. Stay put. Is that you, Jana? Lydia?"

Lydia and Jana were in shock and held each other closely. The girls weren't sure whether to believe their good fortune or if it was a ruse. Could it be that Raul and his henchmen had caught up to them in the tunnel? They were confused and unable to decide on their next move after they heard the shouts in the tunnel.

The water began to seep down from the ceiling; it was much heavier now. The torrential rainstorms had intensified and remained stationary over Nogales, and the flooding plowed across the low-lying areas. Inches of rain fell in a matter of minutes. Water engulfed the flat land and caused flash floods across the region. The water sought refuge, washing out wadis and deluging the flatter plains with nowhere to go. Because of the onslaught of the merciless showers, the land above was becoming inundated. A portion of the torrent streaming above began to filter down through the porous soil above the tunnel.

As they waited for another response from the men behind them, the walls began teeming with water. It was cascading down the walls on both sides of the tunnel. The water pooled in the low areas and was running along the footpath in an increasing flow. The voice rang out again, but it was completely drowned out by the accelerated rush of water. More deluge came, and mud and sand began falling from the sides of the earthen tunnel, which appeared to be losing its integrity.

They moved forward to avoid another cave-in. Simon, Sonny, and the girls slushed through the thick mud and blindly traipsed ahead, fearful of the worsening conditions around them. All at once, the ceiling behind them buckled, and thousands of gallons of rainwater gushed in from ground level, causing a massive flood inside the tunnel. The team of runaways, frightened by the sudden collapse, fled as swiftly as they could given the darkness and untenable walking conditions. They were continually hampered by the mud clinging to their shoes, and the unexpected accumulation of water thwarted their effort to escape as it flooded in from the surface.

Survival instincts spurred the seven, and with superhuman efforts, they plowed forward as the tidal wave exploded on their heels. They heard a loud thud, and the ground shook. They realized the top of the tunnel was collapsing on the pathway only yards behind them. This increased the flow of water even more. As it poured into the abyss, it quickly began to fill the tunnel. The mudslide opened up a crevice, allowing a sliver of light that crept in from the newly opened fissure and gave the escapees some much needed illumination. They fought their way forward frantically, but the water continued its rapid rise.

The discharge of water shot through the tunnel, diverting in both directions and separating the rescuers from the girls. It chased the five policemen in the opposite direction as they tried to avoid being swept under by the flood.

Baez heard the scuffle between Chuy and Simon and released Betsy to pursue Raul's men. The police heard barking and snarling as Betsy fought with one of the cartel soldiers. A whimpering sound was heard and then all went quiet for a few seconds. As they listened for Betsy, shots rang out, then the cave gave way and they were running for their lives. There was no way for Baez to know Betsy's fate or the fate of the girls. The tsunami of rainwater flooded the passageway, quickly rising above their feet and making the escape extremely difficult.

Tatum and his party made it back to the berm caused by the earlier cave-in, squirmed through the niche on top, and fell in a heap of exhaustion behind the wall of sand. The mound blocked the progress of the raging influx of water, redirecting it up the tunnel and toward the girls.

The sand and rock remnants forced the water back up to Jana and Lydia, adding to the deluge the young women were fleeing. The seven hurried from the rising tides and moved as fast as they could, but the water swamped their legs. Light from the fissure began to fade as they moved further up the tunnel, and once again found themselves in darkness. The raging flood significantly impeded their progress as they tried to put distance between them and their new enemy: the water.

The waterlogged bodies of Betsy, Chuy, and Luis' floated along behind the girls, buoyed on the surface and carried along by the flow. The elevation of the tunnel began to increase slightly, but it didn't constrain the tide's momentum. It continued raging up around their thighs.

Jana and Sonny were leading the escape, and Lydia was trailing close behind. The others were struggling, unable to keep up the torrid pace, and Tabitha was slowly falling behind. Simon lost track of her trying to maintain contact with the others. He turned and listened for Tabitha and shouted for her to keep up. He didn't intend to separate himself from the young girl, but he had gotten lost in his own survival effort. She somehow had fallen way behind. It had been a while since he had heard Tabitha. He stopped to listen and heard nothing but the roaring water. Simon was racked with indecision. Should he turn back and look for Tabitha—or try to save himself and catch up with the others? He elected to turn and head back for Tabitha.

The power of the rushing flood made it nearly impossible to fight the force of the current, and his progress was hampered as the water continued to rise. Simon yelled for Tabitha over and over, but all he could hear was the sound of water drowning out his calls. He had no choice but to flee and return to the others and somehow try to escape the rising wall of waves raging above his waist. Guilt consumed Simon. He had accepted the role of Tabitha's protector and then unintentionally abandoned the young girl who always struggled to keep up. Simon was beside himself for letting her down. He wept in frustration, and a wave of dread ripped his soul apart.

As he agonized, Simon felt something bump his hip, floating along the surface and pushed along the passage by the water. It was Tabitha. He immediately pulled Tabitha's head from the water and pulled her up to his shoulder as he continued to move forward with the flow. She was lifeless.

In an attempt to escape the momentum of the water, Simon rushed ahead, hugging Tabitha to his chest and trying to blow air into her lungs.

¤ ¤ ¤

It took the lawmen nearly an hour to make it back to Raul's house, and the five men were dejected and upset about losing contact with the girls. Their minds were fixated on the girls' fates, and they wondered if they were able to make it to safety.

Tatum thought, *If only we could have … if we just could have made it another few …*

The exhausted policemen returned to the basement, dripping wet, soggy and caked with mud. Upon arriving through the double doors, their eyes slowly adjusted to the brightness of the burned-out basement.

Several police officers were snapping photos of evidence and rummaging through the rubble for clues to determine what had transpired in the large prison room.

As Tatum and his team entered the tunnel, the rain was just starting to fall through the open roof, which delayed the efforts to investigate the crime scene. By the time the officers returned, it had ebbed, allowing the investigators to resume their search through the mushy refuse.

¤ ¤ ¤

Jana, Lydia, and Sonny paused for a minute to rest. The roaring rush of the rapids was increasing to waist level, and the water continued to rise as they waited for the others to catch up.

Charlotte and Beth joined the others, completely out of breath, and they waited for Simon and Tabitha. A few minutes later, they heard Simon sloshing along.

When he arrived, Jana said, "Simon, where's Tabitha? Wasn't she with you?"

"She … she didn't make it."

"Why? What happened?" Lydia pressed.

"I thought she was right behind me when everything went crazy.

As we were trying to escape the water, I didn't notice Tabitha had fallen behind. When I stopped, she wasn't there. I went back to look for her and found her floating with her head down in the water. I guess she got taken underwater and didn't have enough energy to fight her way out. She's here with me. I picked her up and tried to resuscitate her, but she was already gone. There was nothing I could do."

"Oh, Tabitha." Beth waded over to hold her.

Simon was dejected and felt miserable that she had drowned before he was able to get to her. He pulled her body alongside the entire distance and let her body float on the water's surface.

The girls gathered around, caressing her lifeless form, holding her head in their hands, and hoping it wasn't true. The girls took turns breathing into her lungs, which were filled with water, and tried to revive their chirpy little friend. After a few minutes, it was obvious the effort was useless; her body was cold and listless. The group encircled her frail body as it bobbed in the stream and said a prayer for Tabatha's passing. The group refused to abandon Tabitha and insisted on escorting her back as part of their team.

"She's coming back with us," Lydia announced. "No one gets left behind. Simon, we'll help you carry her. Let us know when you get tired, and we'll take her for a while.

They agreed to ensure she got a proper burial.

Simon held Tabitha's arm and pulled her behind him, letting the water carry her weight; her body was clammy and stiff.

As the cave's elevation continued to rise, the water level held steady, but large chunks of mud and silt kept spilling down the walls. The tunnel was being assaulted by the flooding and was quickly deteriorating.

Lydia asked the others to take turns pulling Tabitha through the tunnel to give Simon a break. With no one in pursuit, they were able to rest for a few moments when exhaustion set in. Their legs and feet were shot, feeling numb and sore. The team gathered around Tabitha's body, and her lips were parted as if gasping for air. They each said a prayer and asked for her comfort in heaven. No longer would she be subjected to the physical torture and mental abuse of being trapped in the dungeon as a prisoner. Tabitha was finally at peace, surely resting in the arms of her Savior, safe from the physically tormented world she was able to escape.

With water lapping around their waists, Simon and Sonny said their piece, bringing tears to each of the remaining young women. They knew it could have easily been them instead of Tabitha. They wondered why it had to be her. The constant barrage of events had depleted their drive, and even Jana and Lydia were exhausted from the lack of water and food.

If we can just make it a little further, Jana thought.

After a short period of quiet, the team, withered and famished and totally sapped of energy, heard the walls convulsing and then a strong tremor. There was no more time to rest. They heard another rumble downstream, and the cave around them shook, causing more water to stream down. Water and mud fell in globs onto the heads and shoulders of the girls, and the tunnel was rapidly losing its form. The frightened team frantically pressed forward, trying to avoid the falling earth washed down by the flooding aboveground.

Another vibration came from behind Simon, shaking the walls and causing some of the cave's ceiling supports to break loose. The planks reinforcing the tunnel dome fell, banging into the cavern below and dropping tons of soil and water into the tunnel. Giant slabs of earth separated from the walls and fell all around the group.

Jana and Lydia plowed through the water as fast as they could, and the others tried to keep up. Moving in the waist-high water was rigorous, but the fear of being buried alive propelled the group beyond their normal capabilities.

Part of the tunnel imploded and fell within a few feet of Simon. The thunderous collapse resounded through the tunnel, causing Charlotte and Beth to scream in horror, and a huge wave of water submerged them all.

Lydia gasped for air and tried to surface, but the rush of water kept forcing her down.

Jana's body was thrown against the side of the tunnel. The tall blonde was stunned and disoriented, but she was able to claw her way to the surface and grab a breath of air.

Sonny was tossed down the tunnel, riding on top of the cascade, but he was able to stay afloat.

Charlotte and Beth were tossed underwater, banging around on the cave floor, and fought their way back to the surface. As the initial wave subsided, they were able to right themselves and paddle up to the surface and catch a breath.

Simon was the last to appear. He was finally able to make his way out of the water, but he suffered an abrasion on his head when he tumbled underwater against the tunnel floor.

Tabitha was swept along by the tidal wave, but Simon never lost his grip, maintaining his tight hold on her wrist to keep the group intact.

When the rush of water subsided somewhat, the seven tired young men and women hurried forward on their flight to safety. The stability of their environment was deteriorating quickly, and they were aware that the tunnel could go at any moment. To make matters worse, the incline of the tunnel continued to rise, making their escape that much more difficult.

As it steepened, the water levels started to recede. With every few feet, they were able to move faster. Without warning, the roof of the cave shuddered, and a massive load of sediment fell, ripping down several beams with it and partially blocking their path. The upper part of the cave was jammed with the fallen girders. In order to clear the collapse, they would have to swim through the dark murky river below the fallen wooden supports.

As each person took their turn swimming under the debris,

Beth's gown got snagged on a splintered beam below the surface, and she couldn't free herself.

Lydia noticed her thrashing underwater, dove in, and felt her way to where Beth was struggling. She found the obstruction and tore the gown, allowing Beth to pass under the obstruction. They finally surfaced and met the others, gasping to catch their breath. After a short respite, they painfully moved forward. Their weary bodies were being driven by the will to survive.

Simon, Sonny, and the girls pushed forward, moving much slower as the fatigue and darkness sapped their strength. The incline became slippery and treacherous, and the sides of the tunnel continued to disintegrate and fall into the slushy water. Dust and rocks continually fell onto them, and they covered their heads to protect themselves.

As Charlotte was slugging forward, a giant slab of earth separated from the wall and fell on her legs. Simon and Beth heard her scream and went to her aid—followed by Sonny, Jana, and Lydia. The five young adults felt through the darkness where Charlotte was whimpering and worked on pulling her legs free of the broken embankment. As they were digging her out, they felt more rumbles and shaking directly above where they were aiding Charlotte.

Globs of mud began falling and splashing all around Charlotte as she struggled to keep her head above the water. The exhausted group worked feverishly to free her. They finally pulled her clear and helped her to her feet before the tunnel crumbled any further.

Jana put her arm around Charlotte as she limped along on her injured leg away from the damaged area of the passage. A massive block of soil along with the timbers collapsed on the place had they just vacated, which caused more water to be forced up the shoot. The band of escapees were inundated a second time. The underground tributary was causing significant damage all along the tunnel. It was washing away soil from the supports along the walls and on top of the cave.

They were engulfed in the turbulent water, but the team stubbornly pressed on. They tried to stay ahead of the flow, and as the elevation was changing, they were able to slowly climb above the flood. As they ascended, the tunnel continued its upward slope, and after a few hundred yards, the water had subsided to ankle depth. The mud was thick and gummy, causing further stress and weariness. Despite the natural forces inhibiting their movement, they were still able to bring Tabitha along.

Fifty-Three

Wednesday, June 19, 7:00 p.m., Nogales

The climb was arduous with Tabitha, but they somehow continued their slow progress uphill. Little by little, a soft glow of light began to filter into the passageway in the direction they were headed. This allowed them to move much faster and see what was ahead. Every new step seemed to usher in more light, and they finally were able to view their surroundings and measure their progress with safety.

The illumination was coming from a single light bulb hanging from the ceiling. Others were strung along the top of the cave as far away as they could see. Since the lights in that part of the tunnel were working, they assumed it meant they were tied to a circuit on the Mexican side, which was unaffected by the explosion at Raul's.

They had entered Mexico.

The bulbs began shaking violently, and a major upheaval threw them off balance and caused their feet to stumble. The walls trembled, the floor quaked, and more dirt and rocks began falling. The exhausted runaways raised their arms to shield their heads and dodged the falling debris by running as fast as their bodies could move. They continued up the slight increase in elevation to flee the catastrophic implosion in the tunnel.

The entire underground pathway was trembling, and support beams started falling like toothpicks only yards behind Simon. Following the seismic shudder, they heard a blast of thunder.

The floor crumbled and disappeared right in front of Jana's feet, and she nearly fell into a deep, yawning crevice. The men and young women peered down into the gaping hole and looked dejectedly at the new obstacle in their path.

Charlotte dropped to her knees and began to cry, having spent her last reserve of energy. Beth kneeled to comfort her friend. The others sighed and sat down, confounded by their persistent run of bad luck.

Lydia walked over and stood at the precipice as the shuddering continued all around the tunnel. She gauged the depth and heard the sound of dripping water falling far below. It appeared to be at least fifty feet deep and was filled with sludge and a shallow pool of water at the bottom. She stared into the deep cleft, but she couldn't see the bottom clearly. She heard the dripping sound of escaping water flowing inside and then splashing when it hit the bottom.

Had there not been light, Jana and the other girls could have fallen into the crater with no guarantee of ever getting out, especially if the hole continued to expand or collapse. The sinkhole stretched across the width of the tunnel and left no path to climb around. As frazzled as they were, it was difficult to think through the options and come up with a viable way for everyone to cross. Some could make it across without a problem. The men and Lydia and Jana had a good chance of being able to leap across the hole, but there was no certainty that Beth and Charlotte could make it that far.

The only solution they could come up with was to take Sonny's T-shirt and Jana and Lydia's gowns and roll them into a long cord, tie the ends together to make a rope, and toss it over to the remaining girls. To make the rope, Jana and Lydia would need to disrobe, but at this point, there was no shame given their dire circumstances. They agreed to carry on and help their friends in need.

Before they helped Beth and Charlotte, the four who could clear the expanse needed to cross to the other side first. Sonny stepped back ten feet, cleaned off his shoes, and prepared himself for the leap. He jumped to a start and ran as fast as he could toward the opening, shot across the expanse, extended his legs, and landed on the other side.

Now that he showed that it could be done, Simon chose to follow Sonny. The plan was to move both men to the other side where they could utilize their strength in case it was needed to pull the others across. Simon dashed forward, mirroring Sonny's leap, and flew over the gap, landing precariously on the opposite ledge. Sonny grabbed his arm and pulled him forward, away from danger. Even though Simon's jump was short of Sonny's, it was successful nonetheless.

Lydia leaned forward, muscles tensed, and stared at the men on the other side. She flexed her firm thighs and took a few practice steps to get a feel for the ground leading up to the hole. Once readied, Lydia bolted forward, her powerful body leaping over the hole with ease, and landed about where Sonny's feet set down.

This gave Jana confidence that if Lydia could do it, she could, especially with her long legs and uncanny athleticism. Jana stepped back and got in a runner's stance, poised for the leap. Not wanting to waste any more precious time, she ran forward and skyrocketed across, stepping on the front lip of the abyss, hurdling the expanse, and hitting the ground on the opposite side with plenty of room to spare. She stumbled upon landing and teetered backward, off balance. As she started to fall back toward the hole, Sonny grabbed her and pulled her out of harm's way.

The next task, pulling Tabitha's body across, would be more difficult. Sonny took off his shirt, and Jana removed her smock, forgoing modesty, and they began knotting the garments. Sonny couldn't help looking at Jana's body, but he turned away in shame, realizing there were more important tasks at hand. Lives were at stake.

Lydia pulled the dress over her head, gave it to Jana, and they tied the ends together to make a single strand of material. Beth removed Tabitha's gown and pitched it across the expanse to Jana, and they were able to add another two feet of length to the rope.

Simon and Sonny tested the knots to make sure they were secure by stretching them toward each other. They decided to test the makeshift rope by pulling Tabitha's body across before bringing over Beth and Charlotte. It was about ten feet long.

Confident it would hold, Jana threw the knotted cord over to Beth.

Charlotte and Beth tied it around Tabitha's wrist and tightened it snugly. While Simon and Sonny held the rope, Beth and Charlotte slowly lowered her body into the mouth of the drop-off. She dangled precariously over the pit for a moment before the two men were able to pull her up to the opposite side and lift her out.

Beth and Charlotte stood in trepidation. It was time for them to cross. More shaking and rumbling were felt, and soil began to tumble into the deep abyss. The two young women were acutely aware of how much effort it took to clear the space and were worried they wouldn't be able to duplicate the feat of Jana and Lydia. It would prove to be harder now that more of the ledge around the hole had crumbled into the expanse below. The escape from Raul's house and fleeing through the tunnel had depleted their stamina, and the girls' spirits were weak, making the task even more daunting.

Jana and Lydia and the two men on the other side urged them ahead and tried to give them confidence.

Charlotte wrapped her end of the makeshift rope around her wrist to ensure she could maintain her hold and prepared to leap. She was concerned about running on her injured leg, and the time in confinement had sapped her strength, adding to her hesitancy. Charlotte took a few steps back, rushed up to the crater, and jumped as far as she could.

Gravity started pulling her down into the hole.

The four on the other side yanked the tether and were able to pull her over to the slippery bank on the far side of the crater with her feet dangling over the fissure. One hand was holding the bound material, and the other was flailing in the air and searching for someone to help.

Sonny and Simon rushed to Charlotte and grabbed her arms so she wouldn't fall, and Jana and Lydia helped pull her up. Charlotte was safe.

Beth, was frail and more physically wasted. She was concerned about running on her injured feet because of the cuts and bruises picked up making the trek barefoot. She had been weakened by her captivity in Raul's basement for more than a year, which added to her uncertainty. Her brown hair was mussed and matted, and her gown was caked in mud and damp from fleeing the raging river.

They could all feel the tension in her demeanor as she prepared for the jump. It was obvious she understood the difficulty of what she faced and was not very confident she could pull it off. After Charlotte was safely settled, the five waited with great anticipation as the braided line was pitched to Beth.

A sudden rumble interrupted their concentration, and pieces of the cave fell into the deep hole. Distracted by the disturbing sounds of the tunnel, Beth missed it on the first try. The rope fell limply into the pit. They gave it a second try, and she was able to catch it and hold onto it firmly. Beth tried to dry her clammy hands as the perspiration surfaced from her nervousness, but it didn't help much, and they remained damp.

As she gathered the fortitude to jump, the others cheered her on. She ran a few steps and made the leap. Beth's effort was meager, and she fell short of the other side. As she dropped into the hole, the clothesline jerked, but the five on the other side were able to keep her from falling by holding the cord tightly. They began pulling her up to the top of the crater.

Beth thrashed and kicked the wall as she tried to get traction and help them raise her to ground level.

Lydia and Jana grabbed her shoulders, and the men pulled hard on the rope to lift her up. Beth's hands were weak, and she struggled to maintain her grip as the others tried to raise her. She couldn't maintain her grip and finally lost control, letting go of the rope.

With no weight on the cord, the men unexpectedly fell backward, leaving Jana and Lydia as her only lifeline.

Beth panicked and began clawing desperately at the rim of the sinkhole, making Jana's and Lydia's effort to hold Beth that much more difficult, and they fought to maintain their precarious hold on her shoulders. The grip on her gown was tenuous, and Beth's hysteria made it that much more difficult to keep her in their grasp.

Just as they were losing control, Charlotte ran up, reached down, grabbed a handful of Beth's hair, and jerked her forward. This allowed Jana and Lydia to get a cleaner grip, and they began pulling her up.

Sonny and Simon hopped up from the ground and rushed over to help by grabbing Beth's flailing arms and lifting her to the safety of the bank above. As Beth stretched her body over the top, everyone fell into a heap depleted, yet relieved they were able to snatch her from the yawning cavity.

Beth began giggling nervously, which soon turned into relieved laughter, and before long, all six broke into hysterics on the cave floor and laughed until they could laugh no more. As they collected themselves, a massive chunk of the tunnel floor where Beth started her leap broke off and fell into the deep ravine. This shocked the team back to the reality of their plight, and they stood and prepared to run.

Jana and Lydia realized they were still naked and unraveled the clothing and quickly put on their gowns. They dressed Tabitha while Sonny was slipping on his wrinkled shirt.

The fleeing refugees ran as far from the sinkhole as quickly as they could in their exhausted condition. They were beyond feeling tired and were operating on primal instincts, adrenaline, and fear.

The cave floor behind them shook, and as the group looked back, they could see the crater swallowing more and more of the tunnel. Panic ensued, and they bolted up the path, leading farther away from the disintegration. Finally coming to a place that seemed a safe distance from the implosion, the group absolutely had to rest. They fell to the ground, totally exhausted and breathing heavily, and not a word was spoken.

The men and young women had been through the pit of hell to get where they were at that moment, and they wondered if they would ever make it aboveground. The group hadn't rested for but a few short moments when the ground began shuddering again, causing the floor of the cave to rattle and vibrate. Sand and rocks rolled down the slope into the crater. A wooden support above their heads snapped in two and fell with its jagged edges right between Beth's legs. Had it fallen an inch or two either way, it would have crushed her leg. Dust sprayed down on top of the youth from the top of the tunnel covering them in silt.

Without notice, the floor began breaking off in chunks. By that time, they were on their feet, summoning energy to dart away from the falling projectiles. The tunnel was in the throes of destruction, and it was only a matter of time before the entire passageway collapsed. The six were running for their lives, carrying Tabitha up the steep, dusty walkway as the walls buffeted and the ground under their feet shook and heaved like an earthquake.

¤ ¤ ¤

Tatum, Perez, and the detectives huddled on the first floor of Raul's house, trying to make sense of what had happened in the tunnel. The men were visibly disappointed after losing contact with the girls and being so close. The conversation moved into a more constructive state of mind, considering whether there was anything left they could do. No viable solutions surfaced, and they walked around the house, in deep thought as they considered the alternatives.

The forensics team had just arrived, and the last of the fire was being extinguished by the fire department. The exhausted firemen were winding up the hoses, replacing equipment, and readying for departure. The fire inspector was making his rounds, and after concluding their duties, a few of the police officers headed to their cruisers.

Tatum looked up and saw a helicopter circling in the distance. It seemed to be searching for something and loitering in a holding pattern.

Captain Perez got a call from Jesse, his Border Patrol contact, and received an update.

"Hi, Captain. This is Jesse, USBP, how are you?"

"Doing okay under the circumstances. Where are you now?"

"We've been watching the border since your office called to tell us about the situation at the location in Nogales. So far, we haven't seen any activity along the ten-mile stretch of border around Nogales that we've been monitoring. Were the guys at the house members of the cartel?"

"We believe so ... still checking it out, but all indications are that this house is a cartel outpost."

"Captain, the reason I'm calling is that we've been tracking a low-flying chopper that's been hovering for some time right over the border."

"Yeah, I see it."

"It has Mexican registration and doesn't have a flight plan or a manifest to fly in US airspace. The ID on the aircraft hasn't come up on our database and appears to be unauthorized or unknown. That tells us it could possibly be owned by the cartel. Our men in the BP copters have been dogging them all this time, and so far, they've stayed on their side of the border, but it's strange how they're just hanging around."

"Oh yeah?" Perez pondered a minute. "What do you think would happen if your helicopters left the area?"

"Not sure. Why we would do that? They might come into our airspace."

"Is that a bad thing to let them enter, and then once they're in our airspace, we force them to land? Our helicopters could appear as if they were moving somewhere else and be just out of sight of the cartel. If the bad guys come into our space, maybe we could keep them from leaving somehow?"

"That's a little tricky, Captain, but if they do enter our airspace, we could try to box them in with two or three of our aircraft and see if they'll land. We could make an arrest at that point if they're illegal. I'm sure ICE would be interested in talking to them."

"How many eggbeaters do you have locally?"

"Within twenty miles … three."

"So, theoretically, could it be done?"

"Yes, sir. If we can get our copters in place before they can get back across the border, it's possible we could make the pilot do a forced landing. That's assuming they would chance coming over here in the first place."

"I'd like to try it. We have reason to believe they may be connected with a sex trafficking ring here in Nogales and may also be part of a major drug ring too—all under the cartel umbrella."

"Okay. I'll pass this up the chain, and if they give us the thumbs-up, we'll need to clear it with ICE and maybe the FBI."

"All right, do whatever you need to do and get back with me."

"Ten-four."

Perez hung up, and an incoming call from the Nogales hospital chimed in. "Yes? Perez here."

"Hi, Captain. This is Officer Davis at the hospital. Raul Alvarez, the patient we brought in from the fire, is in stable condition. We have an officer in the room and two posted outside the door. Everything here is quiet, and he's not talking a lot. I guess that's no big surprise."

"Yes. I agree. He won't be very talkative, but that's okay. The feds will get their time with him later. Thanks, Davis. I appreciate the update." Perez hung up and rejoined the group of officers from Phoenix. "Any ideas, gentlemen?"

"None that make sense. We're still running through scenarios, but so far, we can't think of anything that will get us through the tunnel, especially with it flooded out. Hate to say it, but we're not even sure they're still alive."

Sad expressions settled on the men. They looked down and brooded for a few seconds, not sure where to turn.

Fifty-Four

Wednesday, June 19, 8:00 P.M., Nogales

The tunnel got brighter and brighter as they ran up the shaft, and the team could see every detail of the long passageway. Simon and Sonny took turns carrying Tabitha's body, and then Jana and Lydia would hoist her limp arms over their shoulders and carry her for a while.

Rocks and sand continued to fall from the top of the tunnel, and they struggled their way forward through the fallen sediment.

About five hundred yards away, they could see what appeared to be a dead end. They followed the string of lights bulbs leading down the shaft that channeled its way forward, abruptly ending at what appeared to be the tunnel's termination point.

As they moved along, the brightness of the bulbs strained their eyes, which had been subjected to the dark for so long. They squinted until their pupils adjusted to the new environment in the lit cave.

The girls' thoughts now focused on where the tunnel came out and where they'd be in Mexico if they were to get out. Other questions surfaced like how they'd be able to return, crossing the border, and trespassing in a foreign country, which led to a different type of anxiety beyond the physical distress they had experienced recently.

As Simon, Sonny, and the girls neared the tunnel's end, the ground began shaking more violently, and their footing was rocked. Soil and stones began tumbling toward the sinkhole, and it seemed as if the entire tunnel was being sucked down into the black hole behind them. Large segments of the tunnel collapsed and plummeted down the path. Sand was raining down from above, covering their heads with silt, and the sturdy wooden supports began collapsing like dominoes behind them.

They grabbed hands to keep from being dragged down by the cascading debris and hurried up the slope.

A significant tremor jolted Simon and Beth to their knees. The implosion caused a vacuum as it sucked up rocks and sand, and the two were caught up in the momentum of the downward draft. They were barely able to struggle to their feet. Simon was desperately holding onto Beth's hand as the cave floor evaporated under their shoes.

Lydia pulled Simon forward, with Beth in tow, and they were able to move ahead on their own. They hurried up the last few yards of the tunnel, bringing the group to a wooden portal with light filtering in through the cracks of a wooden door. The gang of exhausted refugees gathered together for a moment and stared at the tunnel exit.

The ceiling shook, and wooden beams began falling all around them. They pushed on the door hysterically and found it firmly locked from the outside. The rough-hewn door was made of old weathered planks, reinforced by two-by-fours, and worn from the years in the harsh desert climate.

More of the tunnel collapsed, and a piece knocked down Charlotte, dazing her momentarily, and then she scrambled to get up. Sonny lifted her quickly, and then he attacked the aged door.

As more silt and rock were falling on the terrified huddle of young women, Sonny and Simon hastily put a shoulder on each side and drove the full brunt of their bodies against the barrier. The deluge of rock and earth continued to tumble onto them.

More pathway disappeared behind them, and the girls huddled close to the exit, wondering if they'd be able to get out in time. The wooden door split, but it didn't budge. Simon began kicking the door in desperation, and Sonny continued to ram it with his full weight. The men continued to attack the barrier until the door began to break down, and it finally detached from its hinges and fell to the ground.

Another cave-in dropped loads of earth onto the frightened bunch just feet from the outside. It knocked Beth down and partially covered her lower extremities. Sand and rocks pelted her head, and she couldn't see or move from under the accumulation of sediment piling on her legs. Simon turned quickly, reached down, grabbed her firmly, pulled, and was able to dislodge her from the pile of falling rubble. He dragged her forward until she was at the opening of the cave entrance.

As the doors were knocked free, the group flung their bodies headfirst out of the entryway and fell on their bellies onto Mexican soil. As they landed outside, the entire cave collapsed behind them, tumbling into the sinkhole that had grown to enormous proportions as a victim of the monsoon's barrage.

The light temporarily blinded the escapees, and they strained to focus. The exhausted team swiftly crawled away on hands and knees, slopping through the mud to put distance between them and the tunnel's implosion. When the young men and women were safely distanced from the collapse they sat up, turned, and looked at the dust pouring into the sky from the hole they had narrowly escaped. Sand was shooting twenty feet in the air as the cave heaved its last breath.

Outside, the metallic cloud-covered skies partially cloaked the fading sun on the western horizon. The clean, clear air, purified by the rain, was refreshing, and the scent of the outdoors was intoxicating to their senses. As they took in their surroundings, they saw a stand of tall, gnarly shrubs on their right, protecting the cave entrance from view, and then a vast field beyond.

Looking in the other direction, they spotted a pile of old lumber concealing the tunnel. A sign was posted on one of the fallen tunnel doors: "*No entres o te mataremos—El Cartel.*"

They surveyed the area around them to evaluate any possible threats. The rain began to fall again and turned their grubby clothes into wet, muddy rags. With significant effort, they were able to stand, and when they felt sure there wasn't any risk, the girls began wiping their faces with the fresh rain and splashing themselves clean.

Jana and Lydia laid Tabitha's body on the ground outside the entrance, folded her hands on her chest, and closed her eyes. They stood around her body in the rain, seeing her countenance for the first time. The struggle showed frightfully in her face, her lips were purple, and her skin was pearly white. Beyond their friend's body, they took in the beautiful panorama of the bruise-colored sky billowing against the dying sun that was taking one last peek before scurrying on its path to the west. The birds and the warm air gave them a new appreciation for what they once had taken for granted.

Simon and Sonny high-fived, and the girls hugged each other in long embraces. They cried, laughed, and hugged again and again.

The nightmare was over. Jana, Lydia, and the girls looked a mess. Their white gowns were covered with dirt and mud along with a few blood spatters from their run-ins with Raul at the house and with Chuy in the tunnel. Their hair was matted, tangled, and caked with mud, and slime was smeared all over their faces. When they took a moment to finally look at one another, they broke into another fit of laughter, gazing at how filthy and disheveled they were, and the hugging began all over again.

¤ ¤ ¤

The USBP helicopters departed from their respective launch sites amid heavy showers when they got Dunning's order and headed toward the area of confrontation. The choppers' orders were successfully cleared through his chain of command and received the necessary agency approvals with an aim to lure the cartel helicopter into US airspace. The BP helicopter that was bird-dogging the cartel's turned sideways in the air and immediately left the scene after receiving the order.

The cartel pilot's aircraft was being buffeted by horizontal winds, and he fought to maintain his position right over the border, straddling the two countries. He didn't make an attempt to enter US airspace right away, holding his bearing, fluttering up and down in a tight circle, and inspecting the area around the border and then back to his original position.

After the BP copter was out of sight, the cartel pilot decided it was safe to fly over Raul's house and get a glimpse of what was going on at *el jefe*'s home. Raul's headquarters represented the cartel's livelihood, and they had a vested interest in its condition. It was especially important since it was home base for the tunnel that served as its narcotics pipeline into America.

The Mexican aircraft was being battered by the high winds and heavy rain, and the pilot fought to keep the ship level. He stuck its nose over the boundary and hovered for a few minutes to see if the US airships would return. Seeing no threats, the pilot took a quick spin around Raul's home, hovered over it for a few minutes to look inside, and saw the home was decimated from the explosion and was dotted with police cars and firetrucks.

A second man took a few pictures, and the pilot lifted up into the blustery current back toward Mexican airspace. As the chopper levitated over the house to take the photographs, three USBP helicopters appeared out of nowhere and blocked their return home.

The Mexican pilot spotted the US aircraft and tried to take flight. He employed some fancy maneuvers to evade the trap, but each time, the experienced Border Patrol pilots countered and kept him boxed in. After several failed attempts by the Mexican aircraft to elude the US pilots, they pointed to the ground, ordering him to land, and the cartel pilot put up little resistance. He probably had a story prepared about how he accidentally wandered into US airspace, and since they had no contraband, there was no reason for them to expect any harassment from the US officials.

The cartel pilot made an off-balance landing in an open field as he contended with the unpredictable turbulence swirling around him. He landed a few blocks from Raul's home and were followed by the three BP copters watching from above, their rotors spinning amidst the squall.

Agent Dunning and two armed officers left their shelter in the driving rain, ducked under the blades, approached the helicopter, and asked the men to shut down the bird and exit immediately.

The Mexican pilot complied, turning off the motor, and he and the two cartel soldiers climbed out into the gale onto a washed-out, grassy expanse.

The Border Patrol took the men out of the rain into a waiting SUV. During the interrogation, two BP officers searched the helicopter for weapons and drugs. Finding none, they gave the all-clear signal to Dunning.

As the episode was unfolding, Detectives Sharp and Williams and Lieutenant Tatum rode through the sloshy bog to the field with Captain Perez and watched as the members of the cartel stepped into Dunning's Tahoe and shut the door.

¤ ¤ ¤

The girls were ecstatic now that they were finally free. They lifted their arms in a triumphant pose as the rain started falling harder. They were getting thoroughly soaked, but they didn't care. After a short celebration, the group decided to compose themselves and figure out a way home.

Charlotte said, "Wow, this is beautiful. We're outside!"

They looked out at the inundated landscape, dotted with puddles and streaming water as they attempted to determine their whereabouts and the distance to the US border.

Jana pointed north. "That must be the US over there."

Lydia replied, "I think you're right, Jana. That's where we need to go."

They spotted a major highway through the low-hanging clouds, which appeared to be on the US side about a mile away. It made sense that it would be an east-west corridor ending near the border checkpoint. They quickly reasoned that the freeway was north, and Sonny, Simon, and the young women formed a tight cluster. Rain pelted the weary group, and they began walking toward the road ringing wet.

Sonny said, "Let's go this way. It should take us to the border crossing."

They hoped the narrow street would guide them to the

checkpoint, and they could try to reenter through the border gateway. Jana, Lydia, and Simon didn't think it would be a good idea to carry their automatic weapons to the border crossing, and they stacked their guns on the ground.

As the exhausted group made its way to the road, they heard a shrill whistle above the pounding rain coming from behind the pile of lumber by the tunnel entrance. Appearing out of nowhere, hidden behind the stack of wood, five cartel soldiers jumped out with guns aimed directly at the men and young women. They had been waiting for the group to clear the tunnel and were acting on Raul's orders to intercept the runaways as they made their way out. The cartel gunmen carefully approached the six after waiting patiently outside in the rain for two hours. They were cold and wet and in no mood to fool around. The hardened men watched the group as they jumped out of the tunnel, narrowly escaping the implosion. They decided to stay hidden until Jana, Lydia, and Simon dropped their weapons. The cartel men confronted the group. The young men and women were unarmed, and the soldiers slowly advanced toward them. They stared numbly at the cartel goons, and their minds refused to believe what their eyes were seeing.

Jana said, "Oh my God. It can't be."

All the pain and effort, losing two of their friends, and risking their lives over and over—and to now face the reality of being recaptured and returned to another cartel henhouse—was too much to comprehend. It was unthinkable.

Beth fainted and dropped to the ground in a puddle of water.

Charlotte fell to her knees with her hands covering her face and began sobbing. "Oh no. I can't handle this. I don't wanna go back."

"Don't shoot. Don't shoot!" Simon threw up his hands.

Sonny slowly inched his way over to the weapons on the ground, and Jana and Lydia understood his intention of going for the firearms.

The gunmen noticed his movement and lifted their automatic rifles and pointed them directly at Sonny. The girls knew Sonny's fate if he were to go for the guns, and they resorted to the only weapon they had left in their possession to protect him.

"Let's help Sonny, Lydia," Jana whispered.

"Think we should?" Lydia questioned.

"Are you thinking what I'm thinking?"

"Yeah, let's do it."

Jana and Lydia looked at each other, nodded in agreement, and slowly began removing their drenched garments. They lifted the frocks above their heads and stood naked, exposing their breathtaking physiques.

"Hey, guys, over here, look at us!" Lydia shouted.

The beauty of the two young women diverted the cartel's attention for a second, allowing Sonny just enough time to dive for one of the ARs. The men quickly caught on to their ploy and swung back to Sonny, firing in his direction and smattering mud and rocks all around, but they failed to land a killing blow.

Sonny took off running through the rainstorm, bent at the waist, keeping his head down, and zeroed in on an abandoned refrigerator in the field. He leaped forward and slid in the mire until he was able to shield his body and then returned fire.

After being fired upon by Sonny, the cartel members scattered, hiding wherever they could to escape his volley. Once safely in position, they opened fire.

Jana and Lydia picked up their clothes, slipped the drenched gowns back over their heads, and sloshed away in the opposite direction.

The soldiers, angered by the ruse, shot in front of the two girls, splattering watery sludge by their feet.

Jana and Lydia stopped immediately and stood with their hands in the air, afraid the next shots might be closer.

Now totally focused on Sonny, the Mexican mafia discharged their weapons, raking the refrigerator where Sonny was hunkered down. The gangsters tried to chase Sonny out from behind his shelter with their onslaught, but the old metal box held up, and he remained safe even considering the torrid barrage.

While Sonny was pinned down, two of the cartel men ran over and grabbed Jana and Lydia and then collected Simon who was on his knees with this hands up. Raul's men hustled over to where Charlotte tended to Beth. The gunmen violently yanked them up from the ground and dragged them behind the stack of lumber out of the line of fire. When all of the refugees were out of the way, the men dialed in on Sonny. They peppered his shelter and continued to lay into him as he holed up behind the fridge. Sonny was in a desperate situation, pinned down, but he couldn't move with lead flying all around him. The other five escapees felt helpless and could only watch as the goons unleashed hell on Sonny with a nonstop attack, but there was nothing they could do to help their friend.

¤ ¤ ¤

Above the sounds of the torrential downpour, Tatum and the team from Phoenix heard the shots being fired. They became alarmed because it came from across the border, near the site where the officers believed the cartel cave entrance was. The distinct report of AR-15s continually firing meant there was a pitched gun battle in progress. Their immediate reaction was to go to the site, see who was engaged in the gunfire, and check if it had anything to do with the missing girls. The problem they faced was crossing the border into Mexico where the battle was taking place. They weren't certain of their jurisdiction to operate outside of the US. So, they evaluated other solutions.

Detective Sharp came close and whispered into Tatum's ear. "See that chopper over there?"

"Yeah."

"It's a Mexican aircraft, and the pilot apparently has clearance to fly in their airspace even though Dunning's men couldn't find any registration information. What if we were able to take that helicopter over to the location of the gunfire and get a look-see, maybe we'd be able to figure out what's happening. If the cartel's involved in the skirmish, they shouldn't bother with us since they'll recognize the chopper and assume we're part of the brotherhood. That should allow us to get in close. It would only take a few minutes, and if we run into problems, we can always bring the bird back. No harm, no foul. What do ya think?"

"You crazy? Commandeering a Mexican-owned helicopter owned by the cartel and flying it into Mexico to engage Mexican citizens in a firestorm?"

"Yeah, that's about it. Who the heck would know outside of the men here? I think the guys will look the other way if we're using the cartel assets to try to recover some American teenagers involved in sex trafficking. To me, it's worth a shot."

"I don't know, man. That's breaking every rule in the book, and it could get us fired."

"Yes, *if*, anyone were to find out."

The rain was pouring off of Tatum's cap, and he wiped the moisture off of his eyes and looked seriously at Sharp. "Let me talk it over with Perez and Williams."

The four men were getting soaked while they discussed the possible issues of "borrowing" the cartel helicopter for the reconnaissance mission just over the border. Surprisingly Perez didn't object, and Williams bought in too. The men came to a consensus. It could have been that they were more interested in getting out of the deluge to find a dry place to towel off, but whatever the reason, they were all in agreement.

Tatum trotted around large puddles to Dunning's vehicle and tapped on the glass.

The Border Patrol officer cracked the window, trying to keep the rain from coming in, and the two discussed the idea. It meant loaning one of his pilots to fly the cartel chopper, and Dunning had the right to nix the idea before it literally got off the ground.

"I don't know, Tatum. It's not a good idea."

Shielding his eyes with his hand to block the rain, the lieutenant responded, "Trust me. We'll have it over and back in less than fifteen minutes, but I need one of your pilots."

"Tatum, I'm not sure anyone would volunteer for that duty. They're not accustomed to being fired on, and they don't like this kind of weather."

"It's a cartel helicopter. They'll assume we're part of their team, and they won't fire. I know it."

"If you're crazy enough to try it, go right ahead—but without my official permission. At least that's what my story will be. If asked, it'll all be on you."

"I'm willing to take that risk. Thanks, Dunning. You might have just saved some American lives."

Dunning quickly rolled up his window, shutting out the monsoon.

Tatum gave Sharp the thumbs-up, and they ran over to one of the USBP helicopters that was awaiting further orders. They realized it wouldn't be easy finding a pilot willing to fly the cartel whirlybird. More shooting was heard across the border, and the urgency grew. Tatum ran over to the nearest helicopter, stuck his head in the cockpit, and yelled to the pilot, "Hi. I'm Officer Tatum of the Missing Persons Department, Phoenix Police. We're tracking some teenage girls who were kidnapped and are being used by the cartel for sex trafficking. They were last seen trying to escape through an underground tunnel that opens up right over there. We have reason to believe the girls may be trapped by cartel gunmen and need help finding a way out. We want to get them back to their parents. You hear that gunfire over there? We think our female subjects are the target and somehow involved in the battle."

"Yeah, I heard it—so what's that got to do with me?"

"We want you to fly that helicopter over there to where we think the girls may be located. Just to look and see if it's them. If so, we'll try to rescue them."

"That's the most foolhardy thing I've ever been asked to do. No, I don't think so. I value my personal assets too much to risk getting shot at."

"Look, that bird over there is a cartel helicopter. They won't fire at one of their own. Doesn't that sound logical?"

"Maybe, but still. In this rain?"

"You think you can fly that thing?"

"Mister, I can fly anything with a rotor, but I didn't say I would."

"Officer, do you have a family, kids?

"Yes, sir, married with two daughters."

"What if your daughter was stuck over there pinned down by cartel gangsters who intended to sell your daughter to perform sex acts with random men?"

"Well …"

Tatum was dripping water inside the pilot's cabin.

"Well, let's do it, Officer. We'll be back in fifteen minutes, tops."

"This is nuts. Let me ask Sergeant Dunning if it's okay."

"He's already approved—said he's gonna be looking the other way."

"Yeah, right. I've heard that before."

Shutting it down, the pilot stepped out of his helicopter and then dashed with Tatum and Sharp over to the chopper, getting soaked in the process. The pilot jumped in, fiddled with the controls, and got the engine revved up and the prop started to spin.

Williams ran up with weapons and fed them to Tatum—who was seated shotgun in the chopper in case they became involved in the fracas—and the chopper slowly rose in the air and headed over the border.

¤ ¤ ¤

The cartel hit men were peppering Sonny as the sheets of rain slashed across the scrub, slowly beating him down to where he couldn't retaliate. Sonny was running short of ammo and used his shots judiciously, but he kept the cartel on their toes by occasionally firing at their position. Rain was falling so hard that Sonny couldn't focus on his adversaries or keep track of their movement. The cartel henchmen faced the same issue. The girls were screaming, crying, and shouting to get someone's attention for help.

One of the thugs slapped Jana to the ground to keep her quiet. "*Callate, puta.*"

Lydia went to her aid, but a cartel gorilla yanked her by the hair and threw her into the mud.

Sonny finally fired his last round, and all of the hoods soon knew that he was out of ammo. As the rain continued to beat down, the men began plodding toward his location. They divided up and approached him from different angles, slowly tightening the noose.

Sonny leaped from behind the refrigerator and crawled on all fours through the quagmire to where Jana and Lydia had dropped their ARs. He got his hands on one of the weapons, shook off the water, and began firing at the men. He hit two of them who weren't expecting him to fire, and the men dropped, mortally wounded. The other two returned fire immediately, showering Sonny with lead and catching him in the leg and arm.

Sonny dropped in a pool of water, bleeding from his wounds, and tried to sit up and fire again as the cartel hitmen closed the distance. This time, with the moisture in his eyes and being hampered by the wound on his arm, Sonny missed his mark. Sonny was an easy target now kneeling out the open as they returned fire and was hit squarely in the gut. He fell flat on his back, groaning and writhing on the muddy Mexican turf.

As they closed in on Sonny, the helicopter carrying Tatum buzzed right over the gunmen. When they stopped to look up at the chopper, Tatum and Williams spotted the girls cowering behind the stack of wood and Sonny under siege. They prepared themselves to defend the American hostages.

The cartel operatives recognized their own aircraft as it dipped between them and the girls and excitedly waved it off so they could finish their attack on Sonny.

In that moment of hesitation, Sonny weakly leaned up on his elbow and was able to get off a few more rounds, striking down another soldier. The cartel footmen quickly turned their attention back to Sonny, unable to see that Tatum was leaning out of the open cockpit of the chopper as it bounced around in the rain and gusty winds. Tatum tilted his body out of the cabin to get a good angle and surprised the men who were focused on Sonny, spraying several rounds from his automatic weapon at the two remaining commandos. He took one out.

The last of the cartel kinsmen looked around with rain beating down on his face and was confused when he saw his dead comrades. He took off running toward town, hiding behind trees and bushes to cover his escape. The girls watched through the gale-force winds, totally bewildered about what had just taken place.

Once the last soldier ran away, Jana sensed it was safe and rushed over to Sonny. She sat by his side and looked down at man who had bravely put his life on the line to save her and the others. Propping Sonny up, she held him in her lap, hugging him tightly with her arms wrapped around his shoulders. "Sonny, oh, Sonny, don't die. I'm with you. Hold on. Hold on."

He was bleeding profusely from the three wounds sustained from the cartel attack. The loss of blood had rendered him slack and barely conscious. Sonny's eyes were opened slightly, and he gazed up and saw Jana holding him. He forced a smile and winced in pain.

Jana bowed her head in the driving rain and kissed him on the cheek as tears streamed down her face.

Sonny felt Jana's touch on his cheek, and as he was losing consciousness, he stared into her face one last time and closed his eyes. Sonny was lost on that dreary, blustery day in Mexico.

Upon orders from Tatum, the BP pilot landed the cartel helicopter close to the girls. Tatum and Sharp unsnapped their safety belts, hopped out, and ran over to the young ladies.

Seeing the men leave the chopper, Jana returned to her mates, and they huddled together awaiting their arrival.

The four teenagers were disoriented and perplexed at what was unfolding as the men jumped out of the chopper and nervously headed their way. They stood like marble statues, silhouettes in the light rain that was finally beginning to recede. The girls stared blankly with mouths agape and eyes wide open as Tatum and Sharp rushed forward.

Lydia thought the two men didn't appear to be Mexican and wore suits. Her initial assumption that they were more of Raul's band of murderers. So, they stood in place and decided not to run. The young band of hostages were so weary and probably couldn't have tried to escape anyway. They remained flatfooted, arms limply by their side, and their backs slumped in fatigue.

Jana thought, *What's gonna happen next in this awful nightmare? Who are these men—and why are they advancing so quickly? Why is there urgency in their eyes?* She prepared for the worst.

Sharp and Tatum ran splashing through the puddles and stopped in front of the girls. Beads of water flecked their faces as they looked at the girls and Simon. Tatum reached in his pocket, making the girls flinch at his sudden movement, and they looked at the officers expectantly. Tatum flashed his badge in front of the four, and they looked at him, then to Detective Sharp, and then back to Tatum. There was no way the girls could know that these men were the officers who had been working on their case day and night. All of his time and effort led them to where they stood now, hopeful that the case was soon to be resolved. The girls were so disheveled and muddy that Tatum didn't recognize Jana or Lydia from the photos. Tatum scanned the four girls standing before him. "Are any of you Jana?"

Jana was still paralyzed by her trauma and looked at Tatum, but no words left her mouth. She finally pointed a finger to her chest and said, "I am. I'm Jana Lincoln."

The girls finally clued in that they were in the midst of being rescued. Their prayers had finally been answered—and they might be going home.

Lydia said, "And I'm Lydia Cantu, from Phoenix."

"I'm Charlotte from Vegas."

"And I'm Beth. I was kidnapped a year ago. That girl over there is Tabitha, our friend, but she didn't make it.

Simon stepped forward and offered his dirty hand to Tatum and introduced himself. His FedEx uniform was a soiled brown mess, barely discernible. "I'm Simon. We're together. Some cartel guys chased us in the tunnel, and we made it out. We're so glad to see you guys. We thought we were toast."

"Nice to meet you, Simon, and thanks for helping the girls escape. I'm sure they couldn't have done it without you. Young ladies, if you only knew how long and hard we've been searching for you. I must say you were difficult to find, but I'm glad we were finally able to catch up to you. Look, we know you're exhausted, but we're in a hurry. See that chopper over there? We hijacked it from the cartel gang, and we're not supposed to be here. We've been working here across the border illegally—so we need to get over to the bird and leave as soon as possible. Come with us."

The rain had tapered off, and the girls followed Tatum and Sharp to the helicopter and climbed in. The space was limited, and Tatum decided to make two runs. The first would be with the girls, and they'd return to pick up Simon and the bodies of Sonny and Tabitha.

"I can't believe we've been saved, Jana," Lydia whispered.

"Me neither. This has been such a horror story. I can't wait to get home and see my parents."

"Looks like it's over. We made it, girlfriend."

"You and me together, we did it."

Simon flopped down on the ground, legs crossed and hands over his face, and wept uncontrollably, knowing that he would live to see another day.

As the helicopter rose and sped its payload to US soil, Simon walked over and picked up the diminutive Tabitha, the young lady he had tried to protect until nature ripped them apart. He brought Tabitha, laid her next to Sonny's body, and waited for the helicopter to return. Simon still felt grim remorse for letting her drown and vowed to accompany her back home and see to it that her body was returned safely to her parents. He would be certain to share his stories of the young girl's bravery.

After only a few minutes, the chopper softly landed on the US side. The girls unbuckled, and Sharp held each girl's hand, leading them to the ground, setting foot back on Nogales soil, and ducking under the circling blades. The ladies were soaked through and through and sloshed through the messy sludge where they were welcomed by a horde of law enforcement officers. The officers of the various agencies handed them blankets to wrap around their shoulders and escorted the group to waiting squad cars. The girls wouldn't get in the SUVs and insisted on waiting for Simon and their two deceased teammates. They waited outside the black SUVs, watching the helicopter go back to the site of the gun battle, and then Simon helped Sharp load the bodies into the copter.

The men climbed in the chopper, and minutes later, it was back in the air. The pilot lifted up and quickly powered the cartel transport back over the border, landed, and directed Simon to a waiting vehicle. Simon and the girls stood stoically while the law enforcement officers gently removed the two bodies from the chopper, carefully laid Sonny and Tabitha on the ground and covered them with blankets until they could be loaded for transport.

Fifty-Five

Wednesday, June 19, 9:00 p.m. Nogales: Recovered after Eleven Days Twenty-One Hours

The girls were taken to Nogales Police Headquarters, and officers from the FBI, Border Patrol, Missing Persons, Nogales Police, and ATF were all on hand when they arrived. As Simon and the girls left the vehicle, they encountered a long row of officers standing in a line stretching from their car all the way to the front door, clapping and cheering their safe return.

The girls hung their heads to cover their ghastly appearance, but smiles eventually surfaced—and the officers even got a wave from Lydia. The group was directed inside and handed towels so they could use the facilities to shower and clean up. The teenagers were given scrubs to wear after they were finished, and Simon was handed some men's clothes.

As soon as the girls made it to the station, Tatum's first call was to Sylvia Cantu. The two sets of parents had been awaiting word for a couple of days, knowing that Tatum and his team might be closing in on the girls' location.

"Hi, Mrs. Cantu. This is Officer Tatum."

Her voice quivered, and she put him on speaker. "Yes, sir. Any word on our girls?"

"Yes, Mrs. Cantu. We were able to find Lydia, and she's safe in our custody."

"Oh God, oh God, I can't believe it. Praise be to God. Thank you, Officer. Thanks so much!"

"Lieutenant Tatum, my wife and I can't tell you how much we appreciate ..." Al broke down.

Sylvia and Al began crying tears of joy and dropped the phone out of sheer excitement. Sylvia recovered and said, "Officer, we're so grateful. Did you find Jana too?"

"Yes, fortunately they were together, and they're both in good health and preparing for a debrief. Once we dispense with the formalities, we'll have her in the first car back to Phoenix."

"Oh, I can't believe it! We're getting our baby girl back. Thank you, God!"

"Well, I've got another call to make to the Lincolns. We'll be in touch soon to provide our ETA back in Phoenix."

"Okay, thanks again, Lieutenant Tatum, for all your efforts and everyone else who helped out. We don't quite know how to show our appreciation."

"We'll see you soon in Phoenix."

His next call only rang once, and Justine picked up quickly. She and Tom had been counting the minutes until word arrived.

"Mrs. Lincoln, this is Lieutenant Tatum."

"Yes, yes, any word on Jana?"

"Yes. I'm happy to inform you and your husband that we were able to locate Jana, and through the cooperation of many law enforcement individuals, we were able to extract your daughter and Lydia from harm's way. They're in good shape, very tired and certainly worn out, as can be expected, but we have them in our custody and are preparing them for debriefing."

"Oh, Lieutenant Tatum." Justine fainted and fell to the floor.

Tom reached for her phone. "Lieutenant Tatum, hang on. Justine just fainted. Did you find our Jana?"

"Yes, sir. We did. She's at the police station in Nogales, and we'll be bringing her home later tonight or in the morning."

"That's such wonderful news. I don't know what to say! We can't begin to thank you for all of your diligent hard work in locating our girls. You did find Lydia too?"

"Yes, sir. We did. They were together, inseparable, like sisters. Both will be driving back together, and I'm sure they're looking forward to a nice welcome home. These two young ladies are so thankful to be out of their situation and will need a lot of rest."

"Thanks again, Lieutenant. It will never be enough just to say those words. I hope you know that."

"Yes, I do. We appreciate your assistance throughout this ordeal, and I'm so pleased this had a happy ending."

"Me too. Excuse me, but I need to check on Justine. Goodbye."

"Goodbye."

The next day, after returning to his office, Tatum found Charlotte's and Beth's contact information from the missing person's database and made a call to their parents, relaying the news of their rescue and good health status in Nogales. The parents were beside themselves—Beth's in particular since her disappearance was so long ago, and the assumption was that she'd never be seen again. The parents were having a hard time grasping the notion that their young daughters would once again be home, safely rescued from their kidnappers.

Beth was a year older now and had changed in so many ways beyond what their parents realized. Her abuse over such a long time had etched horrible scars on her memory that would never disappear.

Much like Beth's mom and dad, Lydia and Jana's parents didn't realize how diabolically mistreated and constantly sexually exploited they were while away. This would necessitate months of psychological therapy and counseling. It was questionable whether any of these young ladies would be able to sustain a normal relationship for quite some time or be prepared to have any kind of sexual relationship when they grew into adulthood. However, the abuse was over, and the nights of crying and hurting were behind them. The first road to recovery was the ride home. From there, Jana and Lydia will reclaim their lives that were hopelessly lost in Nogales and be able to begin anew as free young women.

Epilogue

Jana and Lydia returned to Phoenix early the next morning. Jana fell into the embrace of her parents and hugged them so tightly they lost their breath. The tears she shed washed clean the many nights of longing to be back in their arms, and the two parents reclaimed their daughter and spent the rest of the morning listening to her trials over the past twelve days. Justine slept with Jana and listened to her daughter tossing and turning, fretting and fighting back the evil that she had grown so accustomed to.

Lydia's parents were equally as excited to have their daughter home, and they hugged throughout the morning until they finally gave in to exhaustion and went to bed. Lydia slept the early morning hours between her parents and had to be touching one of them to make sure she wasn't dreaming.

Beth returned home to her parents, and they noticed how much older she seemed than what they remembered. Because of the long-term trauma and abuse, Beth spent the better part of five years on medication to battle her anxiety. Her nightmares persisted for years, and she didn't allow another man to touch her until her late twenties.

Charlotte returned home to a rousing welcome by her family, friends, and neighbors. She even appeared on news channels and talk shows to talk about her ordeal in Nogales. Charlotte went through countless hours of therapy to ease her anxiety and guilt, but she was never quite the same.

Raul was tried and convicted of more than twenty felonies and received life in prison with no parole at Arizona's Federal Corrections Institution. He was systematically beaten and abused by the many inmates who thought youth sex trafficking was something that deserved payback, and he finally died after a retracted battle with colon cancer. No one attended his funeral, and he was cremated. Not knowing what to do with his remains, the prison officials took his ashes and flushed them down a community toilet at the prison.

Simon went back to work at FedEx and continued his route delivering packages, but he requested and received a change of his territorial assignment. He refused to step foot near West Crawford Street ever again.

Sonny's funeral was five days after the girls were rescued. Jana, Lydia, and their parents drove back to Nogales to attend the ceremony and meet his family. Jana spoke on behalf of her fallen friend, celebrating his courage and bravery and sharing that she wouldn't be around if not for Sonny.

Jana went on to say that she owed her life to this special man and would never let his memory slip from her mind.

Lieutenant Tatum had to deliver the grim news to Tabitha's mother and to Emma's somewhat apathetic father. Tabitha's divorced parents were particularly torn up, waiting and worrying for over two years to hear news about their daughter. Now that it had arrived, they were in shock, especially knowing the other girls with Tabitha were rescued. Even though they had given up hope of finding her, the finality of the news was devastating. Attending Tabitha's funeral brought her parents back together, and they sat together during the service. At the memorial, they caught up and rediscovered the spark that originally brought them together many years ago. They remarried a month later.

Simon spoke at the funeral and expressed how attached they

became in the short period together in the tunnel. His parting statement was that her memory would remain in his heart forever. Emma's father took the news in stride. He had written Emma off as lost or traveled away somewhere. He was fairly disinterested in her story until Tatum explained how Emma sacrificed her life to free the others that day. Tatum went on to describe her daring and heroism by lighting the fire that opened the girls' escape route.

The only thing her father said was, "Uh-huh ... that's my girl."

The four surviving girls remained in touch for many years and talked at least once a month in a bond that no typical friendship could be measured.

Lieutenant Tatum and the detectives worked on many future cases of missing persons and specialized in youth abductions and kidnappings. Occasionally they were successful in finding the missing, and when they did, like in the case with Jana and Lydia, it gave the two lawmen an unbelievable feeling and reminded them of why they worked so hard searching. If they were able to reunite just one girl with her family, it was worth a lifetime of hard work.

Jana and Lydia remained best friends throughout their senior year in high school and played soccer together, accomplishing feats the school had never seen. The young ladies wouldn't let the other go anywhere alone and talked by phone throughout each day.

They both received soccer scholarships to attend Arizona State and excelled on the field as well as in the classroom. They led their team to the university's all-time winning record their sophomore year and were named all-conference athletes twice each.

After hearing from her parents that Jeff Bridgestone was instrumental in providing information leading the police to Raul's house, Jana called Jeff. Jana expressed her gratitude and forgave him for the awkward night in the parking lot outside of Raining Nails. He was embarrassed about revisiting the fateful evening Jana was kidnapped, but he was happy he was able to help the authorities locate the two teenagers. Jeff was surprised when he received a reward check for twenty thousand dollars in the mail, but he promptly endorsed it over as a donation to the Global Alliance Against Trafficking in Women.

After graduation, Lydia was maid of honor at Jana's wedding, and three years later, Jana filled the same shoes at her best friend's wedding. Never did they mention the night Raul forced them together. For all intents and purposes, it was forgotten after that night and remained unspoken even in the most intimate moments with their husbands after they were married. Jana and Lydia left their nightmares in Nogales and seldom revisited the time in confinement. Their experiences were locked away forever and would never be exposed again.

About the Author

Gregory Mack Hasty is a native and fifth-generation Texan born and raised in the Dallas area. While attending David W. Carter High School, he served as sports editor for the high school newspaper, *The Wrangler*. After his journalism teacher threatened to fail him because of his lack of interest to some of the more mundane parts of the curriculum, he was somehow able to pass and decided to major in journalism in college. Gregory attended Texas Tech University in Lubbock and began as a journalism major, writing articles for *The University Daily*. While enrolled, he went on to write articles in his spare time for a local periodical, *American Dawn Magazine*.

The next year, he changed his major to radio and television and began a short career as a disc jockey and music director for local Lubbock radio stations. He wrote and produced radio commercials and public service announcements and conducted numerous in-person interviews with nationally known musicians and bands. Gregory eventually graduated with a BS in communications from University of Texas in Arlington after moving back to the Dallas area with his wife. He landed a job with a large bank in downtown Dallas, which started a forty-year banking career. Although he enjoyed his tenure in the financial world, he longed to use the creative side of his mind, which was neglected for decades while supporting his family.

In 2004, he discovered a surprising talent for painting and has completed more than 150 works in oil and acrylic media. From 2005 until 2008, Gregory wrote album reviews for *Lit Magazine*, covering popular music releases in all genres. Besides writing his autobiography, *No Wasted Motion*, Gregory has written three novels. *Jana and Lydia* is his second full-length novel. His first, *Unsettled Business,* is about a young drug user in West Texas who gets caught up in a web of illegal activity and tries to escape his predators and the local sheriff's office who's determined to bring him to justice. His third, *Woodstuck,* is a fictional account of five teenagers' exhilarating experiences at the Woodstock Music Festival in 1969.

Mr. Hasty has taken a serious interest in sex trafficking and wrote *Jana and Lydia* in hopes of exposing this hideous industry and to raise awareness. His hope is that this book will shine a light into the darkness—on those that make a living from selling our young women and men.